RSØ3

OCT - - 2012

THE LAURELS *of*
LAKE CONSTANCE

D1516858

MARIE CHAIX

THE LAURELS *of* LAKE CONSTANCE

TRANSLATED BY HARRY MATHEWS

DALKEY ARCHIVE PRESS
CHAMPAIGN • DUBLIN • LONDON

Originally published in French as *Les lauriers du lac de Constance* by Editions de Seuil in 1974, and in English as *The Laurels of Lake Constance* by the Viking Press in 1977
Copyright © 1974 by Editions de Seuil
Revised translation © 2012 by Harry Mathews
First Dalkey Archive edition, 2012

Library of Congress Cataloging-in-Publication Data

Chaix, Marie, 1942-
[Lauriers du Lac de Constance. English]
The laurels of Lake Constance / Marie Chaix ; translation by Harry Mathews. -- 1st Dalkey Archive ed.
     p. cm.
Originally published in French as Les lauriers du Lac de Constance by editions du Seuil in 1974.
ISBN 978-1-56478-723-1 (pbk. : alk. paper)
  1. Collaborationists--Fiction. 2. World War, 1939-1945--Fiction. I. Mathews, Harry, 1930- II. Title.
PQ2663.H259L3813 2012
843'.914--dc23
                              2012004232

Partially funded by a grant from the Illinois Arts Council, a state agency

Cet ouvrage a bénéficié du soutien des Programmes d'aide à la publication de l'Institut français/ministère français des affaires étrangères et européennes

This work was supported by the Publications Assistance Programs of the French Institute / French Ministry of Foreign and European Affairs

www.dalkeyarchive.com

Cover: design and composition by Sarah French, photograph by Steve A. Johnson

Printed on permanent/durable acid-free paper and bound in the United States of America

For Juliette

CONTENTS

I

ALBERT AND ALICE

He threw himself into politics heart and soul, at the risk of neglecting everything else in his life.

At the age of thirty, a great craving for action suddenly turned him from the easy path unconditionally laid down for him by his father, a successful man who had fulfilled himself through wealth, business, the stock market, and the Legion of Honor.

In 1936, Albert is a high-ranking executive in the Rhône-Poulenc factories at Péage-de-Roussillon. He is a chemical engineer, a brilliant one: his career is already rich in diplomas, distinctions, and the praise of professors and employers. You have every advantage, his father tells him, don't spoil your chances. You'll make your mark in business.

Then the strikes start. Albert, who has never bothered with politics, discovers a new vocation. He chooses sides: guided by his convictions as Frenchman, Catholic, and soldier's son, he turns ineluctably to the right. He is fascinated by social problems, and he commits himself to the unions' struggle. He knows that nothing in industry works anymore, and he believes that everything must be changed—but in an orderly, disciplined way. He'll fight for the workers he loves and understands (so he claims), against owners who understand nothing but whose minds he can change (so he thinks).

Little by little the Lyons area is paralyzed by strikes. Albert is proud to be running the one factory holding out against the "Reds." They're the ones he hates, and he's already fighting them inside the factory: the Bolsheviks, those drifters, those perverted offspring of France who swear only by Moscow.

Albert's father, Louis, of peasant stock, had graduated from field to factory, and at the end of a long career had found himself in command of workers whose lot he had once shared. For him, this was the only way for anyone to "turn out all right." He had, quite naturally, started his sons down the same promising path into that prosperous new class of self-made men for whom Communists were the very devil.

Alice is sheltered from any such problems. Her husband does not want his little family's comfortable life disturbed. She devotedly raises her three children in their charming house with its flowering balconies, a full-time maid, and every comfort. She has her set day for receiving the wives of other engineers, and she returns their visits, elegant looking, with a smile on her lips, in a silk dress and patent-leather shoes. She is the beautiful, loving wife of a young manager with a promising future. She sympathizes with his vagaries and listens to him, welcomes his friends and listens to them, often feels afraid (and cries, too), but loves him blindly.

When the sounds of the factory at last invade her house—insulting leaflets, hammers and sickles strewn in front of the door in early morning, and whispers behind her back at the baker's and at the pharmacy—when pebbles spatter on the windowpanes, and threats are made to kidnap one of the children of a certain anticommunist engineer who is in league with the bosses, Alice really becomes frightened, locks her doors and windows, and asks a few questions, which as it turns out remain unanswered.

Worried, she settles down to wait. Evenings drag by under the parchment lampshade: knitting and crocheting, Balzac's complete works, the crackling of the radio. He comes home late, nervous, speaking in monosyllables.

"We'll hold out—as long as we can. I won't let myself be intimidated."

"What's going on? Explain it to me."

"I don't want you to worry. Strikes—you know. At the factory. My workers are sticking with me. I'm backing them up. They won't give in. It's getting harder and harder. The others are wrecking everything."

Then one evening he says, "Alice, we've got to leave." Disheveled: his shirt collar open, his tie loose. His voice is trembling slightly. "They've given up. A general strike. The Reds have won. I've lost the first round. But I'll be back. We aren't safe here any more. We've got to leave."

"What are you going to do?"

"First of all, get you to a safe place. After that, go up to Paris. I've been given time off—it seems I need a vacation. In a few months I'll find a house in Lyons. Let's see what happens."

The Citroën sedan left Péage-de-Roussillon on a mild June night in 1936, with the three children asleep.

Albert left his family at his family's house, near Fontainebleau, then took time off to think.

Paris has never known a hotter summer. He wanders through it alone. He retreats to a little hotel room at La Motte-Picquet, not far from the sun-filled building where, under the eye of his parents, he spent his twenties as a student. He seldom goes out. He gives no one his address. Every other day he calls his wife, who is getting worried: My beloved, I need quiet. See you soon. He reads the main right-wing weeklies from front to back, and rediscovers the headlines of his college days as he leans on his balcony in the clear breeze, savoring his morning croissant and watching Paris come to life at his feet.

His dreams have not yet been visited by the goddess of Politics, mounted on her chariot and stretching toward him the sword of social justice, but she is on her way. One thing is sure: the factory is no longer an arena large enough for his ambitions. In some vague way, he is looking for broader horizons: he is longing to play a role in the political life of his country.

The revelation occurs one morning near the end of June.

His favorite paper, *Je suis partout*, announces that Jacques Doriot is founding a new party to "rally the anticommunist ranks." Its program is one of constructive commitment to social welfare.

Albert knows nothing of Doriot as a man. Jacques Doriot, born of working-class parents, is now the mayor of the industrial suburb of Saint-Denis. Once a leading Communist, he was expelled from the Party. He has changed sides now and is ruthlessly pitting himself against his former companions.

On June 28, 1936, Doriot announces a mass meeting in Saint-Denis, to which he invites any and all interested in his struggle: former Communists like himself, but also active members of Action Français and other Rightist groups as well. His slogan: "France will never be a country of slaves." Preaching war against the Bolsheviks, he sets forth a program of "social progress and empire." From this meeting emerges the manifesto of the French People's Party; Albert is overwhelmed by it.

The longed-for path opens in front of him. At last, the combat nurtured in the soul of this budding activist finds words to express itself. The only thing it needs is a face. He sets out for Saint-Denis to meet Doriot.

The new party is bursting with activity and excitement. In one gloomy little office, mail bags are piling up. Doriot, inundated with visitors, is giving only brief interviews. The secretary-general of the FPP accepts Albert's membership.

"Now that you're here, and since for the moment I don't know anyone in Lyons, how would you like to meet with the people down there who have already signed up? Get in touch with them, hold a meeting, appoint a provisional committee."

Albert becomes the FPP's regional delegate.

At Champagne-sur-Seine, when he stopped to kiss the children good-bye, Alice was waiting for him. She finds him lively and alert, is delighted, showers him with questions. Darling, what a lovely surprise! I haven't time to explain, I'm off to Lyons, I have work to do. At the factory?

Yes and no. I'll tell you later, take care of the children, enjoy your vacation. But where will you stay? Will you be safe? What about the Communists? Don't worry, it will all be fine. Laughing, he shows her his FPP membership card. He's excited; he's happy: social program, people's party, Jacques Doriot—sleep well, sweetheart, I'm going to find a house in Lyons, and when everything's ready you'll come and join me there.

Things start to change. Albert's and Alice's parallel lives take wing. For him, a departure toward a new world: the exhilaration of midnight conversations, the comradely exchange of views, a car speeding through the dawn at sixty miles per hour. For her, silence and patience: Chopin waltzes floating through a sleeping house, days flowing by like so many questions.

Politics invades their existence more and more, cutting into evenings, nibbling away at family Sundays. It is still only an undefined presence, something that accompanies a day or a mood. She thinks that politics is for Albert what music is for her: a passion each must pursue in solitude, far from the other. She finds it only just if politics brings him the peace and joy she finds in music, when she is alone between a *lied* and a nocturne; but she is as unaware of the hold politics has on him when he is away as he is unable to guess the rapture music plunges her into when she is alone. He feels that music is essentially feminine, as she believes that politics is the business of men who meet late at night to build a universe for other men.

He never talks to her about what he is doing. She only grasps snatches of conversation when his friends join them for dinner.

With her, he talks about the children, about meals, and, when he thinks of it, about the way she has done her hair; except for certain rare, good-natured evenings when he starts to talk, and, in his ardor, reveals such a dizzying multitude of events and unlikely details that she does not dare interrupt him for fear that he will fall silent once again. She sits there breathless, limp with fatigue, her eyes open to the night, already resigned to the next day's silence.

On a quiet street in Tassin-la-Demi-Lune, Albert has found them a place to live—a large, ungainly country house, with a slate roof and carved wood balconies. Its dovecote and pointed turrets overlook a dense garden where winding paths of gray and pink marble disappear into shrubbery. In summer, three elms, centuries old and choked with ivy, shade the restful cream-colored wicker settees underneath.

The children search for hiding places among the giant elders and horse chestnuts. Jean, Paul, and Anne will spend the best days of their uneasy childhood under the beams of the balcony and among the lilacs along the fence: a maternal, feminine childhood streaked with flashes of light—the ephemeral bright wake left by their father when he strides unexpected through the house, irate, wreathed in the mystery of his secret activities.

A father who is always leaving and never coming back. Tires hiss on the drive, and he goes by in his black Citroën. He never arrives when he is supposed to, but then comes laden with presents when he is no longer expected. This handsome father, with his square shoulders, his aquiline profile, his sleek hair, smelling faintly of lavender—this father, loved with true love, becomes the hero of an everyday life in which he participates less and less.

His words: from the telephone on the little table at the bottom of the stairs, from behind the closed door of the third-floor office (a massive table, boxes of cigars, you tiptoe by)—the voice yelling into the black receiver and making the walls shake, and the other voice, muffled by carpeting, that you strain to catch on the sly: the words, whirling and rebounding, are intercepted in mid-flight by the children, who tirelessly line them up like toy soldiers: FPP—Communists—conference—membership—comrade—speech—meetings—dinner—social platform—Doriot—party—editorials—Marseillaise—left—right—left! Right! *Vive la France!*

Meanwhile Maman lowers her eyes over the "Moonlight Sonata."

He quickly makes his way in politics. He is no longer the faceless member who, because he happened to appear a few days after the party's inauguration, was asked to help get it started in his part of the country. In a short time he has become a hard-working organizer. He visits every corner of the region around Lyons, working around the clock, rallying, recruiting, gathering, and making himself useful to his chief.

He devotes less and less of his time to chemistry. He doesn't dare tell Alice that he has given up his job at the factory (where he is nevertheless still on salary—they don't want to lose him and expect him back). Instead, Albert is getting his district organized and throwing himself headlong into this new task. Alice no longer sees him. A new wind is rising. He's starting to live.

At the end of a few busy months, he founds the FPP's local weekly, which he christens *Attaque*. He becomes its political director. He brashly sets out to win new members and lead the assault against the Reds with fiery editorials, devastating controversy, and rhetorical headlines:

FRENCHMEN, THE CHOICE IS YOURS
SAINT-DENIS AND A FREE FRANCE
OR MOSCOW AND SLAVERY

After One Year of the Popular Front,
Decadence Awaits Us

Echoes of all this reach Alice through the insulation of her manorial life: she is the abandoned lady of the château, roaming in solitude behind closed doors. Her lord has gone off to the crusades. His return will be celebrated with due honor. In the meantime we must sew, embroider, and weep into our cambric handkerchiefs. We must raise our children with a sense of respect for church, family, and fatherland.

One night after she had given up waiting for him but was lying awake, with her bedside lamp turned low, he came in exhausted, but his eyes were shining as he said to her, "It's time to put on your white gown and golden slippers. I'm taking you to Germany." (We'll start a new life. I've found you again, my pretty rosebud. The bridge won't collapse quite yet).

"Why Germany?"

"To make you happy. So that we can take a vacation. So that you can see Alsace again—we'll stop on the way. So that you can speak the language that's so beautiful when you speak it. So that we can love each other. And forget. So that I can meet your family, my darling—write to your cousins. We're leaving in a week."

And be beautiful: she picks out pale coats, sheer stockings, and lace gloves. Everything's ready. Shut your eyes, open your eyes—you're not dreaming.

They're leaving; they've left. A perfumed hand waves good-bye to the children lined up by the gate. The shadow of a beige hat set askew on her forehead hides a little tear quickly dried by the wind.

One morning in June '37, off they went, Albert and Alice, he leading, she following, into the land of National Socialism.

The honeymoon they had never had. She had not seen Alsace since their marriage twelve years before. Storks perch on the roof-tops, the hop fields are aquiver. Summer unfurls before them like a long red carpet beneath Alice's hesitant feet.

I'm coming back. I'm here. I'm going to take you in my arms, old ghosts.

My eyes will blur when I visit my mother's grave in Dornach. Put your arm around my waist—it's Mulhouse, we're passing the town hall. Do you remember, I stumbled down those steps in my bridal gown. The high school! Turn off the motor. I cried so much when I had to leave. Ivy has overgrown the classroom windows. Come, my darling, come onto the little bridge. Strasbourg cathedral is in the background. Don't move. Smile. You've just had your picture taken.

I'll stop in front of each stained glass window and every stone saint. I'll wait for the church clock on the hour. I'll just take one look at the little square third-floor window where Aunt Eugenie used to live, counting the half-timbered beams between the dormer and the attic, and then I'll fly straight up to heaven! Hold me down!

He waits. He waits silently. Let her see everything, recognize everything, breathe in the air, fly away, and come back. He waits impatiently. I don't like pilgrimages. I'm letting you have this summer, but I have no time to waste.

The car crossed the bridge over the Rhine. On the road to Bingen they sipped cool wine; then, driving through heavy-laden vines, they plunged into that brown land.

Albert has little gift for languages and no affinity with this barbarous people: he can't speak a word of German. But everything interests him. He's a farmer's son, and he has never really been weaned from the soil. Mulhouse, where he studied chemistry, was the end of the world, and when Albert introduced his fiancée to his father, the latter wanted to know if she understood French.

She guides his steps. She has to translate everything for him—conversations, newspaper articles, street names, banners. She laughs when he repeats words and mangles them horribly. In taverns they drink huge glasses of beer at rough-hewn tables. They buy postcards in souvenir shops; in one, among portraits of the Führer, she discovers an album of children's songs. He in turn complains about the food and the raspy accents of the passersby.

One Sunday, there are festivities in all the villages they drive through. Blond braids and brown shirts with armbands on their sleeves (with red splotches like wounds) have filled the streets and are singing under the flags. The old people all sing too: less loudly, but with apparent docility and hardly a trace of skepticism. Alice is vaguely amazed by all this rhythm and energy. Voices ring clear. Eyes gaze confidently toward the future.

They walk slowly down the streets, stunned by the moving, noisy crowd: a blond, muscular flood. They turn to stare fascinated at uniformed groups arranged by height: children, adults, old people—Keep in step! As for you who are solitary, silent, on the fringe, the street is no longer yours.

Something is happening on this side of the Rhine that still shocks him (Verdi's operas used to make him cry but he tended to avoid Wagner); yet it etches itself in the depths of his memory, like the dazzling images of a film whose dialogue one doesn't understand. The din of these *Heils* and marches gives him goose pimples. The dark faith of this well-disciplined people intoxicates him with vague unease; like an unfamiliar, untouched brew whose mere fumes have already made you drunk.

After miles of gleaming autobahn, and nights in hotels where they curse the beds that you can't tuck in, the black Citroën stops one misty morning at a hushed garden in Altenburg, the birthplace of Alice's grandfather. The car door slams in the gray air smelling of damp leaves. Her white leather and black patent-leather pumps crunch on the gravel, his tweed trousers go in through the front door. And here are Hildegard, Gerhardt, Erika, and Dorothea! In the pale silence laughter breaks out. Smiles are exchanged, hugs are exchanged, introductions are made. We've never met before! Alice kisses the shy blond children. Heels together, Gerhardt bows from the waist: *Guten Tag!* Alice, where are you, what's he saying?—Let's have some coffee, among the faint greens and dark reds of the drawing room. Let's sink into these antique armchairs.

The cousins' property extends far beyond the shrubbery, trees, bowers, and clear ponds. Sleek black dogs stalk the fir-lined paths. Five young children chase each other among the flowers. Over the three majestically deployed wings of the house spread wisteria and Virginia creeper. Floors creak in the depths of rooms that smell of waxed furniture and herb tea. Baroque fireplaces, great mahogany banisters, hunting trophies, heavy wall hangings.

Alice rediscovers her two cousins, Hildegard and Wilhelmina. They haven't seen each other since childhood. They bring out yellowed snapshots and paste memories together. Albert listens, smiling and attentive. The three murmuring women resurrect the past. Between the enormous fireplace and the carved wooden armchair, he sees Alice as a child with worried eyes, stiff in her dress of dark cloth, her white collar, and her high-laced boots.

The husbands speak little. One wears a monocle. Germanic stiffness; abrupt gestures. To be affable, Albert from time to time punctuates the sentences he cannot understand with a sober smile or a nod of the head that indicates his knowingness. The two men are pharmacists: two life-size stone lions stand watch at the entrance of the most splendid *Apotheke* in Saxony. Gerhardt and Erich are Nazi Party members. On Sunday afternoon, Altenburg decks itself out and the blond children sing beneath its flags.

Alice is happy. The blue room—the best room—has been prepared for them. Unpack the suitcases. We'll stay a few days. Let's limit Germany to this haven of leaves, shrubs, and firs, hang it with garlands, and sing "*Stille Nacht*"?

They left Altenburg in the clear early hours of a morning that promised to turn hot. Smiles, *auf Wiedersehen*, thank you, *es war so schön*, see you soon, *werden wir uns je wiedersehen*, next summer. And send us the children: they'll learn German.

The honeymoon is taking them to Berlin, which is celebrating its seven-hundredth anniversary. Erich has told them to drive straight to the city. There will be a great popular celebration. The houses have been decked out, and all the monuments are illuminated and hung with flags. And on Sunday the Führer will speak. The speaker's platform has been erected in the *Sportpalast*. Make sure not to miss it.

The heat is almost unbearable. Berlin—a city of eastern Europe, a continental beauty, a city stiff with majestic façades and avenues—a distant, proud city that emerges from its stoniness as it stretches out among forests and lakes. Berlin: a green, violent, summer city that simmers and throbs before the oncoming storm.

They stay at the Am Brunnen, a hotel in Charlottenburg gently set in a swerve of greenery: a high-ceilinged room with Gothic windows and balconies sculpted with garlands of fruits and flowers. Her openwork white-leather slippers step across old-gold carpeting and settle side by side under the bedside table, where, between the ashtray and the water pitcher, our Führer keeps watch from a mahogany frame.

She lies down. Weary. Berlin has made her dizzy. Young shoots of Virginia creeper climb around the sides of the open window, clambering toward coolness. Outside, surrounded by white gravel, a trickling fountain empties itself in the sunlight.

Exhaustion. Eyelids closed. I'd rather be strolling around the Wannsee, gliding in a boat over the blue lake, drinking cool wine as we watch the swans drift by. But today he couldn't care less about nature.

"Hurry up. We'll be late."

The bedroom spins. Such heat. I'm coming. I'm ready. The crepe dress twirls; a hat of fine straw; Cinq de Molyneux. Here I am!

The taxi leaves them five hundred yards from the Sportpalast. Nearer, please. *Unmöglich,* madame, crowd too colossal. They lead each other by the hand through a warm tide of people channeled by Brown Shirts. Drawn by the fervent singing of young men, the crowd pours into the red arena.

In the distance, curving around the track, stretches an unmoving wall of scarlet cloth slashed with white bands on which hundreds, thousands of swastikas are outlined. In a clamor of hoarse voices, songs, and shrill orders, the crowd spreads out, filling up the entire stadium.

Caught. Trapped. She looks around the blazing arena. Her temples contract. Waves of noise absorb them.

The steps of the rostrum fill up. Brown shirts, black uniforms, and boots, boots, boots. Decorations on which sunbeams splinter. SS on a black background, swastikas on red.

The crowd stops moving; voices are lowered. The show is about to start. Two groups of Hitlerjugend in formation strike up the *"Horst Wessel Lied."* With sweat running down their faces, they stand stiffly on either side of the rostrum weighed down with flags. The National Socialist anthem rises from thousands of breasts in perfect communion.

On the final note, he appears. Right arm raised, lowered, raised. The response is an outcry: *Heil, heil, heil!* For a few seconds he hops back and forth behind the microphones. Then, with a sweeping, brutal gesture, he imposes silence.

Alice swallows. A veil shrouds her. She turns her head—Albert's face is in sharp profile, chin thrust forward, a faint smile on his lips.

The speaker begins. He erupts into frantic motion cadenced with furious howling. Words burst forth, sentences spat out and shredded as if pulverized by a flamethrower.

Alice shuts her eyes. A bead of sweat runs from her ear down her neck. She drifts off. The voice coming toward her scarcely penetrates the veil of mist.

"Tell me what he's saying!"

The hat droops against Albert's shoulder, the straw caressing his cheek. He shakes her a little, and the hat straightens up.

"Did you hear me? What's he saying?"

She opens her eyes. Through the straw of her hat, the sun casts stippled light and shade on her pink, burning face. In the distance, clouds are piling up and proceeding slowly toward the red wall.

"I can't understand all of it. Anything more than conversation is hard for me—it's a question of style. . . ."

Her faint voice is swept away by the buffeting gale of enthusiasm that sweeps over the circus tiers. She presses against him.

" . . . remember the sound. Tomorrow, I'll translate the words for you in the *Völkischer Beobachter.*"

"You're keeping me from hearing your Führer, Alice von Altenburg! Onkel Erich wouldn't be pleased."

She holds on to the brim of her hat with one hand. A warm wind heavy with rain is rising among the summer frocks, the red faces and banners. She looks at him, outraged.

"You're talking to an Alsatian! Don't mix everything up!" She is shouting. "You're the one who wanted to come, you're . . ."

Her protests cannot be heard over the song of benediction being sung by thousands of grateful throats. The sky is growing dark: a cloud as thick as soot is about to seal the stadium under a low ceiling. It's all over. On the rostrum, hurrying to escape the storm, the Führer distributes a few violent handshakes. The first drops fall on hats, rumpled dresses, and naked shoulders. The crowd bustles and disintegrates as it rushes toward the exits.

A last look at the stadium: in the violently rising wind, flags swell and twist. The crimson wall is breaking up into drenched strips that flap lugubriously. The sky is black.

Before we start dashing wordlessly home tomorrow, let's explore Berlin one last time, my love, and then leave town. It's been raining. The party has been swamped. Garlands of flowers hang pathetically from balconies. Sodden streamers with Gothic lettering wave above porches and shop windows. Our steps lead us down wet sidewalks. The festive flags—huge reddened eyes struck with swastikas—still accompany us: four-story-high slashes on the housefronts of the lovely, gleaming avenue called Unter den Linden. The ensign and its blind eye float in the wind among the columns of the Brandenburger Tor. Our steps echo in the Wilhelmstrasse, and we pass under Hitler's balcony: still these gigantic rags beat the air about our ears.

Let's escape down the embankment of the Spree, let's wander under the mauve sky. Berlin has spread out and forgotten us.

She reminisced to the children nostalgically about the trip. He at once resumed his excursions in the Lyons area. There was no more talk of Germany between them, but he expressly forbade her to attend FPP meetings.

Preparations for the party's first regional convention were under way. *Attaque* announced a "great demonstration of popular enthusiasm and faith in France" to celebrate the new FPP chapter's first full year. She had read it one morning, in the little office that smelled of cigarette ash.

On mornings after late nights, Alice allowed no one else to open the windows, empty the ashtrays, and dust the club chairs. He would leave her a short note: "7:00 A.M. wake me, 7:15 reminder, 7:30 coffee," and she would take his shoulder and shake him gently. It's seven, sweetheart, wake up. A groan, followed by a sigh. At seven-fifteen she would open the curtains with a determined gesture, announcing in a louder voice that the fifteen minutes of grace were up. He would get out of bed without a word, drink his coffee like a sleepwalker, and lock himself in the bathroom.

He would leave in a rush, his brow furrowed. Kiss the children, where are they? Where's my jacket? Where are my keys? Open the gate! As soon as the car had turned the corner, Alice would sigh deeply, climb the wooden stairs, and settle down in the little office. She would take a seat and leaf through a copy of *Attaque* or *L'Émancipation Nationale*. She even dared to retrieve scraps of speeches from the wastebasket, reading them with a slight tremor at the sight of that tiny, regular hand.

That was how she learned of the meeting he had been organizing night after night. It was to take place in the old Buire workyards in Lyons. The FPP regional delegate would speak, as well as several important members of the political committee. At the end the star attraction would appear—Doriot, the chief himself, who was coming down to Lyons to consecrate by his presence the intense activity of the Lyons section.

Forbidden or not, she was going.

Her ears are humming as she arrives at the entrance of the vast, festooned hall. Familiar only with theaters and charity bazaars, she is bewildered: she requests a seat. They ask her name, and then smile and treat her with consideration and sympathy. A bodyguard in a navy-blue shirt and an armband escorts her toward the front rows.

There is a groundswell of shouts, voices, laughter. I avoid the faces. I move forward through a surge of heads. Tricolor standards float in the warm air. F, P, P: the letters leap forward, blur, recede.

At the foot of the high rostrum, sumptuously draped in fabric stamped with the party insignia, a row of FPP-Jugend is flexing its muscles as it proudly flourishes the party's standards. I want to run away and disappear, I want to hide, I want . . . Too late. The pearl-gray dress settles on its pleats, beneath the rostrum, in the front row. A prisoner. I have to live with them. No screaming, no laughing: stay calm. On a merry-go-round, her cheeks ablaze. The glass skylight rumbles. White spotlights pierce the smoky noise. Eyes closed. My temples have caught fire, they're dripping.

Darkness in the hall. You didn't want me to come tonight. A muttering sea. The rostrum is flooded with light. Flags come to life. The anthem begins: the crowd stands up, mouths open round, arms are raised.

> The freedom our forefathers
> Paid for with their blood
> Is threatened by new masters:
> Arise, O people all-powerful!
> Already the Red tyranny,
> Bloody image of inhuman strife,
> Is feasting on our wound.
> Up, Frenchmen! Saint-Denis gives you his hand!
> Set yourself free, France, set yourself free . . .

I am carried away by the tide. What language are they speaking? Wake me up! I see you: features hardened, a cigarette in the corner of your mouth. You smooth down your lank hair with a nervous gesture. Your short-sleeved shirt is already damp with sweat at the armpits. Yet you must have changed it: I put two in your briefcase.

The whole speaker's platform is in shirtsleeves. It's hot. The professional politicians have taken off their jackets. You are sitting next to a fat man in the middle who is a head taller than the others. He is wearing black-rimmed glasses and mopping his brow with his handkerchief. He is talking to you, leaning toward your ear. You listen as you puff on your cigarette. It's him: the chief.

It's not your turn yet. A puny fellow approaches the microphone, taps it, and the murmuring dies down. You raise your eyes: they meet mine. My heart drops into the pit of my stomach. I lower my eyes.

For two hours Alice saw nothing beyond the hairy legs of a young flag bearer in short pants. Words, sentences, shouts, and cheers passed through her head like fever. I can't see any more, I can't hear any more. I didn't want to come, I didn't, I didn't.

By the time the gathering dispersed, Alice had turned to stone. In tears, she stood by herself in the middle of the hall, unseeing amid the scattered, crumpled tracts and the overturned chairs. He took pity on her. He put an arm around her waist and guided her through the near-darkness. Come on, I'll introduce you to the chief.

Albert had made a good speech. The chief had acknowledged the energetic work done by the Lyons chapter. In an elaborate ceremony, he had distributed new flags to the local delegates, who each raised an arm and repeated: "We pledge allegiance to the FPP, to its ideas, and to its chief. We swear to fight communism relentlessly. We will raise this flag everywhere against the bloody banner of Moscow, until at last it flies in its place."

Alice suddenly looked very pretty in her silk dress. He would show them his wife once and for all.

In a white, low-ceilinged room a buffet has been set up. Naked white and red bulbs have been strung on wires hanging at varying heights. A few shabby garlands are scattered here and there on partitions. The busy hands of the party women have set graceless little bouquets on the long tables, which have already been laid to waste and splotched with wine.

It's a scorching night. The flowers droop onto the sandwiches. Alice is floating on a cloud. She is obediently shaking hands, returning smiles, and casting sweet looks. He is leading her by the arm, she has no time to answer questions, and she doesn't understand them anyway, wrapped as she is in wafts of dulled sound that leave her feeling weak. White shirts, loose ties, *pol-it-ics* is all they are talking, and they are drinking a great deal. Yes, that's fine. Thank you, that's enough. Glass in hand, ice cubes clinking, they penetrate a denser group that buzzes around the tall, broad silhouette of Doriot.

He notices her, stops talking, and comes toward her, one hand holding his glass, the other outstretched. His rumpled white shirt slops out above a braided leather belt which, at the apex of his belly, holds up a pair of baggy dark gray pants, with, for added safety, a pair of brown suspenders. His forehead is beaded with sweat, his hand is moist, his smile is warm. Alice feels dwarfed by this noisy, affable giant. She smiles. Her voice fails her. Albert thinks: she's moved at meeting the head of the party.

To make her feel at home, Doriot offers her a pamphlet. On its white cover, the red title reads, *Doriot: The Life of a French Worker,* by Drieu de la Rochelle. Alice smiles, turns the book over in her hands, and nods her thanks. Doriot smiles, takes it back from her, and says, "I'll inscribe it for you."

"To Alice B., whom I had the pleasure of meeting today, in friendship and in honor of her husband's triumph."

She takes the pamphlet, reads the inscription, raises her head, and looks around. The room is spinning. The chief opens his mouth and speaks. She answers in a whisper. He laughs. The rumpled belly shakes with laughter, the black-rimmed glasses revolve like pinwheels. All the rumpled white shirts start laughing, too. Words break loose; sentences take flight. What's wrong, sweetheart? Hold my hand, I'm going to fall down. First one foot, then the other. A little fresh air.

I feel better. I had a wonderful evening.

You scarcely looked at him, that fat man whose booming voice is still quivering in the nape of your neck. In a swoon, the bannered streets of Berlin streak past your eyes, and for an instant the triumphant songs of the Brown Shirts blend with the party anthem. Same feelings. The same thing. The flags snapping. High voices rolling over an expanse of motionless heads. Sweat. The smell of violence. The docile crowd.

Up on your cloud you feel weak. Get away quickly. Shut your front door behind your dripping back. Stop seeing them gesticulating, shouting, applauding, singing their lungs out.

You have experienced the approach of danger without knowing its name: you draw back and hide. Without knowing it, you have met the beast that prowls the roads of Europe from Rome to Berlin. The beast advances, looking for shelter, and finds it whenever it can utter its cry through the mouths of sweaty men.

You do not know its name. Shut your eyes, let it go past. You will still find it at a turning in your path, more alive than ever and more voracious. It will disrupt your life. You modestly call it "politics" and go away, all innocence. It's quite enough for it to devour your days, your sleep, and your love.

Let it pass as far as it can from your garden, without damaging your morning glory, your white iris, and your fragrant boxwood.

Let it go feast on other passions. Violence shall not come near you. Weed your paths, prune your geraniums, practice your scales. In the meantime, doors open, and the beast fattens.

A SOLDIER'S DIARY

The war started. We dreaded it, we didn't want it. Now it's here. Everything has fallen to pieces. Everything has to be started over from scratch.

I'm the regional delegate of the FPP. From June '36 to September '39, I devoted myself entirely to the fight against communism. My family life has suffered—my wife's existence has been tedious, and my children complain of never seeing me. I haven't always been able to make them understand the importance of my task. They must be sheltered from a violence that has nothing to do with them.

Now the war is here. It concerns all of us. It may separate us a little more from one another, because I'm determined to get into it.

The chief called in his delegates to give them his instructions. They are to be transmitted to all party members. "Our course is laid down for us. You don't argue when your country is at war. Get to the front. Fight bravely. Be the best soldiers your country has."

On September 30 the last issue of my newspaper *Attaque* appeared. It reflected the chief's wishes. His words, which were those of a true patriot, woke echoes deep inside me. In the Great War my father distinguished himself at the front, and I was raised by the soldier's code: devotion to one's native soil and love of France.

When called up, I hold the rank of captain in the reserve. All my promotions were earned in the ski troops; but after 1936, the War Ministry, without asking my opinion, had me specially reclassified as a chemical engineer. I'm supposed to become a manager at the munitions factory at Belle Etoile, which belongs to Rhône-Poulenc. This is a humiliating situation. I haven't asked for a cushy job. I want to fight. I have three children, and it's because of them as much as for my professional capabilities that it was thought preferable to keep me on the sidelines. I won't accept it. My work and my fine record at the Saint-Maixent infantry school (I graduated first in my class) weren't meant to get me conscripted for factory work in time of war. I won't be left behind.

Alice is worried. She doesn't understand my longing for combat, for so dangerous a role in the struggle. She speaks little of her feelings, but her looks tell me "Stay." This morning, with her hands on my shoulders, she sang in an undertone, smiling faintly, "Will Albert come marching home again . . . ? A widow and three orphans—doesn't that frighten you?" I console her as best I can.
I immediately send urgent requests to the Ministry, as well as to the 14th Military District and CMI 143, to which I belong. I apply for assignment to a combat unit. Far from concealing my political affiliations, I make a point of them: I can be even more certain of obtaining satisfaction.

I'm mobilized as a volunteer in '39, in a branch that is reputed to be one of the most dangerous.

The children's good-byes were touching. One felt that they sensed the seriousness of the situation. Moved as they were, not a tear was shed. They wished me courage and victory. "Don't worry, we'll take care of Maman." Alice didn't cry. Her wan smile is still with me, as well as her words: Our life is nothing but a succession of departures.

I travel to Depot 145A in Rochemaure. There is a bulletin asking for volunteers: five lieutenants, twenty noncommissioned officers, and a hundred soldiers. Five days later, I learn that we are assigned to the 16th Regiment of Tunisian Riflemen in the Army of the Levant.

The conflict has already been christened the "phony war."

The French front appears to be somnolent, and we sense that in the Middle East we'll have the privilege of actually fighting.

Months have passed, and with them our hopes of combat. And yet as soon as we reached Aleppo, I took my battalion in hand: I made it lead such a life that in a short time it was ready to withstand any assault and perform courageously under fire.

At the start I often missed the ski-troop battalions, where formerly I had had so much useful contact with French workers and farmers. But in the course of these months of training, I learned what a leader can accomplish when he gives himself up wholly to the service of his men, whatever their race may be.

We have left Aleppo for Upper Gezira, on the Turkish frontier. Conditions are very rough, but the desolation of backcountry life has given me insights of inestimable value. Cut off from everything, the radio our only contact with the outside world, contending with overwhelming heat (120° in the shade), we have had to see to the construction of our entire quarters, using only local earth. We must feed our men, get them to do their work in a difficult climate, and provide them as well with a minimum of recreation. We have tarantulas, vipers, and scorpions to contend with. Supplies are barely sufficient, sanitary conditions mediocre, the environment depressing. The Battle of France has made us live through tragic moments. In spite or because of these exceptional circumstances, I have experienced, here in my scorching camp, hours that must be counted among the most intense, rich, and virile of my life.

From the start of the May 10 offensive I had been anxiously following the news that came over the radio. After May 25, I gave orders to pick up only English dispatches. Not knowing the language, my radio operators would be unable to decode or divulge them.

Unfortunately, as the days passed the situation worsened. When I heard on June 11 that Paris had been declared an open city, I could not hold back my tears. My officers knew then that all was lost. During an assembly at Kamashlia I was able to converse with the battalion officers. I learned that a general named de Gaulle, whom no one had heard of, was making almost daily appeals on the London radio: he was asking all Frenchmen still under arms to continue their resistance.

Our decision was made. We would go to Palestine and from there to London. Our departure was scheduled for July 8 to 10.

Then on July 5, like a thunderbolt, came the news of the bombardment at Oran. We were stunned. We could not understand the purpose of the English attack against our fleet, which was, in our view, in conjunction with the colonial army, the factor essential to our recovery.

Had it not been for Oran, I would not have returned to France in 1940. I would have joined de Gaulle's forces.

COLLABORATION:
THE BEGINNINGS

France, November, 1940: France divided and maimed. My country, my beautiful country, you cannot have been so utterly subjugated. On the ship that brings you into port, on the boat that brings you ashore and into the country itself, you keep telling yourself: the old man is outfoxing those Krauts. The game isn't over. There must be something going on underneath it all.

Then you go ashore, and you see that everything is much worse. You talk, you converse, you open your eyes, and you're appalled by the scope of the disaster. Like a film run backward, a dismal skein of events that are now forever part of history unwinds itself to explain the France you have come back to.

Lack of equipment. Deficiency of leadership. Officers usually the first to run; troops abandoned; pell-mell flight to the south. Dunkirk, no air cover, the Maginot Line flops, delays in wartime production (and we were—ha, ha!—the strongest), the Norwegian expedition, we'll cut the line of advance. Crack units wiped out, the exodus. France on the road (a pathetic bombing target), the government panics, Mass in Notre-Dame, we need a miracle, and the *Massilia* sails. Poor France!

When, after you are discharged in Nîmes on November 2, 1940, you see what the country has become and find that there are Frenchmen—many Frenchmen—who are not all that displeased with their lot in this occupied, shamed, and divided land, what do you do?

You weep inwardly. Your determination is unwavering. But you do not make a pilgrimage to Lourdes. You go and see Doriot.

A civilian once again, Albert first stops in Lyons to change his clothes and give his little family a warm embrace. They have been waiting for their captain in the downstairs rooms, where fires can be lit. Albert finds them huddled morosely in the midst of autumn grayness, completely at a loss.

Among the first frosts in their quiet garden, the questions tumble forth. Papa, tell us about the war. Alice, wrapped in her cashmere shawl, asks, Now what are you going to do? What will happen to us? He says nothing, gives no answers. He sleeps little and paces around the cold house, kindling fires in the fireplaces. He tries to regain his footing on uncertain ground and, in the damp twilight of bare pathways, to channel the jumble of thoughts in his head.

One morning near the end of November, ill humored and nervous, stirring the little spoon in his coffee cup—Juliette, do you call this coffee? Sir, we make do with what we have!—he announces:

"I'm leaving for Marseilles."

Doriot has set up his headquarters in Marseilles, over a café called L'Estaque, which belongs to party sympathizers. It's a time of decision. Everything has to be done over again. The party is illegal and no longer exists. The chief spends his time rallying his troops—discharged party members and scattered officials—and, above all, concocting a brand-new political line for them, one rooted in the fall of France as rewritten and brought up to date by Marshal Pétain.

As he stands in the grimy corridor of the train taking him to his chief, Albert knows nothing of Doriot's attitude. Watching the countryside streak past beyond the window amid spurts of sooty smoke, he is trying to work out an eloquent view of things that will persuade Doriot of the full extent of his disappointment as soldier and Frenchman.

Doriot had told his followers: fight. If Albert hadn't fought, it was not because he hadn't wanted to. Doriot had told them: be the best. He had done what he could. While battling desert tarantulas, he had rather forgotten the party. Social action, organizing the Lyons chapter, conventions, *Attaque*—all had sunk to a secondary level of importance. When the foe is at the gates, there is only one language and only one response: the force of arms. He had not engaged in politics among his infantrymen. In the army they make soldiers, not activists.

Doriot had said: fight the Germans bravely—they're also the Reds' allies. Albert had found no difficulty in putting on a uniform, or in adopting a tone of command, or in thrilling to the colors.

But now, but now? The question unfolds to the train's jolts, switchings, stops, and starts. The question speeds down the Rhône valley, carried by a cold wind under a steely sky all the way to

Marseilles. There the former FPP delegate very much hopes for the answer that will reassure him and provide him with wings for some new flight.

The chief hasn't changed: a powerful build, ready smile, and alert eye. Dominating everyone with his exceptional height, he wanders around a makeshift office that seems too small for him. The two men exchange a brotherly embrace. Greetings, comrade. It's too bad, it's terrible, how the times have changed. But we're still here, ready as ever.

Albert sits down. He is moved. A hesitant smile—then he quickly gets hold of himself. He opens his leather cigarette holder, lights a cigarette, inhales several burning lungfuls, and starts to tell his story.

Doriot doesn't budge. He listens, with his hands folded on his desk, a heavy palpitating mass of attention. Albert speaks successively of Syria, of the infantrymen, the camps, the heat, the men's eagerness for combat, the flag. He speaks of defeat, de Gaulle, the mood in the Army of the Levant, Oran, his incredulousness (those English bastards!). Of homecoming, reality, disillusion, and rage. Doriot doesn't budge and scarcely blinks.

Albert concludes his account: "As far as I can tell, the policy of collaboration decided on at Montoire must be a feint to mask the real French course of action: preparing to get even."

Doriot explodes. After his long silence, he cannot contain himself. His glasses fall on the table, his arms flail the oppressively stuffy air, and he shouts:

"Albert! My God! You *haven't understood anything!*"

He gets up, knocking over his chair. He opens a door and yells for coffee—Two cups, boiling hot, we're freezing in here! Then, relieved, he sits down, takes a deep breath of the foul air, and turns a penetrating glance on Albert.

"I'll explain things to you."

For two long hours, Doriot patiently expounds his policy and the direction to be followed by his party, which is now in pieces.

"Politics isn't a question of feelings. You have to see things for what they are and then draw the necessary conclusions. The fact of your not liking the Germans is one of *feeling*. Nobody's asking you to take them in your arms. But the real fact is that they beat us and are occupying our country.

"Another hard truth is that, thanks to Russian support, which allowed them to knock out Poland and France in succession, and thanks to the default of the United States, whose support had to be immediate to be effective, the Germans stand a good chance of winning. Now, you say you don't want to go to England, and even if it's pretty much a sentimental decision, I accept it. So for you that solution is excluded. But we have no right to exclude it for France. In case Germany is beaten and England is the victor, France has got to be represented in the other camp. De Gaulle has taken that road, and that's fine. I know nothing about his political ability—I have no idea whether he can hold out against the English when the time comes. But by then, other Frenchmen will have joined him, and for the moment the main thing is to have France represented in London.

"But if you don't go to London, don't plan on preparing for revenge over here. Aside from the fact that a policy of resistance would aggravate the country's problems, and bring on reprisals as well, you have to face the realities: the greater part of France's industrial potential is controlled by the Germans. If they run into difficulties as the war develops, you must expect them to make ever-increasing demands of France. At the present time, the main problem is to limit the damages caused by our defeat. The Germans are the masters of France. If we assume an attitude of resistance, they'll make the occupation tougher, they'll impose a Gauleiter on us and help themselves to whatever they want without our being able to protest.

"But if we collaborate with them, we'll give them only what we can't possibly refuse."

"So it's still a question of outwitting the Germans?"

"No, absolutely not! That's not our concern. One of our aims is to preserve France's wealth—that must be a cornerstone of our policy. *But another aim is to collaborate in a way that leaves no room for doubt*—I might say, *almost brazenly.* The Germans will certainly feel a natural reticence toward their former enemies: if they have even the slightest impression that we're fooling them, our efforts and sacrifices will be totally wasted. As Marshal Pétain defined it, 'We must collaborate with honor and dignity, but straightforwardly.' Once again, resistance is none of our business. You can't follow two policies at the same time. We have to support Marshal Pétain. As long as his government holds out, the Germans won't impose a government of their own choosing, or, more simply, a Gauleiter."

"Then what will Marshal Pétain's policy be?"

"It's too early to say. There are a lot of people flitting around Vichy that I'd rather weren't there, but that's the way politics is played. We'll see what happens. The one thing to remember is that Marshal Pétain has to stay in power at all costs. Aside from him, I don't know of anyone in France capable of preventing the Germans from governing directly. Furthermore, he's a staunch anticommunist. Now the Communists are trying to benefit from the Hitler-Stalin Pact, which they supported. They want the Germans to recognize their party, with the idea of forming a Communist government. As long as Marshal Pétain holds out, the Germans will exclude the Communists."

"Then if we collaborate, we'll be on the same side as the Communists domestically? And on the same side as the Soviet Union abroad?"

"You're exaggerating. The USSR hasn't gone beyond economic aid to Germany. I know that's more than enough, but I have to accept the fact—and I can do that as long as Germany doesn't encourage Bolshevik policy in France. Within the country, we're only apparently on the Communist side. What they want is an immediate peace, peace at any price, according to the terms decided on in '39 by Molotov and Ribbentrop. We have to occupy a place alongside them to prevent a peace treaty being signed before the war is over."

"What's your attitude toward England?"

"Vichy has broken off diplomatic relations. That's none of our business. It would be absurd to go as far as a declaration of war. The Germans won't ask that of us, because then they'd have to let us have an army—and I doubt they'll trust us to that extent! What would we gain by declaring war on England? They'd have a pretext for taking over our colonies overseas. Our cargo ships from North

Africa would be torpedoed. Maybe one day they'd start bombing us. No, let's not get England's back up, not yet. Let's see what they do. Let's leave it to de Gaulle."

"You'd let de Gaulle recruit and expand his following in France?"

"Let him recruit all he wants! Although it seems to me that not many Frenchmen are eager to start fighting again. If his following grows in France, we'll decide what attitude to take. If he ever starts fighting the Communists, we won't bother him. On the contrary."

"And what about the empire? What's your position on that?"

"Absolutely uncompromising. It's not to be touched. Without an empire, France loses all chance of recovery. That's why it must be defended against anyone who lays hand on it."

"If the Germans are the victors, won't they want to oust us from it?"

"Of course—if we don't collaborate. They'll send in the Wehrmacht, and that is to be avoided at all costs. But if they do assert the right to take it over, then we'll have to fight. Albert, I'm not saying that this policy of collaboration is the best thing in the best of all worlds. I'm saying that to save what can still be saved, we've got to be *political realists*; I'm saying that all risks have to be covered, including that of total German victory. That's the one we can guarantee by collaborating, and that's why the policy has to be tried out."

"If Germany loses the war, won't we be accused of treason?"

"No. We're only following Marshal Pétain: he's the instigator of 'collaboration.' And we'll be able to show those who hold the opposite political view that our own was necessary, that we applied it in good faith and entirely for the sake of a higher national interest. If Germany wins, we can welcome the Gaullists and tell them that we understood how necessary *their* policy was. But you realize that this isn't the moment to say so. On the contrary, we have to get ready for some rough infighting with them. At the moment they're still in London, and here the Communists are making it their business to oppose them.

"Well, one last word. *If there were only a handful of us around Marshal Pétain, that would be treason. But there are several million of us: that's an opinion!*"

Albert is impressed, but he won't admit to being convinced. He mistrusts his liking for Doriot: Doriot, the great chief who harangues crowds so well. Just listening to him makes you feel like jumping into the sea in full uniform. The decision is a serious one. He wants to defer the moment when he officially resumes his high position in the party.

He gets up, crams his felt hat on his head, and warms his hands over the stove. He takes a last cigarette from his case and lights it. He wraps his knitted wool scarf around his neck, smiles, and holds out his hand to Doriot.

"Albert, don't give up your better feelings. And stay in touch with me. Remember, we've already fought side by side. France needs us. The struggle is still going on."

A cigarette between his lips, his hands in his pockets, the little captain goes off, hurrying through the winter and the cold north wind.

Vichy Diary

During January '41, Doriot tells me that Vichy will again try to form a single mass party of pro-collaborationist forces. This will be the second such attempt, and he has high hopes for it. (After the initial failure to form a single party in October, the chief had tried to bring about a *fait accompli* by founding, with the support of the daily *Le Cri du Peuple*, a movement called the "Rally for National Revolution.")

We mustn't forget that on December 13 a palace revolution led to the eviction of Pierre Laval as Prime Minister. We must make up lost ground and reinforce our position against Déat, who is supporting Laval and is Doriot's principal rival.

The chief has delegated two fellow members to represent the party in the discussions that are about to open. He is asking me to join them as observer. (He told me that in this way you can get back in the swim of things in full cognizance of the facts.)

So I've come to Vichy. The first contacts have been disappointing. They have not given me a high idea of the people in office. There are lengthy speeches, interminable parleyings, backstairs conversations, and all kinds of intrigue. Nothing positive, despite the intervention of Marshal Pétain.

And at the very moment that this second attempt is miscarrying in Vichy, Déat outflanks us in Paris. While we are deadlocked, we learn that he has not waited for the end of this laborious and sterile haggling to launch his National Rally of the People. His new party has set itself the goal of restoring Laval to power. It is supported by Abetz, the ambassador of the Reich.

Doriot responds by publishing *In the Steps of Marshal Pétain*, a collection of his most important articles. But Déat remains a dangerous rival.

Peyrouton, then Minister of the Interior, receives me with the words, "Tell your chief that France is done for, that everything is done for, that anything we try is pointless."

I'm so shocked to hear an acting minister express such an opinion that I can't help replying, "Then, sir, may I ask why you remain in office?"

He shows little surprise at my rejoinder. "Oh, I'm ready to get out at the first warning. I keep my bags packed day and night."

Admiral Darlan, the Assistant Prime Minister, receives me. He has great dignity and simplicity and the forthright eye of the soldier or sailor. He at least is determined to show himself equal to his task. He complains of difficulties caused by the endless intrigue and political jockeying of Marshal Pétain's intimates. I ask him about the social program, which is, as I tell him, my main preoccupation. He at once takes from a drawer a fairly long memorandum that he wants to read to me. It's the draft of a constitutional labor law, a kind of compromise between paternalism and corporatism. The divergent tendencies on which the plan is based spoil its overall unity, but it contains many just and desirable things. I tell him so, and he is delighted by my approval.

"Tell Doriot what I'm trying to do, and don't leave Vichy without seeing me again. We'll discuss it some more."

As I leave, he says, "Why don't you stay in Vichy? It would be easy to find you a job. You could do useful work."

I evade the question by saying that without the chief's authorization I cannot commit myself. I leave with the impression that if they offer positions to newcomers so readily, the people in Vichy don't know which way to turn.

At the end of a month I make my first report to Doriot. In it I express my disgust in plain language. He advises me to persevere and not let my critical instinct get the better of me. So I stay in Vichy, and soon find myself miraculously provided (but how?) with orders for a special assignment as attaché to the Assistant Prime Minister. I'm to receive a salary and traveling expenses. The orders allow me to travel freely by car in the occupied zone—a great advantage.

It may not be hard to get a job in Vichy: it is much less easy finding an office, or anything that can be used as one. For a while, Charles Vallin and I share a room that Tixier-Vignancour lets us use at the national radio headquarters, on the top floor of the Hôtel du Parc. (Tixier is then secretary for broadcasting.) The room makes an excellent observation post: Marshal Pétain, the Prime Minister, and their staffs are all settled in this hotel.

One day, Chassaigne appears, just named to a post created specially for him. He is to take charge of "social propaganda on behalf of the national revolution." He asks us to help him in his task. We agree to try, since our role would involve getting in touch with whatever workers' organizations have survived in the unoccupied zone. For me, it's an unhoped-for opportunity. I can investigate the country's state of mind in surroundings that are of special interest to me. Lyons, Roanne, Saint-Etienne, and Chambéry are the cities to be visited—a region I know well.

I withdraw very soon. I can't subscribe to the Vichy social program or appear as its envoy to the workers' organizations. They have understood nothing. They will only succeed in angering the workers and encourage Communist propaganda.

Tixier-Vignancour, for his part, has given up his duties. He is addressing a long letter to the members of parliament in which he scathingly indicts the achievements of the French state—propaganda, social legislation, administration, the youth corps, and the volunteer legion.

He suggests that Vallin and I countersign the letter. Although it wins our complete assent, Vallin wants La Roque's authorization and I Doriot's. The letter in which I solicit this authorization, justifying my request with the most violent possible critique of Vichy, has the honor of being censored. Called in by Dumoulin de la Barthète, I'm given twenty-four hours to get out of town.

I shall not set foot in it again.

In Lyons, to which I return at the end of April, I learn that there is to be a conference of party activists in Paris on May 4. I decide to attend.

Doriot again expounds to his assembled comrades the various points of his policy: it pushes collaboration to its extreme.

Vichy is sticking in my craw. I won't go along. I ask the chief—I can tell that it exasperates him—to approve my position as observer. For the time being I shall be involved, but circumspect.

Not satisfied with irritating him by my reluctance, I ask such questions as: where does the FPP get its money?

The chief answers patiently: "Since December 13, 1940, Marshal Pétain's civilian cabinet has subsidized *Le Cri du Peuple* and *L'Émancipation Nationale*. This guarantees the self-sufficiency of the two papers. As for the party, we have a finance committee whose job is fund-raising. But people are all too happy to invoke business problems and the taxes they pay to Vichy in order to give as little as possible. As soon as we have permission to resume our activities, I think that we can count on a German subsidy."

At this meeting, we agree to organize a convention for the party members in unoccupied France. It will be held in Villeurbanne, a suburb of Lyons, from June 20 to 22. It will use as cover the Friends of National Emancipation, which has been founded in the free zone in anticipation of Vichy's approval.

Until then, I shall engage in no party activity whatsoever. But I agree to draft and present to the convention a work charter that will provide an alternative to Vichy's program.

For this convention—the big event of the summer—a speech must be written, polished, and memorized. The first two days whirl by in a tumult of blue shirts. Order is disrupted on several occasions, either by Communist demonstrators or the Veterans' Legion, which is loyal to Vichy. The Blue Shirts restore calm. The chief is to speak on the third day. An audience of several thousand is expected. For its benefit, Doriot will elaborate his policy of collaboration. It will be a vast gathering, the first since the war. The party must be reborn. Hesitations must be overcome—even in conditions that have not been helped by the former Lyons delegate's withdrawal from his duties.

But he has prepared an extraordinary welcome for his chief. He won't be accused of defeatism. He has not spared flags, pennants, or supervisors—FPP youths, muscular and proud, with armbands on their blue shirts.

And, almost miraculously, history is to play into Doriot's hands: an event that will give him the opportunity to deliver the wildest harangue of his career occurs with impeccable timing.

Lyons, June 22, '41. Out of the blue, the news breaks just before Doriot's appearance on the speaker's platform. *Germany has broken its pact with the Soviet Union. Hitler is launching his Russian campaign.*

Get those Bolsheviks!

They're ecstatic. They hug each other. To hell with scruples—Hitler, FPP, united in one struggle. In a riotous carnival atmosphere, with only the beer and sausages missing, the chief gets up to address six thousand happy, exultant, overexcited Frenchmen. He shows his gift for finding the right word.

"In the attack against bolshevism, Hitler's genius has reached its zenith. He has proved himself this day to be not only the leader of Germany but the leader of all Europe, the great pioneer of modern civilization."

There are moments in life when one should not mince one's words. He immediately inaugurates a Legion of French Volunteers—the LFV. Let the brave men who refuse to be crushed by the Red peril put on German uniforms and hasten to the eastern front to fight side by side with their brothers of the Wehrmacht.

And to set an example, he himself—Doriot, the chief—will be among the first to leave.

Heil!

"This war is now our war. It is a veritable crusade against the number one enemy, not only of France, but of all Europe."

The crusaders gather backstage to exchange toasts and congratulate each other. His eyes blazing under his thick shock of hair, his shirtsleeves rolled up, dripping with sweat, the chief is vigorously shaking hands and slapping the bent, submissive, quivering backs that gather around him. His heart throbbing, he embraces Albert and says to him:

"Comrade, what a joy to learn the great news in your own hometown! I don't imagine you need anything else to make up your mind, right? Can you have any doubts now?"

1942

The little girl was born on February 3. Since a child, even in war-time, requires nine months of preparation, she must have been conceived on a day early in May '41.

He had returned from Syria a beaten man; his fighter's heart broken, he had been fired by Vichy, and landed in an oppressive, gloomy city—Lyons—that was already numb with deprivation, mistrust, and bitterness. But April, unaware of men's torments, burst into bloom. Hearts full of uncertainty and distress were sub-jugated by this season full of sound and song. Without a thought for the dreariness of breadless days, spring raised forsythia, wiste-ria, pink cherry, and white lilac skyward.

The captain from the Middle East was frustrated. The special agent of the French state at Vichy was crestfallen. But when he opened the garden door and felt the gravel crunch beneath his soles; when he saw his wife in her white dress casually raising her ringleted head (her lips geranium red, her eyes green—there you are, there you are!), when he saw his three children running toward him from between burgeoning horse chestnuts, Albert felt life flooding back inside him. He would do something else. He would forget about the war, politics, and Marshal Pétain. He would stand under the arbor, listen to the birds, then rediscover, in the depths of cool sheets, his gentle wife. Amidst lily of the valley and mauve lilac, he fathered a child.

One evening—sweet month of May!—in the glow of a candlelight supper, with the windows opening on the young branches of the lindens, in a fit of springtime tenderness, to the crystalline sound of champagne flutes, he declared, very sure of himself: "I want a son who will never know the meaning of defeat!"

On the summer day when Hitler invaded Russia, Alice had her first dizzy spell. She was secretly hoping for a daughter who, defeated or not, would never go to war.

France might collapse in fear and chaos: she could endure it. He might leave, come back, and leave again: deep within her, she had a hope of being less lonely. While Doriot rallied his partisans in Paris, and Albert rushed off to his men's business, she miraculously rediscovered a true reason for being a woman and for shutting her eyes to the world. Count the months up to nine. Forget the rest.

The pregnancy followed its perilous course among ration cards and rutabagas. The children might fight over a piece of bread, but milk and butter had to be saved "for your little brother." Juliette would say, with unshakable logic, "Times are hard, and that's that." She would patiently cook up little dishes out of nothing—various kinds of colorless vegetable purées and broths that in other times she wouldn't have fed to the cat. They didn't alleviate hunger. Too bad, eat it up, it'll do good where it's going, even if it goes through too fast!

War and its deprivations did not stop the children from building tree houses or playing cops and robbers in the shelter of the garden. They also enjoyed putting out the *Tassin Evening News*, a little newspaper published in an edition of three or four copies on ruled school paper. It related the most recent gossip about Vichy, Lyons, Tassin, and the FPP. Albert provided them with material whenever he appeared. The boys would excitedly ask him a multitude of questions about airplanes, the German army, the Allies, and the eastern front. He would answer them with a smile. The newspaper's header reproduced the party emblem—a little blue and red flag with FPP at the center—and the slogan, "FPP shall triumph!"

Alice would take her big belly to do the shopping. She had priority, and so the meager provisions reached home quicker. She was not worried. She was not the only one. She was carrying a child, and it would be born—a little child of the war. It would be suckled, loved, and rocked in its cradle, and it would turn out all right, like the others. This wasn't the first war, after all.

During the nine months Albert rarely showed up. His activities left him no leisure. He would telephone, find out about the progress of "his son," and cheer up the mother.

Can't come now, sweetheart, but feel very close to you. —What are you doing in Paris, darling? What's happening? Will it be over some day? —Working at it, working at it, we think of nothing else. Coming for Christmas. Bringing huge package, all kinds of food, have certain privileges. —It's cold here, very cold. No coal. No wood. At night we huddle together. I'm sewing and mending. No wool. See you soon, darling.

It was a very harsh winter. Lyons disappeared under snow that piled up in high, frozen ridges. France heated itself as best it could. Wrapped in anything woolen that was available, their feet tied up in socks, strips, and pieces of cloth, the inhabitants of Lyons, like everyone else in France in '42, waited in long lines outdoors. They did not converse. Their noses dripping and their breath white, they passed each other without greeting. You had to save your strength.

The girl was born in the depths of that wicked winter. She almost made her appearance in the taxi that was struggling to reach the hospital. The wrinkled red and blue thing, wrapped in a profusion of pink, made her mother burst into tears. A daughter, a daughter, thank the Lord! She turned it every which way to make sure the shortages had caused no damage: nothing was missing. The thing howled and squirmed, and waved its thin, icy hands.

Albert arrived by chance twenty-four hours after the birth. There had been no way to tell him about it. He found the thing tiny and unbeautiful, but at the sight of his daughter, he was moved. She'll never have to go into the army—fine! Let's celebrate, let's pop the champagne—a little girl is born!

Two days later, the father left home. With Doriot away at the head of the LFV on the eastern front, the subtle, extensive, antlike work of the party's laborious beavers must not slacken. He had to be in Paris for the weekly report. He could not miss the Wehrmacht roll call.

Alice cried a little. Oh no, you're not leaving us already. . . Duty calls, sweetheart. Everything's fine here. Don't worry, nothing's going to happen to me. I'll send you a parcel next week. Look at all these flowers! Our friends have been spoiling you. I'll come back for the christening. Try to find some sugared almonds for it.

There were, of course, none to be found. In the father's absence, the child was baptized a month later with stonelike sweets that the whole family found impossible to chew.

The snow had melted. They gave a little party. Albert's parents had managed to cross the boundary between the zones, in a car bulging with free-range chickens, hams, butter, and potatoes. "It's the Holy Virgin that sent you!" said Juliette, overwhelmed with joy.

Jean, the older brother, was godfather. Paul was jealous. Anne did her hair in ringlets and wore her brown dress with the cream-colored lace collar. Mother wore her navy-blue suit, her veil, her rouge, and her beige leather gloves. She smelled of lavender and orange blossom. The bells rang on and on, and the baby shrieked.

In my embroidered dress and my plain-knit shawl, after being salted, blessed, commended to God, and christened Marie, I was ready to make my cheerful entrance into the world.

I was born in '42. There were other war children: they were given calcium and vitamins so that their milk teeth wouldn't crumble.

But I am a child of Marshal Pétain and collaboration; of Doriot, the Wehrmacht, and anti-Semitism.

I have been born on the right, with the LFV and *Le Cri du Peuple*. My father writes for it. It's the organ of the FPP, restyled. From '40 on, it expresses anti-Semitic views. A dominant theme of the paper is "purification." Doriot supports Vichy's laws against the Jews and Freemasons.

My father follows the line. He is in Paris in '42, while my cheeks are filling out against my mother's breast. He is one of the leaders of the party. He would like to make social problems his only concern, and it's true that he keeps aloof from the other leaders: but he remains close to the chief, and he will be entrusted with ever-weightier responsibilities.

Before leaving for the eastern front, Doriot took Albert aside and opened his heart to him. Comrade, I'm going to make you one of the biggest figures in my party. But don't tell anyone, it will only encourage jealousy.

He then explained what he expected of him.

"Events have singularly accelerated the FPP's destinies. It's now time to settle accounts with communism. Our revolution must be a social one. We have to make the mass of workers forget communism and join us.

"In order to succeed, a revolution must not only be prepared ideologically: it must know how to use men to its advantage. This is a job that must be done in secret, because these men cannot possibly all be found inside the party.

"Albert, you are going to get this project organized for me without wasting a minute. You're going to assemble a file—a huge, secret file. *You're going to construct the framework that the party needs as it moves toward taking power."*

In this way the FPP's secret service was born. Albert devoted himself to it ardently and methodically. But that wasn't all. Doriot asked him to take personal charge of relations with the OKW (*Oberkommando der Wehrmacht*)—a real proof of friendship on the chief's part . . .

Since the Montoire agreement, three main forces dominate the French scene, and every good collaborator has to reckon with them. First, in the diplomatic sector, the German embassy, with Abetz and his staff, who support Laval. The FPP cannot expect much from that quarter; contact is nevertheless maintained. Next, in the National Socialist sector, the all-powerful SD and SS Corps. Doriot is personally in touch with them. Dealings are often tricky: the men of the Gestapo could help the FPP, but they are intrusive and they want compensation. Finally, there is the military section, headed by the OKW. It has great authority in France: the *Militärbefehlshaber* commands all the departments connected with the occupation. It was he who authorized the FPP's activities in December '41.

Here, too, there is a problem of compensation, but in this case Doriot is utterly intransigent. "Get the most for the least" is his motto—and isn't that also a key tenet of our beloved Marshal? Doriot doesn't want to lose his independence as a *French* political leader. The party is not to become an intelligence service for the occupying forces. Anything but that!

Albert, to deal with soldiers we need a soldier. *You* won't let them walk over you. —A tough bird, inflexible, reluctant to mix with Germans: Doriot when he leaves has nothing to worry about. His orders will not be overstepped.

(He never ceased repeating to the chief, Social problems are what interest me. Be patient, Albert, I'll give you a ministry. Meanwhile, on the road to victory, everyone must pitch in. You have to make the best of things.)

So Albert is responsible for liaison with the OKW as well as for the secret service. He is in touch with Colonel R., a soldier of the old school. Doriot has described him as a friend, a fine man with a horror of Frenchmen who don't remain, above all, *French*. Having served in the First War, where he learned to admire the *poilu,* he understands the idea of an alliance against a common enemy but not that of submission to foreigners. He is also the head of counterespionage for Western Europe.

It is agreed that Albert will discuss political matters only with him. Every week he is to see Colonel R. or his executive officer, Count K., and deliver a written report on the party's "general political direction."

To keep the secret service secret, neither the party's political committee nor the military services of the Wehrmacht are to learn of it. (Doriot's policy is a subtle one: to obtain—without informing his comrades—support, backing, and information from the Germans, who in turn are kept ignorant of their use, and who receive in exchange only a brief summary of irrelevant matters.)

They're some Germans, these Germans. Not the brusque, dry Gestapo kind, not at all. These soldiers are agreeable—agreeable and distinguished. A routine is established. Each Monday Albert has an appointment with the colonel, who receives him in his house in Neuilly. He very quickly makes friends with the executive officer, Count K., and sees him frequently. K. is the scion of an old family of Baltic barons that has furnished many members of the Prussian, Polish, and German diplomatic corps. His university years were chiefly spent in Paris. Young, ambitious, widely cultivated, he has set his sights on being German ambassador to France if Doriot comes to power. It does not take Doriot and Albert long to grasp the benefits they can draw from this ambition, and they make of K. a very valuable ally.

"Every two or three days he used to come and see me, bringing me documents, reports, and lists, which I had to copy quickly. He was certainly the person who provided the FPP with most of the information on the resistance that the party gathered between '42 and '44. In return, each week we drew up a synopsis as the chief had ordered. It was a kind of memo the colonel needed to prepare his weekly report on French public opinion for the *Militärbefehlshaber*, who would subsequently transmit it to the Führer's headquarters."

In Paris, in the year 1942, you can be a collaborator and not realize it. You keep up a polite friendship with astonishingly well-bred Germans. You discuss Goethe, Beethoven, and Voltaire. You have tea once a week with a count whose manners are exquisite and chatter daily with him about the drift of "politics," never mentioning a name, never doing anyone any harm. Oh, the Führer must have been enthralled by the reports signed by Albert. As for those hundred thousand francs, why, the Wehrmacht contributed them to the party's charities.

In Paris, in the year 1942, you call your wife. I'm very busy, I'm caught up in my work. I won't come on Sunday but a parcel and ration books are on their way. —Darling, without you Lyons frightens me. I don't go out anymore. Juliette finds anonymous notes in the mailbox in the morning. I want to leave Lyons and these people who call me a German. —Don't worry, the war's almost over, "FPP shall triumph," and we'll build a wonderful, new happy Europe: collaboration rhymes with reconciliation.

It is the summer of 1942, in Lyons. Broiling hot. But in Tassin-la-Demi-Lune, on Chemin des Cerisiers, there is a garden. You find coolness under its boughs, you smell the leaves that stir in the sunshine at a breath of air, you breathe in the evening sky that throbs like the crickets and the glowing smiles of the baby, outdoors in its wicker cradle. In Lyons, one can breathe. Between the cries of the child and the mother's flowered dress, time has stopped. With bent head she fingers the little mother-of-pearl buttons, opens her blouse, and moves the darling's head against her breast. On a lovely July evening, beyond the end of the world, there is a garden suspended in time, and in it dwells a woman rocking a child who will soon fall asleep.

That night, in Paris, French policemen spill out by the truckload onto streets muggy with sleep. They break into houses, knock on the doors of Jews, and cart them off by families in the trucks. They are dumped inside the Vélodrome d'Hiver—the winter sports arena, the "Vel'd'Hiv." They do not know why they are being taken; above all, they do not know where they are being taken. Laval said: the children too. They are Marshal Pétain's first Jews, his first wagonloads. Foreign Jews now, the others later. He has promised as much.

This is Operation "Spring Wind," the great, brilliantly engineered roundup of the night of July 15, '42. It brings more than twelve thousand people to the Vel'd'Hiv. Four thousand of them are children.

They stay there seven days. Waiting there, dying there. Beneath a glass roof, in fierce heat. Some lose all hope; some commit suicide.

They will be packed into Marshal Pétain's railroad cars—the first Jews from France, destination Auschwitz. A handful will come back. *Not one child.*

That night, in Paris, *three to four hundred young men, wearing blue shirts, shoulder-belts, and FPP armbands, have come to lend the police force a hand.*

I was born in '42. Others were children of the roundup, the Vel'd'Hiv, freight cars, Auschwitz. Not me: a pink child, loved, suckled, and cradled. A child spared.

1942.

THE THISTLES

We had to leave Lyons. The summer of '43 drove our little family
out of its slate-roofed house. Much later, the children would miss
the cherry trees and the dense bushes in which they concealed
their playhouses. Their garden, far from grown-ups and the war—
the free, safe place running from one wall to another, where life
could be created with a few boards, a sandpile, and a bicycle.

Much later, with their eyes shut, they would nostalgically re-
trace the outlines of their childhood home, just as earlier they
had drawn pictures of their first house. In pencil or gouache: one
door, two windows (don't forget the shutters), the red roof with
the smoking chimney, the green grass sprinkled with poppies, a
yellow sun, and three festooned clouds.

In front of the house, at the end of the long curved driveway,
a brown wooden gate opens on the world. Through it, on hal-

cyon days, their father's car would burst: reality. Father, don't go away. Come and join us on our green island. France will survive without you.

Behind the house, at the end of the meadow, beyond the apple trees, is a small gate of worm-eaten wood with an ancient rusted lock (there is one in every real garden). It leads through a wall crumbling under ivy and honeysuckle. It creaks when the wind blows. To reach it on autumn mornings your feet get soaked in wet grass and your socks catch on brambles. It is shut against the world. No one passes through it. It is the sluice gate of fantasy.

Between the two gates, one intrusive, the other secret, you make up a hermetic life, a life of leaves and shadows that you will carry with you through the years. Gates that open and shut life—the ones passed through, the ones you forgot to close, and the ones that are locked behind your back. In '43, Jean, Paul, and Anne—sixteen, thirteen, and nine years old—were sheltered, bourgeois children. Two gates sealed off their garden. When they left it, they hadn't realized that their trees, lawns, and games were already frozen in a recess of time, somewhere in their memories, like a dream.

Alice watched them as they gathered their prized possessions, leaping around the boxes and suitcases, eager to experience the thrill of a dangerous journey. The little girl was toddling in the sun-shine, pulling flowers from their beds, tripping on the gravel. Her mother would pick her up silently, console her, and set her down.

Alice walked through the garden, walked through the house. She seemed to be pacing off paths and rooms, counting trees and stairway steps, enclosing within her gaze distances, colors, and spaces, so as to dream of them, afterward, during late evenings alone, in other houses.

She followed the preparations from a distance, her mind elsewhere. Her life was lurching past her, from child to house, from cherry tree to elder, from awaited homecomings to dreaded departures. They had to leave Lyons. Juliette was coming with them—not liking it, but coming.

"I'm not happy about Paris, Madame. But since Monsieur B. says that he's found us a nice apartment, let's try it. I won't have to reheat dinner half a dozen times and then throw it out!"

Perched on a stool, Juliette is taking down the drawing-room curtains. Beside her, Alice gathers them in her upraised arms. The blonde woman turns, looks down, and smiles at the brunette. No, she hasn't gone too far. Alice smiles back, shrugging her shoulders.

"We'll see. Will you help me fold them?"

"Do you think they'll be the right size for the new living room, Madame?"

"How do I know? Will they even get that far?"

Sighing and dropping her arms (which Juliette deftly relieves of the curtains), Alice turns slowly around with a little grimace of indecision, her heels pivoting on the waxed floor. Her circular gaze commits to memory the open beams of the ceiling and the small square windows that give onto linden trees vibrant with soft wings. The furniture has been pulled away from the walls, ready to be packed off. Wood batting spilling out of scattered crates; dust golden in the sunlight; on cream-colored paint, gray marks left by furniture or unhooked pictures.

"You're going to miss your garden, Madame. I don't know Paris. They say there are lots of air-raid warnings."

"He's promised me a brand-new piano. A very beautiful black Steinway grand."

"What about your mother's?"

"There'll be two of them. The apartment is huge. There are two living rooms. I know how I'll spend my evenings between the alerts, I'll run from one living room to the other—to save time, I'll stay on the piano stool and you can roll me!"

They burst out laughing. Juliette has been bending over a packing case, scattering mothballs. She straightens up, red-cheeked, and takes Alice by the wrists.

"Well, I certainly like it better when you laugh."

Alice hides her face in her hands. The laugh has frozen. She looks at Juliette through her fingers and with the tip of her forefinger wipes away a small tear, then rushes out of the room.

"I'm going to take a look at the children. I'll be back."

Resignedly, Juliette returns to the trunks, singing softly to herself. She never forgets to sing. She sings tunes from operettas or nursery rhymes. Time passes when you're singing, Madame, and the work gets done by itself. Or she talks to herself: Cheers me up, Madame. It does help. —We're leaving tomorrow, Juliette, hurry up. Just keep packing and don't bother about anything else.

The furniture, linen, and dishes would be shipped to Paris. The family will be spending the summer at their grandfather Louis's house in Champagne-sur-Seine—a holiday interval before the city.

Louis is waiting for them anxiously. What are they doing? They should be here by now. Their passes are in order. Albert drives fast. With stiff, decisive steps, shoulders thrown back, hands in the pockets of his gray flannel trousers, he paces back and forth along the front steps between white stone columns. Stopping, he draws a gold watch from his waistcoat pocket. Under his bushy eyebrows, his eyes look down through the lenses of his little round gold-rimmed bifocals. He repockets the watch. His hand slides over his shiny dome, still bordered at the nape by a thin wreath of silver-gray hair.

Louis resumes his measured pacing, muttering to himself. A light breeze swells the wide sleeves of his shirt, white finely striped with blue, with a stiff collar under the soldierly chin.

Germaine suddenly appears at the foot of the steps. She looks awkward despite the smartness of her little white flounced apron, tied loosely around her ample rump.

"Madame asks Monsieur if by chance Monsieur would care to lunch with Madame."

Germaine is about thirty-five years old, slightly deaf, a hard-working girl recently exiled from the Burgundian village whence the master of the house has uprooted her. With her big feet she runs diligently and submissively from floor to floor, amazed by the profusion of luxury—the silver, the glass, the embroidered sheets. She makes it a point of honor to speak in the distinguished style of servants employed by the best families.

He has not seen her coming. He jumps, turns around, and re-buffs her with a gesture that sends her flying.

"Germaine! Where are you running off like that? Tell my wife to eat without us if she can't wait any longer. Just a minute! You've made rabbit for lunch? Good. The rooms are ready? Good. Which sheets did you use? Good, that's fine." (His hand now gestures more mildly—"leave me alone" rather than "get out of here.") Nervous and frowning, he resumes pacing back and forth.

Louis had been an extremely handsome man. Still bright and cheerful, he carried his seventy years proudly. He rose early and washed in ice-cold water, healthy habits kept from a harsh farm life that he had only briefly known. In the morning, bent over a porcelain basin and singing *Rigoletto,* he would douse his half-naked body with cold water to start things moving. The central heating, necessary for appearances, was turned on only when the frozen pipes were in actual danger of bursting. Fifty degrees seemed a good room temperature; and in any case, in winter he never left the kitchen, where Germaine kept a fire burning in the old-fashioned stove. He took his naps there, sitting in his old Voltaire armchair (a solitary survivor among the hideous modern furnishings) with his feet in the oven, and, when it was really cold, his nightcap pulled down over his eyes.

Noon by his watch. Standing erect at the center of the steps, his hand shading his lenses, he scans the empty horizon of the plain at his feet. His gaze stops at the huge factory wall, far off beyond the railroad tracks: he makes sure that the two vertical hands of its clock agree with him. He breathes deeply, then sunders the still air with several calisthenic movements of the arms. Up, breathe in; down, breathe out. Notices with satisfaction that he isn't sweating, and that his supple joints haven't cracked. Chest out. Everything's fine. Let's walk a little more.

He was never sick. Look at my teeth, all thirty-two of them. Never been to the dentist—but then I never ate sweets. Health ran in the family. Except for those he had seen disappear as a child, decimated by an epidemic of croup, they had all become fine old men, gnarled and erect, who rose with the sun, walked from village to town to get to market, ignored the weather, and drank their liquor straight.

One of them, his grandfather—he liked recalling his wisecracks at the end of copious Sunday lunches—was going to be the first hundred-year-old in the village. But he spoiled the party. On the eve of the great day, when garlands had already been strung between the lindens in the village square and a banquet table set up in the middle of his field, the old man, sensing the approach of death, summoned his daughter and said to her, "Madeleine, they aren't going to get me alive. They'll have to dance on my grave. Now take me to my armchair, I don't want to die in bed."

Every time he finished this story, Louis grew pensive, as though already reflecting on his own death. He envied his grandfather, even if he himself would have preferred to die on his feet. Since the opportunity of falling on the battlefield—the only ending worthy of the name—was no longer open to him, he hoped that death would at least not catch him unawares. He wanted his death to be a success, even in bed. He liked to imagine himself as a rich tiller of the soil who, feeling his end near, gathers his sorrowing family around his bed and addresses them in the most poignant terms. (That mongrel bitch would catch up with him just like everybody else; his children and grandfather would line up at the head of his bed; but—horror of horrors!—a stroke would leave him speechless!)

With the sun at its zenith, the factory siren unlooses its moan through the shimmering air. A flight of startled birds breaks from the lindens with a whir of ruffled leaves. Louis's eye follows their chirping into the cloudless sky, and he wonders about a possible alert. Wait, no: the droning attains its most strident pitch, then lessens and sinks onto the plain, where it fades away. A glance at his watch—normal enough, it's twelve-thirty. The birds return to their roosts. Louis accompanies his steps with nervous little tappings on the seams of his trousers.

They aren't here. Albert knows very well that I hate waiting. But he's always late. The devil take summer, the heat, and the war. Weary of counting his strides along the colonnade supporting the overhanging balcony, he goes down the steps. His shoes crunch their way through the gravel as far as the open door of the garage. A sweeping glance around the roughcast walls, where sets of every sort of tool are neatly displayed. Satisfied, he walks around the Citroën 15, checks the whitewall tires, opens the door (it does not squeak), and sits down behind the wheel, in a silence laden with gas fumes. He runs his hand over the gleaming black dashboard—not a speck of dust. Saint Christopher sparkles reassuringly on his polished medal.

No one was allowed to touch the car. He would put on his overalls, take gloves from the many pairs that hung over the work bench, and look after it himself, shining it and polishing it for hours on end. It had to be ready at all times, with a full tank, starting up at the first turn of the key.

He often took trips. Whether it was to stock up at his farm, buy a leg of lamb in Fontainebleau after Sunday Mass, or visit his parents' grave on All Saints' Day, it was always a major outing.

A black leather suitcase stamped with his monogram never left the trunk. In it he had carefully packed a specially fitted black suit; a white shirt, starched and finely pleated; a stiff collar; solid gold cuff links; and a new pair of patent leather shoes. Pinned to the lid of the suitcase were precise, sealed instructions that gave the address of the cemetery and a plan of the crypt. He'd had this final resting place excavated in the Burgundian village of his birth and lined it with the costliest marble. He had done himself proud: there was room for sixteen. Life is so short.

One of his great pleasures was to visit his old village in his car, which he drove like a maniac. He traveled across Burgundy like a feudal lord touring his domain. He would stop in the vineyards and silently observe a moment of bareheaded homage to the *grands crus*. Then he would call on his wartime companions. Spruced up, rosy-cheeked, in a suit from the finest tailor, he would brake to a stop at their door in a cloud of dust.

"My poor old friend, I didn't even recognize you! Things not going too well, eh?"

Leaving the other man seething with hatred, he'd drive away delighted. Clean-shaven and discreetly perfumed, he would mercilessly visit the girls (now old maids) whom he had once courted and who at the time would have nothing to do with him. "Poor Jeanne! Old age is so hard when you're poor!"

Long before he was rich, little Marie had not turned him down. She had borne him two sons. She remained in the background, with her embroidery and her sewing, complaining gently to her husband about his delusions of grandeur—she herself would have been content with a thatched roof and his heart. Docile and humble, she spent her days recreating a little life of her own within the splendor erected about her by her Gargantua (as she used to call him with tenderness, respect, and bitterness). Her wifely modesty had been frustrated and, unable to keep up with the frenetic pace of her insatiable husband's ascent, she had sought refuge in naïve sanctimoniousness and vulgar piety. She collected plaster virgins, crucifixes, rosaries, and holy water from Lourdes; she had her charity cases; she visited with well-mannered priests; she never missed a pilgrimage. Louis scolded her and made fun of her gimcrack religion, but every Sunday he followed her to Mass.

"Marie, put on some jewelry and make yourself beautiful."

Afraid of being conspicuous, she would hesitate and then put on her gray or her lavender dress with the lace collar and cuffs, her veil, and, to please him, her necklace of amethysts, which she partially hid within her bodice. She would lightly rest her hand on her husband's sleeve, glancing proudly at his hat of pale gray felt and at the little red decoration on his lapel. Her Louis was a fine-looking man. Taking him to church was the best thing in her life.

Marie adored her daughter-in-law. No doubt she saw reflected in her the kind of love and patience she herself had experienced. She used to pray for her in secret and wish her fortitude. Ever since her awe-inspiring son had soared into the spheres of war and politics, his excesses seemed to surpass anything she had previously known. When he came to visit her and bent over her, wrapping his arms around her delicately so as not to snap her in two, she would utter a thin little laugh, tapping the back of his neck or pinching his ear as though saying, You're giving us a hard time, son, but I forgive you completely.

The Citroën door clicks gently shut: his hand has carefully accompanied its well-oiled course. At the door of the garage he stops, arms akimbo, and through squinting lids gazes triumphantly at the imposing, symmetrical mass of his dwelling. He likes it best from this angle. The metallic glint in his gray eye signifies: I built this, and this is what I'm bequeathing to you, you poor little things.

Louis liked to tell his grandchildren: Without me, you'd be tending cows in some place no one ever heard of. And it was true. Stubborn and ambitious, the young farmer had lifted his family out of their rut, which was circumscribed by vineyard, field, farm, and steeple. He wanted *success*. Over the years he worked hard, became a "gentleman," raised himself as he used to say by his own bootstraps to the top of the social ladder. He became manager of the naval shipyards at Saint-Nazaire, and he ended his career producing the tanks and other war materiel that Marshal Pétain was handing over to the occupying forces.

He liked to run things. As master he was feared, respected, and obeyed. He flew into unforgettable, thundering rages. He loathed contradiction. He liked money and the smell of gold. He played the stock market, made a fortune, and bought up farmland. He would have liked to see his success passed on to his son, but Albert apparently had other ideas on the subject; Louis lamented the fact.

He has gone back to his sentry post, bemused. His son worries him. I don't understand it. He had an excellent job. He's proven himself as leader and soldier. He loves his country. He has a lovely wife and four fine children. What has he gone into politics for? Some people, it's true, do make a success of it. But he's too pigheaded. And where does he get all the money he spends? Isn't that dangerous? Doriot—I hardly know him; saw him once, in Lyons. He has an imposing presence, and he's a sensible man, no doubt of that. And he supports Pétain, which is a point in his favor. But where is it all leading? And what about this big reception he's asked me to organize, here, in my own house, with all the trimmings! Doriot and his German friends: I killed quite a few of them at the front in '14—what am I supposed to talk to them about? The invaders seated at my table, in my house, drinking my wine! He says, you'll see, they're nice people. Just the same, does he realize what he's making me do?

In the middle of the steps, between two of the white columns that support the second-floor balcony, Louis stops. At his back is the heavy wrought-iron door that leads into the vestibule. At his feet, the granite-flagged pathway dividing the lawn of the bare garden. The black iron fence is high; the gate is colossal. Beyond them, the road. Then the lower orchard, whose espaliers and rows of apple, plum, and pear extend down the plain until they disappear from view. At the bottom of the orchard, set among pathetic little gardens, a flock of small, ugly suburban houses faces the passing trains. And at last, with the Seine and the distant forest for background, the haughty, grandiose, hideous profile of the factory rises between Fontainebleau and Moret-sur-Loing. It is the only truly ugly site on the Seine for thirty miles around, at least.

This was where he had to create his family seat, his château, his pyramid: the bare, stony ground on top of this knoll. He drew the plans himself. He wore out three architects, not letting them erect a partition without throwing a fit. The fourth took his orders lying down and saw to it that they were executed.

The costliest materials were brought in: faultless hewn stone; unalloyed copper for the pipes; top-grade mosaic flooring; marble and rare woods for the reception rooms. The house had to be weatherproof, to last at least five generations, and to survive war and earthquake without budging. It had to be beautiful, sturdy, and visible from afar.

By being a nuisance he got what he wanted: a square house of unadorned hewn stone, a gleaming chalk block perched on a rise in the middle of a flowerless garden, with two covered balconies running the length of its front on massive columns. It could be seen for miles around. Irreverent locals called it "the château." To make things perfect, Louis gave his masterpiece the pleasant name of "The Thistles."

Tired of waiting, Louis has sat down in the shade of a column. Germaine has just set a little silver tray on the pedestal table in front of him: the champagne still quivers in the slender cut-crystal flute. Louis cocks an ear—surely that's a motor he's heard.

A car is taking the curve just this side of the railroad bridge.

"Germaine! Tie up the dog! Call my wife! Open the gate! Move!"

Suitcases strapped to its roof, the overloaded Citroën 11 glides along the black iron fence and stops. The gate scrapes over stones that are hot from the sun. The children burst squealing from the car.

"They're not going to start making all that racket. Marie! She's not here, as usual. She hasn't heard a thing."

Having struggled up the rise, the car brakes on the gravel. Louis kisses the children, who have taken the front steps four at a time. "Easy, easy. There." He pats them on the neck. Alice gets out with the little girl in her arms. Juliette follows. Their dresses are creased, their faces tired. Last of all, Albert, with a cigarette between his lips. Grandmother arrives at a run: You're finally here. How the little girl has changed!

"Hello, my boy—you're very late. No trouble on the way? Good. We'll talk later. Park your car in the shade. Michel will unload it. Now let's go in to lunch. Children, go wash your hands. We're lunching in the cellar these days, it's cooler."

Alice looks at Juliette in distress. We're already being drilled. Not even time to freshen up. Grandfather has his timetable, we're already behind schedule, don't waste a minute, just follow orders.

The little girl is crying and squirming in her arms.

"Father, excuse me a moment, I'm going to put the baby to bed. She's done too much traveling. I'll join you."

The main group sets out for the family table, walking around the house to a little ground-level door behind the house. Two steps down into the cellar: a large, dark, cool room with a tile floor, the gloomy summer dining room for guestless lunches. Louis seats them. An embarrassed Germaine waddles in, smiling the full breadth of her bleached moustache. Juliette follows her unenthusiastically into the kitchen and returns with an apron hastily tied about her, carrying a platter of eggs mimosa. Everything is in order. The meal can begin. Louis serves the wine. —Albert, you smoke too much. Children, not so loud. Germaine, the salt.

Wearily crooning soothing words to her last-born child, who is going limp on her shoulder, Alice climbs the sixteen front steps, then the two that lead to the wrought-iron door. She automatically wipes her feet on the doormat sunk into the mosaic paving of the vast entrance. She catches her breath. To the left, the brown and beige drawing room; to the right, the dining room. Both are paneled in Norway birch; both open onto the entrance through broad symmetrical openings fitted with waist-high swinging doors; they are decorated with openwork chrome arabesques identical with those on the stairway banister. The same pattern adorns the mosaic pavement and the old rose rug that covers it.

Alice walks across the fifteen yards of rug to the white marble stairway, which is carpeted in red and leads to the upstairs bedrooms. With a mournful look she once again counts the Cariffas—the only painter who has had the honors of the château. Not a wall has been spared. She smiles in spite of herself.

Louis's taste in art had not developed with his fortune. He had not lingered over questions of decoration. You disguise empty walls with mirrors or with paintings. He gave up the idea of a hall of mirrors and asked Monsieur Cariffa to paint him as many pictures as there were empty spaces. Albert had crossed the Atlantic on the *Normandie*, which had been decorated with works by this artist. Perhaps a horizon of apple trees in blossom happened to distract him from the surrounding billows—on his return, he must have mentioned the painter's name in passing. This was enough for Louis to draw a parallel between the gigantic steamship and his ridiculous house. Landscapes of unromantic mountains; greenish glaciers and streams; tidy cottages on the shores of Swiss lakes; elaborate, lusterless flower arrangements—they were everywhere. Out of breath, she climbs the majestic stairway that is embellished every four steps with a stately bronze statue—*Diana at the Hunt*, Rodin's *Thinker*, or Michelangelo's *David*, depending on the gifts of considerate friends. On the second floor, she crosses another old rose rug with brown and green spirals; enters her room; catches her breath.

She is oppressed by the weight of the ebony wainscoting on the walls. The crimson velvet curtains are drawn. One lively note: the large pastel ceramic crucifix over the bed. Alice had suggested old prints or botanical illustrations as more soothing: a categorical refusal. So be it. She lays the child down on her bed, at the foot of the larger one. (The baby was the only one without her very own room: she had been conceived after the blueprints.) Alice drifts into the bathroom with its clinical white tiles, squints, lowers the blinds. Brings her feverish face close to the three-sided mirror, which she adjusts to show three faces reflecting to infinity: raises her eyebrows, crosses her eyes, sticks out her tongue. She takes off her rings. Turns on the tap. Looks for her box of rice powder—there, with its pink swansdown puff and its familiar scent. Brushes her hair, replaces the tortoise-shell brush, and tiptoes out.

The rabbit *chasseur* is steaming on the table. Red wine follows white. The children are eating ravenously. Grandmother watches them, smiling: I'm going to fatten them up, my little city chicks. Passing behind her, Alice strokes her silver hair.

"I'm glad to be here, Mother. No, Albert is leaving tonight. They urgently need him in Paris. Yes, he does smoke too much—tell him, if you can manage it. She's sleeping, don't worry."

During the meal, in front of the children, Louis talks about raising chickens, phylloxera, and the propagation of bees. After dessert, he gets up, clears his throat, and as he folds his napkin says to his son, "Come on, Albert. We have things to discuss. Come along to my office. Germaine, we'll have our coffee there."

Alice has just lit a cigarette at the end of her long russet amber holder. Squinting behind the cloud of smoke from her first puff, she watches the two men as they climb the concrete stairs. Same build, same gait. She imagines herself twenty years from now, when her eyes (mauve circles making them shine brighter in the depths of their sockets) will follow the same bald head, the straight shoulders, the resolute step, in the same house: a retired husband who raises rabbits, gathers his apples, makes his own cider, and collects stamps. Twenty years—like one year, or tomorrow. She closes her eyes amid the hum of voices. To leap over the years: to overcome time. Find rest in a gentle old age. Be a pretty old lady in plum-colored taffeta, mitts of cream-colored lace, a little velvet ribbon under her chin, with snow-white hair. Sitting in the rustling folds of a long gown, in a bright wicker easy chair, unearthing with the tip of a silver-knobbed cane the crab grass choking a tuft of primroses. Resting from life in surroundings from an English novel.

"Maman, are you asleep?"

She starts, then delicately sweeps away the ash that has fallen on the red and white checked tablecloth. She draws a last puff from her Camel before crushing it out in the pewter ashtray.

"I'm going to unpack. Be good."

On her way, she passes the closed door of the office and stops for a moment. She barely lowers her head before proceeding briskly, her steps muffled by the beige carpeting of the corridor.

Office doors are always shut. Behind them, men talk in lowered voices about politics and war; while women open suitcases, put away linen in cupboards redolent of mothballs, and watch their child sleep.

The dark little office smells of polished wood and Havanas. Albert's astonished gaze rests on the fancy box of fifty cigars that lies between an Empire inkstand and a desk pen upright in its green marble holder.

"A present. Have the first one. You know that isn't one of my vices."

Albert helps himself and reverently deciphers the colored ring. "The best there is." From his waistcoat pocket he takes a little chromed cigar cutter, nips the end of the cigar, and into it gently inserts half a matchstick, which he grips between his teeth. Before sitting down, Louis opens the windows inside the closed shutters. Sunlight seeps through the slats. Beyond, children's happy voices.

Louis wants to talk. His son resigns himself to silence. A light knock on the door: coffee is served in Limoges cups.

"Albert, I'm worried. I don't have to tell you that the bombings are becoming more and more frequent. So far, this region has been spared. And it's true that we lead a life that's almost normal—we're privileged. I'm glad the children are staying here. But all I know is what the radio and the newspapers tell me every day. You're better placed—what's our situation? What do you foresee?"

Albert looks up at his father. On a library shelf, just above his gleaming pate, reigns a portrait of Marshal Pétain, now floating in a nimbus of cigar smoke.

"Don't worry. We may be having a bad time right now, but the game's not over."

Louis shifts in his leather armchair. He tries not to raise his voice.

"Everything you tell me is vague. Are you trying to spare my advanced years? Do you think I'm senile?"

Albert makes a small gesture of denial. In a thin ray of sunlight, his cigar traces a spangled arabesque.

"Father, it's difficult to tell you more than what you already know. The path the Allies have chosen is criminal. They're bombing, and their bombs rarely reach their objectives. The results are appalling. Thousands of innocent people have already died. For the moment we can do nothing about it but be patient. The situation will brighten up."

Albert looks down at his cigar, which is on the point of going out. What more can he communicate, except uncertainty?

Louis emphasizes his words: "Brighten up? Your party is that influential? In France?"

"We're going through difficult times—"

"You said that already."

"Doriot has been in Paris for the last three days. He turned up unexpectedly from the eastern front. His absence is keenly felt, he knows that. Events move fast. Plots are being hatched. There's a state of permanent conflict among the various pro-German groups in Paris."

He pauses, catches his breath, wipes his damp forehead, puts his handkerchief back in his trouser pocket.

"At the beginning of the year, as you know, Déat was advocating a National Revolutionary Front. To Doriot, this looked suspiciously like a plan devised by his rival against him: for over a year, Déat had been promoting a single party, in which he would play the influential queen to Abetz's king. Doriot—you know how intransigent he is—avoided this course like the plague. He is adamant about the absolute independence of his party. But his repeated absences haven't made his relations with the occupying forces any easier or helped the party in the negotiations for taking power.

"I've hardly seen him since he arrived. You understand why I'm so anxious to get back to Paris tonight."

Louis finishes his coffee and puts his cup down on the tray. He opens a little ivory box and takes out a toothpick.

"Albert, tell me, what's your position in the party?"

"Very simple. I limit myself strictly to the role Doriot assigned me: secret service and liaison with the OKW's representatives. My problems with the members of the political committee are doubtless the result of my lack of conviviality. I don't feel much affinity with them anymore, I don't hide the fact, and this irritates them. They resent me for the privileged relationship they suspect me of enjoying with Doriot."

Louis nods his head. He wants to hear more.

"Don't you feel you're sometimes in danger? Shouldn't you be worried about what the ones who don't agree with you may do?"

"Not yet. I keep my eyes open. One of the most serious problems—it gets steadily worse during the weeks the chief is away—is the virtually autonomous activity of the so-called Action Groups. I know that Doriot didn't want them to develop in this way, but at the start he shut his eyes to it, and the infection is spreading. I'm fighting to keep the party's real efforts from being sullied by these vigilante groups—they use the pretext of attacking Communist resistance groups to indulge in looting and murder. But it's becoming harder and harder to control the party's gangrenous spread in the provinces. Before Doriot leaves, I want to have him agree to plan a purge. But I know that for the past three days he's been monopolized by the very people who stand to benefit from the existence of these groups."

"What do you mean?"

"Certain people are thinking about their future. As long as they make a fortune, it doesn't matter much where the money comes from"

"I see. Be careful. I don't like the smell of it."

Albert looks at his watch. He has to get away from the country, away from the shimmering silence of this summer afternoon, suspended between the children's laughter and the sound of women's voices in the kitchen. Get away from this comforting room, with the antique planisphere, the ten-volume Larousse, and the Havana cigars. Get away from this uneasy father, from his silences, his questions, and his advice. Get back into the blast furnace: bare offices, smoke of cheap cigarettes, sweating men.

"I've got to be going. I'm leaving Alice and the children in your hands. I'll phone you and confirm the date of the reception I'm counting on its giving here. I spoke to you about it."

"Is it really necessary?"

"It's *imperative!*"

He shoots up like a spring, lays both hands flat on the glass top of his father's desk, and bends over the skeptical Louis.

"I'm going to tell you something else. Unlike several of my colleagues who receive money from undisclosed sources, I have only the monthly salary that my employer—Doriot—sets aside for me. I handle lots of money, it's true. But it's not even party money—I don't have access to those funds. It's the special budget allotted to the secret service. Only Doriot and I know about it. It's used to finance my work."

Albert straightens up and adjusts the belt of his trousers. He watches the motions of a fly beating against a windowpane in quest of the sun.

"All right. It so happens that for more than a year I've been in touch with two Germans, Colonel R. and his deputy, Count K. The latter, whom incidentally I've grown very fond of, has been making proposals to me for the last few weeks. He'd like me to accept some money, on my own account, in acknowledgment of services rendered, I suppose. I've absolutely refused to take it."

"So what?"

"*So what?*"

(Alice hears this "So what?" on the floor above.)

Albert wipes his hand across his damp forehead. He starts walking back and forth between his armchair and the window: three paces one way, about-face, three paces back. Louis watches him, his hands folded on his stomach.

"So, I don't like it. Against my principles. Especially as they're starting to insist and don't understand my attitude at all. I told Doriot. It made him laugh. 'Albert, you're awfully naïve—these people are doing their job, you can't blame them for that. But your scruples do you credit,' and so forth. Anyway, this reception was his idea: 'to show these gentlemen that you don't need their money.' Doriot likes putting on a show, and he thinks that your house makes a perfect setting. Father, you've got to give them the works. Don't spare any effort. Go down into your cellar and choose your finest bottles. Take them on your tour of France. *Erste Klasse!* Impress them. Show them what it means to be a real Frenchman."

They laugh, Albert happy to have let the tension out of the air, Louis reassured.

"I understand better now. Don't worry about anything. We'll outdo ourselves."

THE BIG DAY

It was a radiant Sunday in July. The white hive has been humming since sunrise. In the bedrooms, in the shadow of shutters, women's perfumes float like clouds. Cinq de Molyneux, Vol de Nuit—a smooth screen set between soft skin and the world. Get ready for July 25 and the big parade. Put on your white gown and your golden slippers for the summer ball, and we'll all go a-roving. Be beautiful, my sweetheart. I'm bringing you my friends. You always complain of being left out: here you will be at the very heart of things. Don't be afraid, relax and talk to them about the Black Forest, about Ludwig II of Bavaria, about the Lorelei. *Ja, von Weihnachten, vom Familienleben in Deutschland und von Blümchen die ewig blühen, ja, ich weiss.*

In the mirror of the armoire, Alice sees herself full length: beautiful. She swivels round, leans her head (chin on round shoulder) to look at her tanned back, bare to the waist. She turns on her patent-leather heels, twirling the dress of Lyons silk, white strewn with wildflowers. The arch of her fine eyebrows is marked with a line of dark gray. Her lips are carmine. She gravely paints her oval nails. She looks up at her dressing-table mirror. Tightening her nostrils, sweeping the hair back from her forehead, sucking the flesh of her cheeks between her teeth, she turns herself into Marlene. Her laugh wells up and ripples through the warm morning. How comical all this would seem if she didn't have a secret presentiment that she is playing a small part in a drama whose ending she cannot foresee.

In the kitchen, Marie, in full ceremonial dress, with all her pearls in evidence, her thick nose slightly overpowdered, is putting the final touches on the pastries now emerging from the ovens; while the maids—agitated, cheeks blazing, shiny as new pennies in their black crepe dresses and scalloped aprons—baste birds, stir sauces, and polish silver platters.

At eleven o'clock, at the moment when Juliette is feeding the children in the basement (since eight o'clock the upstairs has been out of bounds to them), Louis, looking very dapper, gives the reception rooms their final inspection. The sun streams in through the wide-open windows, and showers gaily over the silver, the plates finely chased with gold, and the crystal glasses. There are four kinds, from the long-stemmed *flûtes* for Alsatian wine to the iridescent goblets for old burgundy (you can almost bury your face in them). In a shaded spot on the sideboard, red wine gleams darkly in dusty bottles, their labels frayed and faded, left there since dawn.

Five minutes before noon, the whole family is mustered and lined up on the porch. Paul wonders why flags haven't been broken out. His older brother digs his elbow into his ribs and raises his eyes to a heaven of dazzling blue.

"No time for jokes. See how worried Grandfather looks? He'll feel better after the brandy."

"Well, I hope they're wearing uniforms, and we can take our coats off soon."

High noon

Two black cars slow down as they pass the iron fence. Juliette, who has heard the motors, smooths her apron, fixes her hair, and picks up a tray laden with little dishes that are piled high with hors d'oeuvres.

"I'll take this in now. I have to see what's going on."

"Better wait till he rings for us."

"Not likely. I want to see the *Boches* arrive, and the big chief too. I know *him*—he used to come all the time in Lyons. He was always nice to me."

12:10

"Well, Germaine, you know, those Germans look all right. If I hadn't been told who they were, I never would have guessed it. OK, they're blond. But no boots, no uniforms. Gray suits, white shirts, very polite. They smiled and bowed very low to everybody. The children were impressed. The little girl didn't want to say hello, except to Monsieur Doriot—he grabbed her in his arms and laughed very loud. He hasn't changed. Still enjoying life, still fat and jolly.

Naturally he's too hot already, he's wiping off his forehead every other minute. He's wearing a short-sleeved shirt and the same old suspenders. Doesn't bother with the niceties, not him, and he's right. But that didn't stop him from kissing the ladies' hands. I forgot to tell you, the three Germans have a driver, a little soldier who doesn't seem to speak French. Michel was using signs to get him to park the car behind the house. Hey—there they are! We'll have to feed him downstairs. Is Michel ever making a face! Imagine, being Polish . . ."

12:15—the bell rings

"Cocktails! You're on, Germaine. The trolley's in the corridor. Don't catch your foot on the rug. What's wrong? Why are you making those big eyes at me?"

"You go. I'm not used to it. I'll do something stupid."

"My girl, we have our assignments. Monsieur would be furious if the help started improvising."

12:30

"So, feeling a little less shaky?"

"I'm all right. I didn't spill anything. From now on, I'm sticking to the ovens."

"Did you have a look at them—the *Herren?*"

"Not much. About all I saw was their feet. Monsieur Doriot, he's the fat one with the glasses? He gave me a big smile. That cheered me up."

"And none too soon. Keep an eye on the lamb. I'm going to see the little man downstairs. He looks pretty cute. Must be missing his mommy. Still and all, it's no fun thinking of them eating here while we have people starving in their jails. Monsieur better not hear that! Well, I'm probably too stupid to understand their politics."

One o'clock: the bell rings

"It's for me. Oh, I almost forgot—I finally get to say 'Lunch is served, Madame.' It's only for important occasions. This is no time to muff it. Meanwhile, Germaine, take in the platter of charcuterie and put it on the sideboard. Let's go."

1:15

"We're on our way. They're all comfortably settled down in their chairs. Monsieur Doriot seems to be in good form. My Alice is really beautiful between her two Germans. She seems to be to their liking. The one on her right has put on his monocle—the older one, that must be the colonel. He speaks French very well. The other one too, on her left—young and distinguished-looking. The third one looks like a baby. He doesn't say much, but his eyes were like saucers taking in the glasses and the gold plates. He almost didn't dare put his hands on the embroidered tablecloth."

"Are they eating?"

"Lord, that's what they're here for! Monsieur is playing wine steward, and loving it. He'll be able to talk about his cellar and tell stories about all his wines. They don't have anything like *that* where they come from."

1:45

"Operation Fish successfully carried out. Monsieur is very proud of his jellied hake. They've polished off the five bottles of Alsace, they're starting in on the Sancerre. Very relaxed atmosphere. Monsieur Doriot asked me to touch glasses with him—he's so funny! Right now the conversation is about Monsieur's pig. In Germany, they're supposed to be fatter. Monsieur is *very* surprised."

"The little man downstairs knocked back *his* bottle of Alsace without any trouble. He's working on the chicken."

"Thanks for reminding me. It's like a wedding party today. Send in the truffled fowl! Specialty of the house! Help me carve these little things. Tell me, Germaine, don't you think people around here are going to talk?"

"I don't like it. We didn't care for them in our part of the country. Marshal Pétain, that's different. Never a word said against him. But Marshal Pétain—he doesn't invite Germans home, does he?"

"I don't know. Anyway, it's none of our business, poor little Germaine. We have our bosses, and we'd better think the way they do or get out, right? Watch it! You're dropping the drumstick. Never mind, there's the bell—you'd better come and give me a hand."

2:15

"So, did you take a look at the festive board? My chicken has them licking their fingers, 'literally and figuratively,' as they used to say in school. And how about the big chief? He ate one all by himself."

"Well, a man his size . . ."

"I'll say—big as a barrel! Even in here you can still hear him. They're only at the Clos-Vougeot, but they're warming up. Watch out for the Chambertin!

"Doriot making a speech—that was something. I went once, in Lyons, before the war. It was really worth it. Thousands of people. The party was getting talked about, it was starting to move. And real people came to listen, not just the rich ones. I never understood it all, just that he wanted a better life for the workers, for the little people, you know, like us. But now, with the war, what's it add up to, all of that? I don't get it. It's fine flirting with the Krauts, but then what if it all falls apart, and their colonels and counts and so forth say to hell with them, then we'll be sitting pretty! Well, thank heaven for Marshal Pétain. Poor man—he's certainly earning his retirement, isn't he?"

Bell

"Meanwhile, this crowd isn't having any supply problems. All right, all right. Get the lamb ready."

Three o'clock

"Seems they haven't eaten a leg of lamb this good since they've been in France. Doesn't that make us happy! She's hardly eaten at all, my little Alice. Doesn't stop talking with her admirers. Listen, is that the children?"

"No, they're upstairs playing ping-pong with Michel. It's only Jean. He's downstairs having a talk with that young soldier."

"Naturally. He never misses a chance to practice his German. Everything's interesting when you're his age. You should see him when his father's telling stories—can't keep his eyes off him. There are lots more things he'd like to know, that boy. But his father doesn't want him getting mixed up in politics. How's the driver doing?"

"Cheese, and one bottle of Chambertin. He drank it like pop."

"The Wehrmacht is going to have quite a trip home tonight."

"Whew! Dessert, at last. Madame said she would pass the liqueurs. As for Monsieur, he's telling them the history of the last war. I might have known. Albert isn't too amused, but the big chief is doubled over. You know, he's got to that part where he's in the trench about to fall asleep from exhaustion. Then a shell suddenly wakes him up, it's a miracle, he's still alive, under a pile of corpses—"

"What are the *Herren* going to say?"

"Don't worry. They're going to pay homage to the French soldier and then they'll drink a toast in memory of the Great War . . . Come on, we'll clear the dining room. There isn't a bottle left. Their German friends can certainly drink. —Did you see? The little soldier's playing ping-pong with Jean. And Michel's refereeing! He'll have a lot to tell his Polish friends."

It was a warm evening in July. The two black cars drive off under a pink sky. Lined up on the porch, the French family waves its guests good-bye. Alice, her eyelashes blinking, with a prompt gesture removes her ruby flowerets; they leave red marks on her tender earlobes. She shivers. With her little girl trotting behind her, she slowly climbs the white marble stairs.

The next day, Albert telephoned his father to thank him and to tell him that everything had gone just as Doriot hoped it would. Alice received a huge sheaf of flowers, which she arranged with indifference in the large Sèvres vase in the drawing room. No one ever heard German spoken at The Thistles again.

THE BLUE SHIRTS

It's the bluish-gray dawn of August 8, 1943, in Paris. He hasn't had much rest, but his speech for the afternoon's big rally is ready. He marches his large frame up and down the room, into which thin warm sunlight is trickling. His LFV uniform has been hanging on the back of an armchair ever since his return from the eastern front. Outside, the disturbing early morning quiet of empty streets fills a sleeping, joyless city.

In the bathroom he blows his nose and splashes his face with cold water. He shakes himself. In his undershirt, already fitted with his suspenders, he shaves. His eyes are wide-awake behind the two disks of his black-rimmed glasses. A cigarette between his lips, he looks at himself in the flawed mirror.

In a while they'll be here, in the capital of occupied France. They are gathering from all the provinces to hear their chief. They'll have come by the thousand—my Blue Shirts, my "French Guards," my party's police force.

He wipes his ample cheeks with a honeycomb towel and straightens up. He cups his hands and throws water over his thick hair, which he combs into straight, flat furrows. He lowers his suspenders, slips on a short-sleeved shirt, replaces the suspenders.

Soon his Blue Shirts will be there by the thousand. Marching in step with raised arms, they will parade in front of their chief in his tight-fitting *LFV-Kostüm*.

He puts on a brown jacket, picks up the uniform and tosses it into a canvas bag. He'll get into it just before making his entrance. He slams the door and goes down into the sunny Paris streets, now coming to life.

Lines of long-faced housewives in print dresses are already stretching out in front of closed shops. At the party headquarters on Rue des Pyramides, the regional delegates wait for their chief. A radiant summer day begins.

Four thousand Frenchmen have assembled in the Vélodrome d'Hiver. They fan themselves with newspapers and with the leaflets handed to them at the door by the FPP Youth.

Exactly a year, a summer ago, they had been twelve thousand strong in the Vélodrome d'Hiver. They were hot. The same Blue Shirts had watched the yellow Stars of David as they trooped in. A year, already. Since then, the "Vel'd'Hiv" has been cleaned up. No trace remains of the damage done by the Stars of David, or of the filth, urine, and blood. It has been disinfected. Oceans of bleach have been poured onto the tiers of the Vel'd'Hiv so that French-men could come and sit there without being soiled.

Today a lofty rostrum has been erected and draped in black. Behind it, an immense black screen slashed with a double *S* and flanked by two monumental blood-red hangings.

The great volunteer, the one who was the first to go, the French officer, the soldier from the frontiers of the east appears, a little uncomfortable in his tight, handsome uniform. For when he re-turned from the front, great was his hunger, and great his thirst. (On warm Paris evenings, you can easily find friendly restaurants where it's pleasant to sit back and recount the exploits of the Wehr-macht.) His arm stretched out, his garrison belt pulled tight, he presents his broad, soberly decorated breast to the crowd. Cheers shake the glass vault. To unshackle his powerful lungs, he snaps open the top two buttons of his blouse with precision. The two *S*s seem to flash from his own brow. To the left, at the foot of the rostrum, in the shadow of the swastika, is Albert.

The *französischer Führer* is making a long speech. He is telling them, Look, I am a soldier, I have returned and I shall go back: fol-low me. He is telling them, Nothing else matters but this combat. The blood we shed in the east will open the gateways of Europe to us. He is telling them, The Wehrmacht has sustained military setbacks, it's true, but the Red Army cannot possibly hold out.

Exactly a year, a summer ago, they were packed, streaming with sweat, under the scorching glass roof and along the airless stands of the Vel'd'Hiv. No one spoke to them. No one explained to them. There was no one on the speaker's platform. At the entrances, they were prevented from leaving. After a week, the Blue Shirts helped the police push them into trucks and later railroad cars. Men to one side, women to the other, the children by themselves.

Since then, the Vel'd'Hiv has been aired out, so that Frenchmen could come and spend sunny afternoons there without being troubled by the smells of excrement and death that still hung under the glass roof after the Stars of David had left.

When the great meeting of this eighth of August has disbanded, twenty-five hundred Blue Shirts will parade behind their flags in front of their chief. Grouped by provinces they march toward the Arc de Triomphe: a fine parade of blue through an indifferent and silent city.

> *Order of the Day: Entry of the French Guards into Paris*
> The date of August 8 may now be numbered among the great days of our party. Every possible obstacle barred our path. Each was surmounted in masterly fashion. The FPP has given the people of Paris and all France new proof of its discipline, its determination, and its strength. The absolute order and calm that prevailed throughout these gatherings are a sign of the political maturity of our great party. From the Arc de Triomphe to Rue des Pyramides, more than one hundred thousand Parisians saluted our glorious flags. Men of the French Guards, men and women of the party, I am pleased with you. Onward to new battles against bolshevism and against our country's enemies. France will live. FPP will triumph!
>
> JACQUES DORIOT

A few days later, having left his instructions with his faithful subordinates, he set out once more on the roads to the east.

On a gray September morning, the Citroën stops in front of a fashionable building on Avenue Rodin. Albert has no time. He drops off his family with their suitcases and packages. He points to the seventh-floor apartment and hands Juliette the keys.

"I'm late. Go ahead and move in. I'll be there for dinner. The concierges know you're coming, they'll give you a hand."

"Here we go again," Juliette mutters. "Don't be upset, Madame. Come on, children. Let's go visit your new château."

They have seen almost nothing of Paris. Bicycle hurries after bicycle down great empty thoroughfares. On the sidewalks, scowling pedestrians ignore the black car full of curious eyes that brushes past them in the dull morning rain.

The elevator fascinates these children from the provinces who have never lived on an upper floor. They emerge on an austere landing with red carpeting and a dying potted plant. By working a fancy little brass handle, they sound a faint bell. Her heart beating fast, Alice turns the key in the lock and pushes the door open.

The troop of children sends the dust flying. Juliette stands paralyzed on the threshold, gazing at all the work "we'll have to do ourselves, Madame." The resonant floor of the seven-room apartment is strewn with crates, cartons, trunks, rolled-up rugs, and furniture that has been set down at random. Nothing has been moved since it arrived from Lyons. Large bare windows cast a wan light on the accumulated disorder. Several telephones have been left on the floor with their wires tangled. Unemptied ashtrays are scattered here and there. Alice identifies the bedroom by the unmade bed where Albert must have spent his brief nights. The ground is littered with cups containing stagnant residues of coffee. Dirty laundry is stacked in one corner, empty bottles in another. Ahead of her, a perspective of glass doors gradually opens into the larger, circular living room. It is furnished with one huge, draped object. Alice rushes over to it and lifts up the covering. There it is: the gleaming, black, sumptuous Steinway. She hesitantly opens the keyboard. A folded note falls to the floor. She picks it up and unfolds it.

"For you. So that you'll be less lonely. I love you. A."

In the gray Paris morning of 1943, with her children lined up at the end of the Steinway and the little girl sitting on the dust-silvered black cover where Jean has set her and now keeps her from beating her feet, Alice, thinking of Alsace, timidly strikes up her favorite Chopin waltz.

Swathed in a long blue apron, Juliette waits in the doorway for the waltz to end.

"And now, children, we have work to do. If you want to eat and sleep tonight in a place that doesn't look like a railroad station, you have to give me a hand."

"Yes, my darlings, let's give Father a surprise this evening. We'll un-pack everything and put it away and make ourselves a new home."

It was a cheerful day, and no warning siren interrupted it. The children were like industrious dwarfs, laughing as they skidded down the corridors with the little girl behind them, giggling under a shower of packing shavings, or whimpering to them in turn, ill at ease in this confining house without garden or foliage. Juliette dusted, polished, swept, and never stopped singing. Alice uttered kindly orders or kept silently busy, gliding across the floors, filling closets, putting away her little cups, her little jars, her china, her lace. Answering the telephone, maybe that's him, no, it's her sister wanting to know if everything is all right, there's nothing you need? We'll come by one of these days and give you a hug. Yes, there are frequent alerts in Suresnes but so far, no damage. You know where the nearest shelter is? Good. See you soon.

In very little time the furniture was arranged, the rugs unrolled, and most of the curtains hung. The apartment was emptier than ever. We'll get used to it, Madame.

At eight o'clock, the children are bathed and combed. Alice gets into a clean dress and puts on perfume. The table is set in the middle of the pretentious dining room. The telephone rings.

"Good evening, sweetheart, how far along are you?"

"Everything's fine. We're waiting for you."

"That's just it. I'm busy for dinner. Don't be sad—it's important. I can't get out of it. I won't be home late."

"The children will be disappointed. Good-bye."

Amid curfews, ruined dinners, alerts, and outings in the park, life on Avenue Rodin goes on for a few months much as it had elsewhere, much as it always had. Alice feels anguish rising in her, it feels as though it would burst from her lips, but she keeps her peace. She clings to the dark daily round of these final months of '43, in an empty, horrifying Paris whose hostile reaches she has no desire to know. She does not leave her zone of well-to-do houses: Rue de la Tour, Rue de la Pompe, Ranelagh, Muette. Behind closed doors, she paces through rooms and corridors, rarely touching the keyboard of her Steinway grand, thumbing through the yellowing scores her mother used to play from in other times.

You are in Paris; he is in Paris; you're alone. He is no more present in Paris than in Lyons. Every day his place is set, every day Juliette reheats the meal, and at last you say, let's eat. As you smoke your Camels, both elbows on the table, you concoct a smile; and your gaze brushes past the children's heads to meet your reflection in the panes of the dining-room door. As for him, he has forgotten you between the time he disappears down the stairs in the morning (I'll be home for lunch!) and noon, when he never appears. He takes all his meals at the Hôtel du Louvre.

At night, you listen for the elevator. You pretend to be asleep when he lies down beside you. He turns off the light. You listen to his breathing for a long time before sinking into sluggish dreams.

You're in Paris, and you're bored. With the tips of your lacquered nails you caress the silk or crepe dresses that fill your closets. You try them on in secret, and your reflection twirls in the bedroom mirror. Not once has he asked you to go out with him. You hate Paris.

You're afraid. Sleek and sad, you raise your children and protect them from the nightmare: but can't you see what's happening? And yet you know about the war—out there. Is it possible that a luxurious seventh-floor apartment has replaced the watercolor hues of your garden in Lyons without changing your outlook? After Chemin des Cerisiers comes fashionable Avenue Rodin, and you're still the same anxious, ignorant woman clinging to your unflinching expectation and love. While the world collapses and Allied planes drone overhead, your smooth white fingers still stroke the shiny keys of your dream piano: can't you hear what's happening?

Juliette is grumbling. These huge rooms, all these panes to polish. The house was different, with its nooks and crannies; it was more human.

And these endless corridors from the service entrance to the back stairs! At the beginning it never occurred to her to use them, but then one day on the red carpeting a Madame de Something-or-other had a few words with her. All right, no point in attracting attention, I agree—I'll risk my life in their death trap for the faithful servants of fine families!

And shopping, what a chore! The glorious summer at Champagne, where you only had to bend over to pick up a chicken or a head of lettuce, had made her forget the long lines in Lyons. It's all very well to be privileged and have two or three sets of ration books, you still wait for hours.

And Monsieur Albert—more and more thin and irritable, dashing in and out, telephoning ten times a day to give orders and then cancel them, warning us about air raids that don't happen: and when there is one, he's never there. Will it all end some day?

While waiting for it all to end, she takes the children to the park. It's a stretch of countryside like any other—if you have nothing better. Anne and Paul perched on their roller skates and the little girl in her perambulator are pretty, well-mannered children in gray overcoats and white shoes.

In the evening, the lights go out early. The boys have turned their beds into underground caverns so that they can read by flashlight without as much as a glow showing through the sheets.

Sometimes, at night, a long ascending wail rises over the city. You have to move fast. Alice and Juliette meet by the door to make sure all the children are there; the little girl has been hastily wrapped up in a blanket. On the stairs, they join a procession of disheveled, whispering figures in bathrobes, all hurrying toward the cellars. There the blind herd crowds under dark vaults and waits—often for a long time—for the alert to end.

For months, Juliette has been dragging a suitcase downstairs with her. It soon made her conspicuous. It was not a large suitcase, but it seemed to weigh a ton, and Juliette carried it so unwillingly that you could notice no one else. There were any number of those who took with them a precious box or a mysterious packet that they clutched to their bosom, or a dog, or a canary in a cage; but the suitcase had people talking. Among the concierges in the neighborhood, rumor had it that the maid was toting her master's gold ingots. And where do you suppose he got them . . . ?

It was his stamp collection. Albert, who had started it when he was a child, had entrusted it to Juliette: it's my most precious possession, the rest can burn. The stamps were taken to all the cellars in the neighborhood and down many an uncertain path. They were later sold for a song.

Jean rarely took part in these nocturnal forays. Since his arrival in Paris, in spite of his father's reluctance, he had become more and more enthralled by the events of the time. He had been an avid Scout. Now, at sixteen, he wanted to get into the fight, do something useful, and no longer be treated like a child. Albert finally allowed him to join the FPP Youth, who helped in clearing the rubble after the bombings. (He refused, however, to let him take a propaganda course.)

Jean became a first-aid worker. He would put on his armband and race away to smoking ruins in distant Paris suburbs. Alice did not oppose this vocation. She waited, trembling, until morning, when he would return home exhausted.

He was very gentle and had great admiration for his father. If he tended the wounded, there might be fewer of them. If he risked his life in the flames, other lives might be saved. And if his father showed him a path to follow, it was surely the only one that might lead somewhere.

Paris '44. The final summer. It's almost time for the fireworks. The party's industrious ants go on digging obscure passageways, laying paths, and raising shelters in the midst of the ruins. The June 6 landing does nothing to diminish their ardor. Always ready for the fray, these knights in search of crusades extend their horizon to include stricken Normandy. Burning mills, your saviors are coming, the Blue Shirts have taken the offensive! After the eastern front, the warriors turn to new battlefields: Western front, we are here!

No later than June 15, the indefatigable chief has submitted to Abetz and the SS staff a request for assignment to the Normandy front. He wishes to "see what measures the French government is taking with regard to the refugees assembled behind our lines." During the days following the invasion, they have fled by the thousand from their bombarded towns and villages along roads that are perpetually being strafed. The FPP is duty bound to assist these unfortunates who, surrounded by panic and death, are not liable to look favorably on the liberators from across the Channel.

On Rue des Pyramides, an information bureau has been opened where refugees can consult lists of victims and get in touch with their families. The reports from the WCIA—the Workers' Committee for Immediate Aid, set up by the FPP a year earlier—spell disaster: administrative breakdown, plundering, and acts of violence, politically motivated and otherwise.

Warned by Abetz, Monsieur Laval categorically refuses to sanction Doriot's planned trip.

So Normandy is now a war zone? So it's completely controlled by the Wehrmacht? Don't let that stop anyone! The chief asks his faithful Albert to make use of his connections at OKW. Albert does so at once, and the answer is not long in coming. "It is not within the competence of the Wehrmacht to authorize Monsieur Doriot to visit the Normandy front as a political leader. On the other hand, the Wehrmacht is able to authorize the visit of LFV Lieutenant Doriot to the western front, where the field division staffs will receive him with pleasure."

During the day of June 29, Doriot tells me, "Make sure you're free for dinner this evening. We have to talk." He has given me no explanation. He rarely does.

Arriving at the Tao Bar restaurant on Rue Gaillon, where the owner is a party member, the chief says to me, "I've asked a few of our comrades to dine with us." I realize that he is setting the stage and will soon be manipulating his puppets, as he is so fond of doing. At the time, my relations with the political committee were very bad. I no longer attended its meetings because of a disagreement with B. and C., two of the comrades present. They had been the initiators of the Action Groups.

Doriot immediately starts discussing his trip to Normandy, scheduled for July 1. He asks C. questions about our total strength in the five departments that comprise the war zone. C., who is often overoptimistic in his reports, cites impossibly high figures. I express my doubts and in passing point out that everything has been disrupted by the bombardments.

The discussion soon becomes acrimonious and I lose patience.

"I imagine the chief would like to know what forces and which party officials he can count on during his trip. By giving him assurances that you know are unfounded, I feel you're putting him in a disagreeable position with the Germans who'll be escorting him."

Doriot then takes me to task. Once again he reproaches me for systematically criticizing whatever my comrades do. The disagreement is music to my friends' ears. The discussion continues without me.

Doriot explains how the party must make an exceptional effort in Normandy to compensate for the government's deficiencies, especially in the realm of social welfare.

"On my return, I'll give you detailed instructions, but right now you must alert your sections and mobilize all the forces we still have on the spot."

As we leave, Doriot says to me, "I'll drive you home." He has no sooner climbed into his car than he starts berating me.

"You'll never change. Are you trying to please them by forcing me to say unpleasant things to you?" Then, casting an irate glance at me, he says nothing for a few seconds.

"All right, it's settled. You're taking charge of Normandy. I suppose that if you made such a fuss, it's because your personnel is in good shape. Put them on immediate alert so that we can send them into action in a fortnight. Till then, not a word, not to anybody. Just let the people you're sure of know enough to get your work done while you're away."

"Away?"

"You're coming with me to Normandy. Do what needs to be done about your papers right away. We're leaving the day after tomorrow."

Next morning I went to OKW to obtain the permits, only to be reminded that no civilian could be authorized by the Wehrmacht to enter the war zone. The matter thus appeared to be settled, but Doriot did not see it that way. He told Count K., who had delivered the message, "I have the right to be accompanied by an aide-de-camp, and that will be Albert."

K. responded, "How can a lieutenant have a captain as aide-de-camp!"

"If that's the only problem, he can be a second lieutenant for a change."

I intervened, "If it's a question of disguise, I don't care what insignia I wear. But the disguise must be complete."

It was decided that papers would be issued to Second Lieutenant Paul D.

You did it! You said, Chief, I'm your man. We're off to Normandy, the divisional staffs are waiting for us. You went to the headquarters of the Wehrmacht and tried on your new outfit. Your friend Count

K. took your measurements: I've got what you need, don't move. He came back with a beautiful, brand new uniform, made to order, nothing to alter besides the little tricolor shield with the word *France* across the top. (My wife will sew it on, don't waste your time on that.) You came home. Children, come see Father's pretty new clothes! You looked at yourself in the mirror from the back, in profile, and facing front. Alice watched you pensively. You said to her, Allow me to introduce Paul D. She couldn't believe her ears—poor Paul, her mother's cousin, the missionary in Martinique. If that servant of God could see himself in this getup! She giggled nervously.

You did it. You were proud to be a captain, you were a patriot, you were your father's son, and you went through with it. For France! You became second lieutenant and standard-bearer to Big Jacques and put on your LFV uniform. On the brink of universal disaster, you put on fancy dress. You scurry off under the bombs to spread the true word of the dying FPP. You preach in the Norman desert. You indoctrinate startled families and explain to them that Our Father Doriot wishes their salvation, while France's Allies are out for their blood.

Albert, deck yourself out, help me onto Rocinante, and together we'll wheel our steeds through the Norman thickets in quest of our faithful blue soldiers. Don't listen to the storm that's sweeping the world, I'm naming you Commissar! There is none but you, Albert, you and your men, to save what is left of our fair country. I'm giving you Normandy, soon they'll give me France. Because they're going to win this war. They're the strongest.

You believed him. When you're just a small drop in the ocean of mud flooding the earth, when everything is toppling, your head is high, your heart is light, you put on fancy dress! You kiss your wife good-bye, and you pat your children's heads. If Paris burns, go down to the cellar, I won't be back for dinner.

You did it.

DEPARTURE

Albert came back from Normandy on July 14. Came back—at a time when, having no word from him, she was imagining the worst. On this holiday evening, one with no sound of dancing, she has stretched out on the living-room couch. The apartment is asleep. Her gaze follows the arabesques of her glowing cigarette tip or stares into the darkness. She hears the lock and runs into the hall, scarcely having to feel her way in the dark, the wide pleats of her satin dressing gown rustling about her.

In the churchly red glow of a night-light, she sees them come in: two dead-weary LFV officers dragging their feet. Albert embraces her. With a tired smile, Doriot takes her delicate hand and holds it for a few seconds between his two broad palms. She leads them into the smaller living room and in the shelter of the thick, dark yellow velvet curtains, silently gives each of them a drink.

"Dear Alice, don't think we feel as dejected as we look! Just tired out by two weeks under fire. But we have great things planned."

She has never seen Doriot so calm, never heard him speak so softly. She smiles, lights two candles, and sits down on the edge of a chair, waiting for Albert to tell her: Sweetheart, we have to talk, you must be tired, I'll be right in.

But to her great surprise the two men have begun conversing in hushed voices, as if picking up an interrupted dialogue. They pay no attention to her, or rather—so it seems to her as the night wears on—they are soothed by her silent, scented presence. She doesn't move. She smokes, amazed to be hearing so much, hanging on to the words of these two conspirators gone astray in a fashionable living room.

"If you'd had enough time ahead of you—if the front was substantial enough to give you a few sure months—you could have developed activity on broad social lines, you could have brought in trained members under you from all over France and built up a solid organization."

"But you saw—the German defenses are weak, they haven't any depth. There's the possibility of an early Allied breakthrough. We have to act fast."

". . . you could have convinced your men that the party had to be purged and openly realigned with the non-Communist resistance forces. Even—I know it's a big step—even if this meant fighting the Germans."

"But to do all that, we needed time, and we aren't going to get it. Can the Germans still win the war? And is our policy of 'presence' still necessary?"

"The main question is: is their policy being effectively carried out by Marshal Pétain and Laval? The best thing would have been to talk it over with them. But how can you trust Laval when he tells Abetz everything? And how can you explain things to the Marshal without everyone in the Hôtel du Parc knowing about it?"

"But if their talk of a secret weapon is true, chief, they can still do a lot of damage—and if they can't win the war, at least secure a negotiated peace."

"In which case we must stay on the scene. Because neither Laval nor Marshal Pétain will have enough authority to parley with the Germans, and in the other camp I don't think Giraud's or de Gaulle's prestige is great enough."

"If there are negotiations, does that mean war with Russia? And when?"

"That's the crucial point. If that war is postponed, there will be a Communist uprising and de Gaulle will be thrown out. Giraud's the one to back against the Communists. And for the FPP to do that, he has to take a stand. That's where your work is vital."

"And if Germany loses the war?"

"Your operation would be even more useful. But the Communists are going to infiltrate everywhere, thanks to the opportunities de Gaulle has given them; and they'll be out to destroy us. They'll accuse everyone of treason."

The candle flames barely waver. Ice cubes clink in the glasses. For a long while they remain silent, in the black Paris night. She dares not uncross her damp legs under the satin dressing gown. In his exhaustion, Doriot seems to be subsiding into his chair. Behind the glasses, his eyelids close. Albert looks at her through a mist: There you are—what can you understand, and what does it matter now?

In a whisper, watching the glass revolving in his hand, his voice hoarse, Doriot resumes: "I'm afraid we made a bad mistake. In November '42 we should have gone right over to Giraud. But how could one imagine that Pétain would let Laval make so many blunders? Laval couldn't stop the workers being sent to Germany, and so the Maquis got established. This is now the Communist Party's greatest asset. In addition, it has turned a large segment of the French people against our policy. In social matters, the government has never known what stand to take. Laval hasn't ever understood the first thing about fighting the Communists. He thinks they can be blocked by backstage maneuvering. All that is going to hurt—really hurt. If the Germans retreat, the Communists will be in charge. De Gaulle too made the mistake of thinking you could do business with them. They'll eat him up. The only thing to do is hope the Anglo-Americans become aware in time of the Bolshevik menace, and that after escorting the Germans home, they'll enlist them as soldiers for Europe. On the other hand, if they make the mistake of wiping out Germany completely and letting the Russians win, then all Europe will be Bolshevized."

He stood up in the smoky room as if emerging from a dream and held out his arms to Alice.

"My friends, I'm leaving. You need to rest."

After seeing him out, Albert came back and took his wife in his arms.

"I have a lot of work ahead of me. You'd all be better off in the country. I'll drive you out to The Thistles tomorrow."

And then, in the middle of this final summer, everything went very fast. The unsuccessful attempt of July 20 on Hitler's life threw the services of the Wehrmacht into confusion. Colonel R., involved in the plot, was relieved of his duties.

Count K. stayed on. Albert kept stubbornly pressing him to authorize his illusory activities in the west. He counseled prudence and moderation: the Wehrmacht, disloyal to Hitler, was being destroyed by Himmler and his SS, who were brutally taking control of the occupation.

The Americans were advancing in Normandy. Unable to keep still, Albert put on his LFV uniform and once again visited the war zone. But on August 8, he abruptly returned from the front with American shells exploding at his heels. Farewell, Normandy. Are we losing France?

On August 9, Doriot summoned his lieutenants to review the situation with them.

"We're entering a new phase that leaves us no room for choice. We must start urgently preparing to combat an armed Communist uprising. When it breaks out, as it cannot fail to do once the Germans have left, we shall while we fight extend a hand to all those who rise up to resist, whatever their background.

"There's no question of staying in Paris. Our security cannot be guaranteed here. The central organs of the party will withdraw to the east. I shall immediately begin discussions with a view to installing new headquarters in either Strasbourg or Metz. Our principal officials must bring their families with them: they must not be left as hostages in Communist hands. For the time being I have ordered our active members to remain in their zones. They need only take certain precautions in the days following the liberation. If they have followed my instructions to the letter and haven't engaged in any 'direct' collaboration, they won't be in danger.

"As for you, Albert, set up whatever contacts your section needs, and, above all, get ready to have your records shipped out. They must be saved at all costs. Your family should be ready to leave the moment the signal is given."

Albert sees his chief again the next day. They have a heated argument.

"I've had my records collected and packed, and I've found trucks and gas. My own intention is to stay here."

"I hope you're joking."

"Listen: I have nothing to be ashamed of. All I have to do is survive the disturbances that will follow the liberation for a few days. If there's a Communist uprising, I'll round up our comrades and persuade them to form a union with all the other Frenchmen who are opposed to a Red dictatorship. And if there's no uprising, I'll hide out for whatever time is necessary. If I'm arrested, I'll know how to explain my actions without implicating anyone else. I solemnly swear it."

Doriot cannot believe his ears. He loses his temper.

"You're out of your mind. In the first place, I need you, and your duty is to the party. Aside from that, they'll find you through your family and use you as a hostage. Then we'd be sitting pretty— paralyzed, on account of you! Come on, get a hold of yourself. There's only one solution for you: to *leave*. And if you care about your family's safety, you'll take them with you."

"My family has nothing to do with this. They've never been mixed up in my political activity in any way."

"You poor fool, you're losing your mind. Your family's crime will be bearing your name."

For the last few days, Grandfather had been very nervous. He shut himself into his office and listened to the radio.

"If our own future was clear," he told Alice, "how excited I'd be by this Allied drive on Paris! They aren't far away. You'll see, they'll be here any day. Alice, if I were thirty years younger, and if I hadn't made such a mistake, I wouldn't be afraid of their arriving, these liberators of ours!"

She lowered her eyes, cold inside, and did not move, as if the better to listen to her father-in-law's remarks. He was ordinarily little given to speaking his thoughts.

"They went too far. I shouldn't have kept so quiet. What good would it have done? Nothing could hold him down. Alice, you'd better be prepared. Anything can happen now."

On the morning of August 13, the Citroën 11 glides past the iron fence of The Thistles. Albert leaps out of the car and kisses his mother and his wife. Anne won't let go of his neck. I clutch my mother's hand. Jean watches him silently. And Juliette comes running up, smelling disaster.

"Don't ask questions. We're going back to Paris. Hurry, the roads aren't too safe."

Louis asks him to explain.

"Things are happening fast. The party headquarters is moving to the east. I can't be separated from Alice and the children."

"You poor man, where are you taking them?"

"We're falling back on Nancy."

"And you're abandoning us!"

"Father, I'm very worried about leaving you here. But it would be even crazier for all ten of us to take to the road. So what can we do? Let's try not to be too pessimistic."

Louis shakes his head disapprovingly, as he has done for the past eight years. His glance reveals neither anxiety nor mistrust; rather, a certain weariness. He mutely takes his son by the shoulders.

"Come, have a drink."

"Juliette, Alice: the suitcases must be ready in half an hour. Bring only the bare minimum."

Louis lowers his head. He tells himself that he will load his gun, wall up the wine cellar, and take down the photograph of Marshal Pétain. Then he will put on his best suit and wait for them. Today or tomorrow, they will surely come and jeer at him—the patriarch of the "château," the old man who had Germans as guests in his house.

The parting is heartrending but brief: unnecessary emotions are not appreciated in the family. Albert will never see his mother again. She stands there—small, submissive, and ignorant—watching her beloved children drive away toward Paris and the blazing roads to the east. She waves her embroidered handkerchief, smiling tremulously between one tear and the next.

I'm sitting on Mother's lap. Her silk dress will be wrinkled. She thinks she has forgotten her jersey and her pearl necklace on the table in the bathroom. She furtively dreams of a bomb that would blow up the whole carful.

At Avenue Rodin, on August 16, everything is in an uproar. Since coming back from The Thistles, they have slept either in the cellar or out of their suitcases. Father had said, "Pack your bags"—they're already packed—"we're leaving tonight. Take as little as possible. We're going to Nancy." At noon he shouts, "Unpack your bags, we're not leaving." Weary of rushing around, Mother sits down at the piano, opens the keyboard, and silently strokes the dusty keys. Juliette, fed up, takes me in her arms and starts muttering. They'll never make up their minds. It's no fun for me, either, having to sneak out of Paris. Monsieur has gone haywire. Madame doesn't want it to show but she's getting hysterical. The children won't let go of my apron strings . . .

At four in the afternoon, in the heavy, threatening Paris heat, Albert telephones: "I'm on my way, don't anyone go out." He hangs up. Alice doesn't know any more—this isn't the first time. She slips into her silk stockings, brushes her hair, and puts on her suit of navy-blue rep with the white daisies.

"Juliette, get the children dressed."

"It's very hot, Madame."

"We're leaving this evening. The night may be chilly."

After buttoning me into my coat of fine tan serge, Juliette dumps me on the little mauve velvet couch in the living room. Be a nice girl, here's a piece of candy, we're waiting for Father. I am a nice girl. Anne is clutching to her bosom a doll and its suitcase full of clothes, which I'm dying to yank out of her hands. Paul jumps around annoyingly, fidgeting, bursting with impatience: "We're leaving! Our car will zoom into the east through curtains of fire, and we'll jump into ditches to get away from the bombs—" Jean paces the hallway, lost in thought. He is waiting for his father.

"Children, this is serious. It's no time for giggling or day-dreaming."

He's there when evening falls. His face is tense. He is sweating; he takes out his handkerchief. He dashes to the ringing telephone. He learns that the two cars the party had put at his disposal have disappeared. There are still the trucks loaded with archives and a few party stalwarts. He has to leave tonight. Count K. urgently recommends it.

Sitting on the flowered armchair in the hall, I look at my white bootees and suck my thumb. Father paces the floor, in one door and out another, smoking cigarette after cigarette, going from the hall to the living room, from the living room to the dining room. Mother draws long puffs from her cigarette holder and looks at him as he walks by. She sits with crossed legs on the living-room sofa, swinging one foot back and forth over the rug. He avoids her eyes. He stops, shakes his head, starts off again, talks to himself: ". . . get you all involved! It's insane. Stole both cars! Oh, these fine French-men, trying to see who can be first off the ship! I could find other cars. No, it's an omen."

He kneels down in front of Mother and takes her hands in his. The green eyes reveal nothing.

"Listen to me. I've made up my mind. I'm leaving alone. It's too dangerous."

"Whatever you want."

He stands up. Mother looks at me and smiles. He runs to the telephone and calls our Uncle Pierre in Suresnes: the situation is serious, I can't stay, I'm leaving them with you, I'm entrusting them to you—take them under your wing, take them under your roof. When things calm down, I'll be back to straighten matters out. Good-bye and thanks.

Now everyone is crying. Soon it was time for departure—only for a while, no choice, the party (the records, the chief, the files, the Communists, the alerts, the resistance), be careful (not a word, innocence), God bless you. Alice and Albert embrace. He is leaving yes I'm leaving, she is staying behind yes I'm staying behind, you'll come back, yes of course I will don't say such things. Juliette lays her left arm on Alice's shoulder and her right arm on Albert's: you're leaving, and we're staying. I'll be here with you, Madame.

Jean goes up to his father and firmly tells him, "Father, you're taking me with you."

The green eyes are flooded. Jean—my little Jean! She could shout out, Jean, don't do it! That time is past. She no longer knows how to beseech or demand. She obeys.

She watches them go off, the slender boy following the man. She hasn't moved. She hasn't fallen down. She didn't want him to leave—she didn't, she didn't.

We too set out on a journey: we had to cross the Bois de Boulogne (our very own park) on that night of August 16. No night for a child to be out. A sputtering of gunfire: in the greenwood blood is shed. In their flight the occupying forces kill, and kill again. Dead hostages are piled up under the trees, at the turnings of pathways, behind the cool waterfall.

Good Uncle Pierre, our savior, arrived very quickly. He crossed the park on a bicycle, towing a little trailer for our luggage. He is tall, calm, and smiling.

"Greetings to my refugees. Yes, Alice; Alice, I know. Don't worry. You can tell me everything later. Come on now, kids. All aboard for the ride around the pond."

Mother and Juliette scarcely have time to gather up a few essential things—the silver, the stamps; and sheets, tablecloths, dish towels, curios, odds and ends of the most disparate kind, everything small and easily accessible to hand or eye before the exodus.

"Don't take too much. It's not wise to hang around this neighborhood tonight. I'll come in a few days and do some looting. You can give me a list."

What was saved that night by the efforts of two compulsive women provided for posterity fragments for a museum of the pre-Liberation period. For years afterward, I heard magic pronouncements: "Don't break the Lalique vase—your father gave it to me for our tenth wedding anniversary, it's from Avenue Rodin," or: "You see, Madame, I was right—we're still using the napkins from Avenue Rodin."

I had only vague memories of that apartment. Later, I reconstructed it out of bits of incredible stories I heard told about it. One evening in August '44, each of us had left some prized possession there, which in times of trouble would be recalled in lyrical-tragical tones. I used to imagine a great abandoned ship that had, as it sank, dragged armchairs, rare books, pianos, lace, dolls, and closets full of dresses to the bottom for all time. And we—the castaways of this huge and splendid vessel—had been left stranded on the cramped island of Suresnes.

From her doorstep, the bushy-haired concierge watches our departure with a distressed expression. As we pass by she whispers timid reassurances and genteel condolences. "Poor lady! Cheer up, you're doing the right thing by leaving. You never can tell. I could let you know if something turns up—"

Pierre interrupts her before the secret word "Suresnes" slips from imprudent lips: "Don't worry about it, I'll come by and let you know how the family's doing."

Juliette lays me in my perambulator. I'm sleeping like a lamb. Pierre leads our convoy, with Paul at his side. The other two follow Indian file, holding hands. (Hurry. Don't look back. Forget our grief, forget our name, forget tomorrow.)

At a turning near the waterfall, a high mound appears in silhouette. Curious, Pierre and Paul approach it. At the sight of the piled corpses they come back at a run. "It's nothing, ladies," Paul says. "Keep going. Things will be better on the other side of the Seine."

They crossed the wood, the wolf was elsewhere. On Rue de Bellevue in Suresnes, Mother's sister Mathilde is waiting for us: none too overjoyed to have our band of dubious exiles surge with their misfortunes into the thick of her life—her garden, her habits, and her cats. On a gossipy little suburban street, you can expect the worst when you suddenly have to take in the family of a collaborator on the run.

She asks, "Where's Jean?" Pierre says, "Shut up." On the top of the stairs in the little gray house, the two sisters fall into each other's arms. Juliette goes into the kitchen to make coffee. Mattresses are laid out on the floor. The refugees move in.

The grass is greener on the other side of the summer: Aunt Mathilde adopts the lost family. She was pregnant and tired, and Juliette would be a help to her; Alice had some money; and besides, it wouldn't last forever!

At dawn, Avenue Rodin was visited by a group of armed youths in search of traitors.

FLIGHT

Jean—Jean, my little boy, why did I bring you with me? For the rest of my life this will be my bitterest regret. Was I afraid of being alone?

A few hours before leaving, I'd had violent arguments with the chief and the leading members of the party. I pointed out certain inadmissible facts concerning the way the evacuation of the party had been organized. My reproaches were very poorly received and widened the gap that already existed between me and the FPP. I felt myself moving at ever-increasing speed away from the men who had been my comrades-in-arms since '36. Was it the feeling that I was now alone and isolated in a hostile country that made me want my son's company? Did I give in to his plea because of the confusion of farewells, flight, and tears?

Was I afraid that in my absence they would revenge themselves on him? Was I apprehensive about his reactions in case there was a Communist uprising? Didn't I yield to the pride of having this son I loved so much near me at a time that promised to be not only important but decisive? Didn't I yield as well to the joy of having his support at so black a moment, when we were obliged to look forward to exile and perhaps banishment?

Was I afraid of being alone?

August 17

Having left at four in the morning, we make our first halt at Châlons-sur-Marne and are in Nancy a day later. I took care to find transportation for my colleagues and personnel. In my opinion, we must form an indivisible unit ready to go to work the moment the chief needs us.

No farther on than Châlons, I learn that I am the only party official to entertain such a notion. The others had their papers packed in numbered crates, and there their task ended. Subordinates then took charge of the material. They are bringing it by truck and taking their own sweet time about it. As for those "in charge," they all made sure of arranging for cars in which to stow their families and personal luggage. They were next seen at Châlons for their allowance of gas. After that they disappeared.

Narrow escape from a bombing attack at Saint-Dizier; arrival in Nancy late at night. After many difficulties, I succeed in having the pre-requisitioned classrooms of a convent allocated to me, and it is there that I billet my men.

August 19

A conflict has broken out between me and the secretary-general. FPP members are streaming in from all over France and joining the group we had originally planned for. The majority of these men must have worked with the German authorities and thus engaged in the "direct collaboration" forbidden by the chief. My advice is to send them back to the Germans without further ceremony. Accepting men who only remember the party when they need it makes us accomplices of the Gestapo. Victor does not share my view. I have decided not to bother with party headquarters anymore.

I have been lucky enough to find a large house near the station in Nancy. I'm moving into it with my son and my loyal party members.

August 20

The chief has arrived in Nancy. I present my grievances to him.

"Leave Victor be—and don't lose that uncompromising attitude of yours! When the permanent party headquarters are set up, we'll proceed with whatever sorting out is necessary."

"When will I next see you?"

"I'll send a courier every other day. He'll give you your orders, you'll give him your report. I'm going to Sarrebourg, where I'm counting on Brückel's influence at Hitler's GHQ to get authorization to move into Metz or Strasbourg. Try using your own connections to make contact again with OKW."

August 22

At eleven o'clock at night I am alerted by a telephone call from the prefecture. The prefect's chief of staff comes on the line.

"The prefect wishes to see you at once for a message of the highest importance."

As my car reaches the prefecture, the barred gates open. They are expecting me. The chief of staff introduces himself as I step out of the car and leads me to the offices of the prefect. The latter receives me with exaggerated deference.

"The German authorities have asked me to inform Monsieur Doriot that Chancellor Hitler requests his presence at General Headquarters. A plane is waiting for him in Frankfurt as of midnight tonight. I have been instructed to expedite his journey by every possible means. I am furthermore required to notify the German authorities the moment I have been able to make contact with your chief."

I cannot help smiling at the fear that a single wish of Hitler inspires in the prefect.

"Sir, since my chief is for the time being no longer an officer of the LFV, it is the French statesman whom the Führer is addressing. I am not authorized to reveal where Doriot is to be found. But I shall do everything in my power to reach him as quickly as possible. I shall keep you advised."

Next day, the prefect grows impatient and calls me every two hours. I remain impassive. The fact is that the chief, whom I was able to notify at once, has told me, "I'm not under Monsieur Hitler's orders. He waited until his armies were on the run before expressing a desire to meet me. He must need us. Let him wait."

Only next day is Doriot officially informed of Hitler's invitation. The delay has allowed him to prepare his position. He reaches GHQ at a time when Déat, Darnand, de Brinon, and Marion have been cooling their heels for three days. Hitler has not wanted to receive them until all were in attendance.

August 25

Groups organized as virtual combat units have reached Nancy. They have to be seen to be believed.

First, there are Simon S.'s men, who fought against the resistance forces in the Rhône valley. Then a jubilant team of men with bags and baggage—money in bills by the tens of thousands, bundles of securities looted from banks, gold bars, and furs and jewelry displayed by these gentlemen's mistresses. One of them—their "chief"—is carrying more than two hundred million francs' worth of assets in his car.

I have an extremely violent row with Victor and warn him that in future, as long as these hoodlums are welcomed into the core of the party, it should consider me and my men as outside the FPP. I shall inform Doriot of this and go my own way.

Mathilde was three years older than Alice. The two sisters were fond of each other. They were like night and day: Alice passionate and secretive, Mathilde shrewder and less concerned with details. She was apt to shrug her shoulders whenever she thought of her little sister's tendency to play the victim. When they were adolescents in Mulhouse, Mathilde used to joke with the boys, while Alice lowered her eyes. She had been one of the first in her class to cut her hair short; Alice won Albert wearing two thick coils around her ears.

Mathilde felt no affinity with her brother-in-law, whom she considered totally insane. Look at the mess he's got you into! What am I going to do with all of you? You know I'll have to let you stay here.

Pierre, who is from the Vosges, a solitary kind of man, has hunkered down until the war ends, often helping people out in his neighborhood. (He found this nothing to boast about.) He has followed Albert's adventures from a distance. He makes no comments and never tries to know more than what he sees—a family that has fallen to pieces. He has picked them up. He has opened his house to us as if it were the most natural thing in the world, helping us feel comfortable, and making himself the good-natured master of our lives, our pastimes, and our changeable seasons. He will defend us passionately against the backwash of hatred—Alice, if people want to talk, let them talk; but after four years of shortages, they must have other fish to fry. They're nice people in the neighborhood. They'll leave you in peace.

It's summer—let's play vacation. The children are not allowed to go outside the garden. Alice doesn't leave the house. She steps out on the balcony whenever she no longer hears them talking and laughing. She jumps when a door slams or the telephone rings. She is waiting, in a haze of expectancy into which she sinks helplessly, the way a body yields to creeping paralysis. She has always been waiting, she repeats this reassuringly to herself. But it had never been this obtrusive twilight that is subtly choking her with its smell of finality.

The slowly elapsing summer no longer signals the end of a nightmare; rather the end of a reprieve. The Liberation that others long for, holding their breath to get through the last difficult days, is for her a return to reality, the inevitable resurgence of years smoldering under ashes. Is it time to begin to understand? Not yet. First, wait and fill up the time with daily living. Notice that there are three children and not four, but don't cry about it. Above all, don't stumble and fall.

Juliette is there to shake off your anxieties. She gets up at dawn, scrubs, washes, does the shopping, counts the food stamps, sings while she prepares the meals, and plays with the children. Madame, you have to eat. Madame, you must get some sleep. Don't worry, Madame, they'll come back!

In her daze, Alice is aware of Pierre's cries of enthusiasm as he follows the advance of General Patton and the Third Army up the Seine. On August 25, there is an outburst of rejoicing in every home, and bells ring from every steeple. General Leclerc's Second Armored Division has entered Paris. Paris is saved. Paris will not be destroyed. Alice is convinced she will never go back there. If Avenue Rodin burns, what does it matter?

How can she say, "All is lost," while Frenchmen are jubilantly emerging from the darkness of four years of occupation? Inside her, everything may falter and collapse, but there is no question of showing it. The gentle heart of the mother and wife must draw on the months of endurance, on the reserves of devotion and fierce strength that she has stored up in the dark. Her suffering is inadmissible.

Pierre says nothing. From time to time, he clumsily takes her in his arms, or puts a hand on her shoulder, as if to say, in a few weeks we'll understand better, for the moment it's a good thing he's not here: he wouldn't get much of a break.

To distract her—to do something that might change the expression on her face, even for a minute—he decides to find out what's happening on Avenue Rodin. Always ready for excitement, Juliette goes along with him. They set off through the Bois de Boulogne on their bicycles, with the little trailer in tow.

The concierge takes them upstairs. She has up-to-date news for them. "You've had visitors quite a few times. I couldn't keep them out. The last ones have been Americans, and they seem to have moved in. There are lots of girls in the evening, and the pianos are getting a workout. They're noisy, but nice."

With his friendly looks and a good American accent, Pierre is welcomed with open arms by a gum-chewing young officer who immediately offers him a cigarette. Juliette, wide-eyed and appreciative, follows them into the living room, where she almost trips on one of the rugs rolled up in a corner. Magazines, tin cans, and beer bottles are strewn over the floor. On the piano, glasses stand in little puddles of soda water; butts spill from ashtrays; other glasses have been knocked over on the open keyboard.

After a lively and apparently friendly conversation, Pierre stands up.

"Juliette, let's go. I've been laying it on thick, so we should get moving before any of the others come back. Go through the closets, take everything you can. Leave them a few plates all the same."

Thus were salvaged *in extremis* the last vestiges of a splendor we were never to know again: a Limoges service, a few crystal glasses not yet broken by the liberators, a handful of souvenirs, some toys, the complete works of Victor Hugo and Léon Bloy, and Mother's silver foxes.

Alice welcomes the two thieves with a smile, but bids her Steinway farewell.

August 28

We have to begin evacuating and move on to Metz. It is impossible to confer with the chief, who is still with Hitler. I don't concern myself about the party but simply prepare my group for departure. There are more than a hundred of us.

A difficulty arises. Since we are traveling separately from the party, I have no papers of any sort to cover the movements of my convoy.

We can take care of that in Metz. For the last few days the withdrawal of the Wehrmacht and the occupation personnel has produced such intense traffic on the roads of eastern France that we should manage to pass in the crush.

August 31

Our convoy has already moved out of the convent and is lining up for departure when help unexpectedly appears. A party member who once worked for me and whom I haven't seen in months steps out of a car in front of me. He says that he is traveling with an OKW officer, Sonderführer Galger, whom he introduces to me. Apprised of my difficulties, Galger says, "I'm cut off from my section and in no great hurry to catch up with it. If you're willing to take me in your convoy, I have papers that will solve all your travel problems." It's no time to be fussy. I accept. He lists our vehicles and the strength of our group on his permit. Everything is in order.

The convoy leaves Nancy around eight in the evening, heading toward Metz via Thionville. We have little trouble slipping into the unbroken procession of military vehicles driving eastward. We are slowed down by the congested roads, but for twenty miles or so everything goes without a hitch. At nightfall we begin to worry. More and more vehicles are passing in the opposite direction. Then our line, which has been slowing down for some time, comes to a halt. The roads are cut off. It's impossible to reach Metz. Then all hell breaks loose—but an organized, German hell. The Feldengendarmerie gets into the act, and soon the entire column, which has been getting more and more ensnarled, has to make a U-turn and follow the "one way" indicated. Any vehicle with driving problems is ruthlessly toppled into the ditch.

We cannot regroup before Château-Salins. But there, as well, orders have been issued for evacuation. No way through to Metz. It's a mass retreat of Wehrmacht units—they pass by without respite, to the sound of artillery firing nearby. The front has been broken through again.

September 1

I decide to move on to Sarrebourg as soon as possible and look for Doriot. We arrive about eleven in the morning. We crossed the border without being checked at all, immersed in the flood of vehicles streaming toward Germany.

Sarrebourg, now in the war zone, has been emptied of its civilian administration and its police. With Galger's help, I make inquiries here and there. No trace of Doriot.

You must not go out. You must not speak. You must wait.

To neighbors and shopkeepers listening and sniffing hard, Mathilde has said, "She's my sister. She's come with her children to spend her vacation with us." But no matter how discreet we are, no matter how fanatically Juliette watches to see that not one imprudent word escapes our lips, we attract attention.

And one day two black Citröens stop in front of the house. Armed men get out at a run and surround the garden. There is violent knocking at the door. Juliette answers and finds a gun pointed at her stomach. She says very calmly, "Why, come in, don't be so formal. You probably want to see Monsieur Pierre?"

Pierre is right there. He knows one of the men. (So who's afraid of the big bad wolf?)

"We're looking for a traitor. Your brother-in-law."

"Hey, not so fast! He isn't here. He's left—ran out on his wife and children. So put down the gun, junior, and make a little less noise—the poor woman has enough on her mind already. Take me along if you like, but don't lay a finger on any of them."

They took him along. Mother had collapsed in a corner. Mathilde said nothing. They brought him back two hours later.

That was the last we saw of them.

September 2

I must find Doriot. Being in Germany acutely complicates the situation. Everything is rigorously controlled, and staying here means being subject to strict supervision. I can only assume temporary responsibility for a section of the party. For the future I need the chief's official instructions.

He had previously spoken of working out of Metz or Strasbourg. That seems a long time ago. Our journey has brought us to the small town of Alzey. I have found quarters for my comrades on the premises of a religious community. No later than tomorrow I shall try to obtain information through the administrative services of the Nazi party.

September 5

The authorities whom I approached with Galger were extremely responsive to my request for help in finding Doriot. After two days of inquiries, we learn that he has gone to Berlin. It has not been possible to learn the date of his return, supposedly to Neustadt, where the FPP has assembled. (That's enough to dissuade me from going there.)

But a solution must be found. Once again, Galger comes to my rescue. He has had news of his unit. It is stationed in Wiesbaden; and he offers to take me there and help me track down the OKW officers with whom I was in contact in Paris.

In Wiesbaden, there is no news of Colonel R. or Count K. But I manage to find shelter for my men in the outbuildings of the château at Hohenbuchau, six miles from Wiesbaden. I take rooms with Jean at a hotel in town, the Schwarzer Bock.

September 12

We are still waiting for orders from the chief. While my comrades divide their time between calisthenics and talking politics, I have shut myself in to take stock of myself and do some quiet thinking.

During my last meeting with him, I had raised the possibility of having to go to Germany. I had told him how appalled I would be to sink so low. Here I am, in Germany.

"The chances of a German victory are now very slim," Doriot said, "but even if there is a single chance left, it is our duty to keep France's options open for such a possibility. *We have gone too far not to see it through to the end.* If bolshevism is the victor, we shall be harried until we are totally destroyed. We shall then have only one expedient left: to die fighting."

But I am in Germany, and this makes me continually uneasy. Leaving France was and will remain an act of flight.

September 17

Having reached Neustadt at eleven, I go directly to the Gauleitung, where I know I can find him: impossible to get to see him. At noon, I catch a glimpse of him in a corridor. He tells me, Come for lunch. We'll have a talk. But at his table I find him engaged in a dalliance and speaking to him is out of the question. He notices my irritation.

"Something wrong? Come and see me this evening. We'll be alone."

During the afternoon, I go into town. The FPP is everywhere. Nearly three thousand of its members have gathered here. They have nothing to do except wander about the streets. One is soon aware of their priorities—where to buy lingerie, clothes, and shoes; where and how to obtain permits, coupons, and tickets; where to find wine, liquor, and tobacco; in which restaurants, cafés, and Konditorei you can eat your fill. And how do you go about getting access to party funds . . . ? Not a word about the political situation, or the steps that need to be taken to keep our exile from being transformed into a sordid disaster. They're people on vacation. They're happy to have escaped danger and anxious to settle down comfortably in a situation that they try to set in the least disagreeable light.

The war? Not our worry—that's what Germany is for. As for them, just living gives them enough trouble. Those who haven't managed to find rooms in hotels or private houses are quartered in the large buildings of the *Gymnasium*. I go there. The courtyard is being used as a parking lot, the classrooms as barracks. The entire premises are supervised by former members of the Action Groups. Not only have they been allowed to attach themselves to the party, they have been asked to maintain discipline: it is, unquestionably, being enforced, with fists and billy clubs.

I go back to my hotel to draft a letter of resignation, in which I express my desire to return immediately with my son to France.

September 18

After depositing my letter at Doriot's office, I return to Wiesbaden. I inform my comrades of my decision. They are ready to join me in my withdrawal.

September 20

A special courier from Neustadt brings me Doriot's answer: a long letter in which he tries to convince me that I'm too idealistic, and that once again I have let myself be carried away by "feelings that are politically irrelevant."

September 21

I return to Neustadt for a long, long discussion with him. He makes these points:

1. Dirty laundry should be washed at home: no point in publicizing our internal quarrels, especially abroad.

2. There is no more political committee, no more party leadership, no more secretary-general. There is the chief, and that's it: I'm taking control of the party. But I want one party, not several.

3. I saw Hitler. I was much struck by his faith in his "secret weapons." He isn't counting on them to beat the Anglo-Ameri-

cans. He wants to frighten them and then induce them to abandon the Russians and form an alliance with him against Stalin.

He has apparently given up his plans for a German Europe: he has decided to give each nation greater autonomy as long as it continues to provide solid anti-Bolshevik support.

4.   The restructuring of the party is to be carried out on two levels. First, there is to be an organization called the FPP Germany: its goal will be an intense campaign of anti-Bolshevik and social propaganda throughout Germany. Second, an illegal FPP France, with its headquarters in Neustadt, whose functions will comprise the undercover reconstruction of the party, the creation of illegal cadres, and preparation for militant anti-Communist combat.

These two organizations will form the framework of a French Committee of Liberation. I have been assured of receiving full material support. There is to be a newspaper for the French in Germany, *Le Petit Parisien*, and a radio station, *Radio Patrie*, for propaganda in France.

5.   There is no question of my accepting your resignation. To reconstitute the party illegally, we must train suitable cadres for this sort of work. You will take charge of that. I myself shall decide on the curriculum, appoint instructors, and have instruction manuals prepared by experts in clandestine action.

You will ask your men which of them wants to volunteer for these activities. The rest must go to work in factories or enlist in the Charlemagne Division. I cannot have people on vacation in a country that is in a state of total mobilization.

I accept.

Our "vacation" is coming to an end. October seemed so far away in August. We must open our eyes to the world outside. We must go out the door, down the steps, and onto the uneven cobblestones of Rue de Bellevue. We must say hello to the neighbors. We must move forward step by step, getting autumn organized, then winter. Find a school for the children, buy their textbooks, and take them right to the door. Father away. Have received no news. So life must go on.

One day, after interminable inquiries, we learn that the FPP has fled across the border into Germany. They are in Germany.

Germany!—"Yes, Madame, I heard you. And no reason why it should stop there, at this point. Here we are putting out flags and chasing the Krauts, and there they are, in Germany. It's not to say anything against Monsieur B., but he's gone a little too far with that Doriot of his! Oh, we women, we're such idiots, we just wait for it all to end. You women can't understand, but war is war. Of course. But what sort of war is *he* fighting? In Germany! That was all we needed."

"They probably had no choice. It's only for the time being. They'll come back."

Little by little, Alice is learning about things. She listens to conversations, she reads the newspapers. On the postwar merry-go-round with its summary trials, accusations, and vendettas, surrounded by a plethora of news, true and false, revelations, denunciations, and enthusiastic pronouncements, she is still groping her way. The gentle blue Germany of childhood—the trees at Jena, the lions at Altenburg—floats at night through her obscure dreams. She wakes up on the edge of a pit that deepens with each morning's lack of news. Will they escape from that fiery furnace?

Waiting, listening, dispelling the veils of mist gently—so as not to be blinded by a reality so different from its image in her own mind. The time has come to pay for what she has never understood: for the party's secret service, the Normandy front, the OKW, the contacts; for the bombings, the torture, the concentration camps; for everything she didn't know; while she waits for a sign from the region beyond the inferno into which they have plunged.

At night I sleep in my mother's bed. Her sobbing wakes me up—a pretty, cooing sound that rocks the mattress. To keep her company, I join in. With my eyes closed, I sing the chorus of brief tears: three notes followed by four rests. She stops and laughs into her handkerchief. She hugs me. I go back to sleep.

Winter is here, bringing no message. Winter quarters follow summer quarters on Rue de Bellevue. The provisional is unfolding into a foreseeable permanence. A little boy cousin is born just before Christmas: we cannot go on camping out at Aunt Mathilde's. On the ground floor, there is a tiny apartment piled high with dust and furniture. Pierre decides to clear it out and settle his wards there.

Paul is fifteen. The pampered child has turned into an increasingly gloomy adolescent. For him, the war had been an adventure lived in the shadow of a father-hero, who on well-disposed days would tell him fantastic stories in which he played the leading role. But one August evening his father ran off, taking his beloved older brother with him. Since then, life has had nothing heroic about it. He has had to open his eyes to a topsy-turvy world, relearn French history, and keep silent.

Paul has never forgiven his brother's departure, and he has locked himself into the anger of a child who has grown up too fast. He resents all of us for his being the only man in the family. We are depriving him from shouting out loud the rage that he lets seep down silently into himself. —Paul, why are you making such a face? Paul, say something!

He was handsome, green-eyed, and tall, but his health was weak. He never spoke, bowed his shoulders, and in his frailness sought refuge in his one great passion: building miniature radios. For hours on end he would shut himself up in the room Mathilde had lent him, soldering iron in hand, his tousled head bent over the silver tubes and the tangles of multicolored wire in strange metal frames: the only things for which he showed any fondness.

I was fascinated and frightened by this grown-up boy, this unfamiliar brother who never asked me questions but who held my hand tightly in his on the way to school. I used to lightly knock twice on his door and cautiously slip into the room, taking care that the edge of my smock didn't spill the tubes with a musical crackle or upset the unstable edifice of cartons filled with infinitesimal colored parts. I would squat in a corner and delightedly breathe in the mingled smells of stale tobacco and hot metal. His profile would be silhouetted against the blaze of a naked bulb hung an inch above the table. From time to time, raising his nose from the depths of his exacting assemblage, he would look at me with his beautiful deep glance and nod his head, with the hint of a smile. I loved him.

At Champagne-sur-Seine, armed young men have not forgotten to pay Grandfather Louis a visit. He was expecting them; he received them courteously. Yes, I have a son who worked with the enemy. No, he isn't here; but if you'd like to have a look around the house, please don't hesitate. They searched everywhere. They didn't drink his wine, they didn't break the windows; but they took him off, together with his wife, Marie.

They did a few things like shoving them into cells with rifle butts, and then they were interrogated. Marie kept saying her rosary, and Louis told the little he knew. But when they said to him, Your son sold out to the Gestapo, he replied vehemently, No, a thousand times no.

On their return three months later, there were a few rugs and spoons missing; but the Cariffas were still there. Grass had grown up between the flagstones on the paths, and Grandmother was limping from an attack of lumbago. Louis had to carry her up the front steps.

She is soon unable to walk at all. She is in pain. She takes to her bed. Louis brings her to a specialist in Paris who is going to save her. When they are through with her at the hospital, they send her to us, in Suresnes. She could not have made it any farther.

They settled Grandmother on the couch in the dining room-cum-sleeping parlor. Lovingly tended by Alice and Juliette, she spent her last days in a dream, surrounded by her grandchildren. (Jean, my little Jean, will I see you again?)

She died with the first buds of spring; as discreetly as she had lived, making so little fuss that Louis, who had not sensed the moment of her death, shook her poor body and shouted, Marie, you can't do this to me! Marie, do you hear me, Marie, you stay here! For the first time, she disobeyed him.

He withdrew into a speechlessness lasting several years, sunk in bitter, resentful mourning behind the iron fence of his empty citadel, with his dog, his maid, his wine, and the gold coins buried at the foot of the big linden tree.

Resignation refused. Refusal of resignation accepted.

Albert has been promoted to inspector-general. He will be responsible for running the FPP's four technical schools. Each has a body of about a hundred students who have been dispersed at random under whatever roofs are still standing on German soil. The schools have been agreeably named after flowers: Rose, Violet, Marigold, and Daisy. They are no innovation for the FPP—from its founding in 1936, it has followed the Communist example by training its active members—but they must now be adapted to "current conditions" and made to function in a country that is now in a state of total war.

Since Doriot's unchanged objective is to seize power in France, the party must be developed on a clandestine basis and made ready to resist a Communist uprising. Confident after his conversations at General Headquarters of obtaining all he needs to carry out his program, Doriot plans to use the schools, which will receive new recruits every two months, to provide rapid training for the future cadres of the illegal FPP.

In the curriculum are such subjects as intelligence, infiltration, military instruction, radio transmission, and sabotage. Nothing surprising in that: won't the FPP agents be parachuted into the midst of a resistance movement that is armed to the teeth? They can't be sent in empty-handed.

The OKW is to finance the organization: its considerable matérial, locations, and transportation—a very expensive proposition. When Doriot submits to the OKW's representatives his list of indispensable supplies, he is told that compensations are expected. In exchange for marks, he must promise that the agents parachuted at the Wehrmacht's expense will supply military information. Doriot makes it clear to his inspector-general that "promise" does not mean "hand over." Albert, we have to play for time. Let's get those subsidies first, and above all, let's not lose our comrades to the Germans so that they can use them entirely for their own benefit.

The schools will remain active for little more than four months. Political training is provided by veteran members of the party, military training by German officers. For want of time, no agents will ever be parachuted.

The weeks pass. Albert's task becomes more complicated as the Wehrmacht is ousted by Himmler and the Gestapo, who are progressively taking control of Germany. Albert's main business, it seems, is ferreting out spies that the Gestapo has introduced into the FPP ranks. Their purpose is to detect the anti-Nazi aims of Doriot's followers and, if necessary, to convert them to their cause.

Albert is too busy with his new duties to be able to keep Jean with him. Sending him back across the border is unthinkable. Albert dispatches him to his cousins in Altenburg.

At first Jean is welcomed with open arms. But time passes and the eastern front falters. His National Socialist cousins let him know that a young man his age cannot sit idly by while the entire youth of Germany is being hacked to bits protecting Europe from the Bolshevik onslaught.

Weary of allusions to his uselessness in the European struggle, he gets a job in a factory. He spends eight hours a day fastening taillights to trucks that will send his German cousins to have their heads blown off by the dirty Reds.

But when the snows started and Christmas neared, Jean had had enough of trucks for the Reich. He wrote his father, "I'm on my way," and arrived the same day as his letter.

DEATH IN FEBRUARY

The island of Mainau is a large garden of almost five hundred acres set in the waters of Lake Constance. About a hundred yards distant from the shore, it is connected to the mainland by a footbridge wide enough to allow cars to pass. A huge park surrounds the château. Long pathways wind among the rarest species of trees, tall greenhouses in which lush vegetation flourishes, and fragrant rose gardens.

The island of Mainau—its name so lovely when pronounced in a singsong accent—is a haven of peace, an out-of-the-way excursion where nothing has as yet been demolished by bombs. In the middle of the park, commanding the meadows, the vineyards, the grainfields, and the lake, rises the château. The part that dates from the last century spreads out in numerous luxuriously appointed rooms. Near the château there is a fine inn that in peacetime received tourists. Nowadays a staff of Ukrainians prepares meals there for the lucky exiles of the FPP and for the members of the German diplomatic delegation assigned to Doriot, who occupies one wing of the château.

The island of Mainau is the property of the Swedish crown. For the first time since the beginning of the war it is occupied. By Frenchmen: that is why Sweden has agreed to it. Since December Jacques Doriot and his retinue have been settled in the Mainau château. He has installed the editors of his newspaper here and all the members of his political committee, with their families, their secretaries, their servants, and their clowns. Doriot—the worker's son, the excommunicated Communist, the mayor of Saint-Denis, the chief of the people's party of France—will live his last weeks of flight in fairy-tale splendor, surrounded by his guard of honor and his Wehrmacht henchmen.

On the Isle of Mainau, the survivors of the FPP are leading the good life. The ladies receive their guests under the king of Sweden's crystal chandeliers. The gentlemen court them, get tipsy, gamble, prattle, and in the depths of brocaded sofas forget their hard party days. Candlelight suppers are served by plump Ukrainian girls on little tables draped with lace, in the huge ground-floor reception rooms that suggest an Art Nouveau palace. The suppers end in costume balls on the glassed-in terrace, or in amateur theatricals in the little theater. How exciting to be dancing on a volcano! You don't do any harm. You innocently drown your cares in wine. You have a good time.

The Isle of Mainau has become Ali Baba's treasure cave. The wealth transported by car over the scorched roads of eastern

France has filled up the château's secret nooks as if by magic. One dips into trunks full of banknotes to procure brandies, old wine, and the rare provender that soon will spill onto the intimate buffets of this elegant assembly. Trucks arrive regularly from Italy loaded with choice supplies. Make the most of them—isn't life hanging by thread, at the mercy of one stray bomb?

At noon on January 15, Albert, his son, his records, his staff, and a few faithful followers make their appearance on the scene of this comic opera. He is flabbergasted. What is he doing in this madhouse? He wants no part of it. His dour face makes a poor impression on the little world at play, and the few acid greetings he dispenses do nothing to relieve the atmosphere. He notices Claude J., the editor of *Le Petit Parisien*, and his wife, the only ones who seem somewhat ill at ease. He does not even see the others.

He asks for the chief. His chief. Chief, this can't be happening!

"Good old Albert—always the puritan!"

Doriot is strolling among his little Louis XVI tables and his Dresden china, in the blue and gold parlor that he uses as an office. An agreeable warmth pervades the room. With his hands behind his back (that broad, reassuring back), he walks silently to and fro, stops by a window, and with a sigh gazes out at the frost-whitened terraces that lead down to the dark green lake. He coughs; he turns around. Garlands of cherubs soar about his powerful head, which seems to have been set once and for all on top of the thick gray wool scarf that he has knotted beneath his chin.

"So for the past two months these poor people have been cowering here, waiting for the war to end in agonies of deprivation and despair."

"Enough moralizing, thank you. I was offered a sumptuous refuge, and I wasn't going to turn it down."

"It's disgusting."

"Albert, you and your killjoy attitude are getting on my nerves. These people aren't bothering anyone, and nothing's keeping us from working. We're putting out the newspaper—it's printed in Constance. We broadcast several times a day. I've been having increasingly complicated problems in my relations with GHQ because of constant surveillance by Himmler and his gang. Everything's happening very fast—I'll tell you about it in detail when you're feeling more kindly disposed toward me. Now move in, and get your unit installed. Room has been set aside for you."

"No doubt. I ran into your private secretary. He let me know that I was welcome to stay in the château, but that my son and my 'entourage' would have to be satisfied with the outbuildings. If you need me, you'll find me there too."

"Is that all you have to say to me?"

"I can't think of anything else. Good evening."

That afternoon, while his friends and assistants install their January quarters in four bright, icy rooms, Albert wanders among the bare trees, down paths crackling with frost, to work off his rage. Jean follows close behind, shivering in his great navy-blue cape, his beret pulled down over his ears. They soon warm up. Their white breaths mingle. The father talks and talks, explaining to his son, telling everything from the beginning.

Albert and his son spent four close weeks together. They shared the same room filled with winter sun. They took their meals together at the island inn. They walked for hours through a world aquiver with hoarfrost that wrapped them in pearl-white peace, far from the disasters of war. Four weeks of happiness spent drinking hot grog, their noses red, or warming their numb fingers as they blithely set fire to the party's secret archives.

They imagine a future life, far from Germany and the harsh world. They prepare for their return home. We'll live in a vast, quiet garden. You'll help me plant rosebushes. And we'll rest, all of us, in the shade of an arbor, all of us together once again.

On February 21, 1945, the chief sends Albert an invitation to dinner at the château that same evening. The invitation stipulates that his presence is absolutely necessary. Doriot has news of the highest importance to communicate to his colleagues. He wants Albert there, whether or not he has resigned. It's an order.

February 21 is also Albert's birthday. Forty-two years old. A little party is planned in their building for his close friends, and particularly for Jean. The lack of news from France has been keenly felt—birthdays had always been celebrated at home. Tonight, my beloved Jean, we will cling to one another harder than ever, we will think of them and soften our melancholy a little when we blow out the candles and smile at one another through a glass of champagne. We'll send them kisses across the sky.

For the past month, Albert had not participated in any FPP activity. His letter of resignation had been acknowledged without comment. Doriot was absorbed by the increasing difficulties caused by his poor relations with Himmler's SS; the rest of the time he had been caught up in the happy whirl of the château's night life. He had not tried to discuss matters with his renegade—

waiting, no doubt, for a new opportunity to charm him. Albert, for his part, had avoided him assiduously. He had taken care of routine work and prepared his hypothetical return to France.

With the invitation in his pocket, he resolves to confront the lion in his cage. He will explain in person why he is not attending the dinner, and then say a final good-bye.

Doriot receives him cordially. He seems in fine fettle.

"Albert, are you by any chance having one of your bad days? Your gloom is about to be dispelled. I have extraordinary things to reveal to you, and I'm anxious to tell you about them before this evening."

"I won't be there this evening—"

"Not again!"

"No—listen, tonight's my birthday."

Doriot jumps up, and his towering mass turns around on the waxed floor: almost lifting the bewildered Albert off the ground, he embraces him.

"Old friend, that's wonderful news! Many happy returns! We're going to celebrate that right now. Champagne! Sit down, and let's drink to your health, to the end of our worries, and to soon being back in France! You're excused for this evening. But now listen to what I have to say.

"While you were being proud and withdrawn, I haven't been sitting still. You know that I made agreements with Hitler and Ribbentrop. The latter's signature is on one copy that I always have with me. It's thanks to them that we're here. But Himmler and his SS jackals are calling all the shots, and they're throwing one monkey wrench after another into my plans. They've cooped me up here—I can't even get gas any more. They're obstructing my political activities. They're censoring my newspaper. What these gentlemen blame me for is not providing FPP members for military missions and not letting them run things. The Wehrmacht is only a ghost army now. The ones left are afraid of compromising themselves—more of them are liquidated every day. Everyone is working with a gun in his back.

"The fact is that the SS are supporting Darnand and the militia. *They*'ll do anything. I haven't let myself be intimidated. Four days ago I even sent Himmler a warning letting him clearly understand that I would appeal matters to the Führer if he went on sabotaging my French policy. The shot must have hit the mark, because last night I learned that the objections to the creation of a French Committee of Liberation have all been withdrawn. They've finally understood that the only solution for France is a program carried out by Frenchmen who know the country's real needs. I'll be given every means of realizing my objectives. I'm meeting Déat tomorrow in Mengen to put the finishing touches on our agreement for getting the committee started."

He pauses and smiles. Raising his glass, he continues: "The war is over. Germany has been bled dry. But we'll be sitting in the front row when the time comes to seize power from the Communists. The Anglo-Americans will soon see through Stalin's motives and turn against him, at our side, to drive the Bolsheviks out of the country. From now on we must pursue a subtle and flexible policy to achieve a fusion with every non-Communist element in France. Will we have to justify our policies of the past four years? I'll take care of that!

"Albert, the real struggle is only beginning. You're going to take charge of the Liberation Committee's clandestine activities. You can choose your own men, inside or outside the party. My only condition is: no factionalism! First and foremost, union against bolshevism, and a brotherly fight for social peace."

"Let me think about it. Perhaps there are some internal problems we should clear up first. I told you in my last letter that I wouldn't tolerate—"

"We'll make a clean sweep!"

With a great burst of laughter, he stands up. "Happy birthday, Albert! Drink a toast to my health and to our success. Set your mind at ease—you'll see your family soon. It's your best friend's wish."

It is at noon on February 22 that Doriot is to meet Déat in Mengen, near Siegmaringen. The time and place have been chosen by Reinebek, the German minister. Mengen is about sixty miles from Constance. There is not a single gallon of gas remaining at Mainau. On the morning of the 22nd, Doriot is informed that the general staff cannot supply gasoline, but an official car will be dispatched for him by their diplomatic service.

Since his arrival in Germany, Doriot has never used any car but his own. He drives it himself, always following routes that he chooses at the last moment. He arranges all his own appointments.

So when the car arrives with a German soldier at the wheel he is hesitant. But the atmosphere at Mainau is euphoric. A bright sun heralds spring. Doriot shrugs his shoulders.

"I don't like it. But the exception proves the rule. It won't kill me."

The car rolls over the lake across the footbridge. Hands wave—
Good-bye, chief, bon voyage!

After fifteen miles, as they drive through a village, peasants
point skyward at the moment the car is passing. The driver slows
down and cuts the engine. There is the sound of planes, growing
fainter. They're gone. Drive on.

Six miles farther, their itinerary takes them along the edge of a
military airfield. Two planes abruptly appear, very low, and as they
fly over the road, they swoop toward the car. The driver brakes,
and Doriot puts his hand on the door handle, ready to jump out—
but the driver says, "No danger, they're Germans. I'm sure of it.
I see them all the time. Anyway, we just passed the air base and
there was no alert."

A few minutes later, the car is driving along an absolutely
straight road with empty fields on either side. As if coming from
nowhere, the two planes reappear and fire an initial burst. An
exploding bullet wounds Doriot in the knee. The driver brakes;
the secretary screams. The planes have already returned. They let
loose their burst simultaneously.

Doriot was hit by eleven bullets, seven of them fatal; the driver,
by an exploding bullet in the leg; and the secretary, by some miracle, climbed out of the bullet-ridden car unhurt.

The planes have disappeared. The soldier cannot stop repeating,
"They were German planes." Five minutes later, a car arrives with
two high-ranking officers who roughly order him to keep quiet.
They turn peremptorily to the secretary and make sure that she
understands no German. Another car arrives, two other officers
get out. The first pair seems to be expecting them. They salute.

Hastily they inspect the car and take possession of Doriot's briefcase and all the documents he has on him. They leave. Soon after, two ambulances arrive. One transports Doriot's body to Mengen; the other carries away the wounded driver.

Count K. was at Siegmaringen in Heyraud's office (he was responsible for police supervision of the French delegation) when a telephone call from Mengen announced "the strafing of Monsieur Doriot's car by an Allied plane." K. left for Mengen at once. He set out to look for the officers who had been the first on the scene, found them, and talked to them. It was only on the following morning that, as a member of the chief's liaison staff, he was able to recover the documents taken from the car and from the dead man's body.

K. brought the documents to Mainau, and there told Albert: "We are obliged to accept the official explanation—'an Allied plane strafed the car.' For your personal safety, let me give you some very friendly advice. Be satisfied with this explanation. But between the two of us, I can tell you this: within minutes after the disaster, four officers were on the scene 'by accident.' All four are veteran members of the SS, and all four belong to the central bureaus of the *Reichssicherheitshauptamt* (RSHA). Your chief's documents and identification papers were returned to me only this morning. I wanted to see the driver: he had, I was told, expressly stated that he had recognized two German planes. Well, the driver has disappeared. At Siegmaringen, as soon as his wounds were dressed, he was taken elsewhere. I have been unable to learn his name, either at the hospital where he was treated (and where according to regulations he should have been registered) or at the foreign ministry, where I was ungraciously informed that the army had provided him for the occasion and that his name and unit were unknown. I could not continue what would have looked like an investigation. I'm a German officer, subject to control by the RSHA, and I cannot allow myself to draw conclusions. I can only advise you, again, to be prudent and discreet."

It was impossible to know if any documents had been taken from the chief's briefcase. Plainly, however, the copy of the agreement drawn up with Ribbentrop and countersigned by Hitler was not among them. Yet Doriot had wanted to transmit it to Déat.

Novak, the head of the liaison staff assigned to Doriot, was absent. On February 20, he had suddenly found it necessary to take a week's trip to Italy.

Later, Albert had occasion to ask the CIC of the American Seventh Army to make inquiries about strafing attacks in the Mengen area on February 22. No Allied plane had operated in the Constance-Mengen-Siegmaringen sector at any time during that day.

It was absolutely necessary to get in touch with the schools and give them their necessary instructions. Albert could not leave Mainau. He had to attend Doriot's funeral; and he did not want to miss the spectacle of the putative heirs to the throne squabbling over the remains of the beheaded party.

It was Jean who left instead. (Jean, my little Jean: in this winter of Germany's exhaustion, in your great navy-blue cape, with your wide beret pulled down over your ears, looking like a bewildered spaniel!) Albert let him go.

Jean had been insistent. Father, let me deliver your orders to the schools. I'll be careful. I'll take local trains that are in no danger of being bombed. I'll take whatever time I need. Father: trust me.

His first mission! After having been scrupulously kept clear of all political action: at eighteen, this adventure. Father, take me with you. Be a man, my son.

(I went a little way with him, he kissed me good-bye with the words, "Don't worry," then left. Ten yards farther on he turned back, waved to me, and shouted, "Of course I'm supposed to come home as soon as possible!"—a last smile, a weak, sad smile, because for the last two days we had been going through such turmoil. I watched him stride away.)

Albert carried his chief to his grave and never saw his son again. And although all organizations were alerted—the army, the antiaircraft battalions, the various police forces, the railroads, town councils, civilian defense agencies, hospitals—the telegrams and radio messages that accumulated by handfuls for two weeks finally came down to this: nothing had been found, nothing at all. Every air-raid warning, strafing, and bombing that had occurred in a four-day period between Wiesbaden and Constance was identified, and the authorities capable of providing any information about it consulted.

Jean's itinerary was reconstructed as best it could.

One day a train between Heidelberg and Ulm arrived—in utterly exceptional fashion, such a thing not having happened in months—punctually on time. It was this train, so it seems, that left my brother at the station in Ulm that 1st of March at ten-thirty in the morning. A connection leaving at twelve-ten would have brought him to Mainau—miracle of miracles—that afternoon.

Up until now, Ulm has been subject only to minor harassing raids. The railroad station is of no strategic importance, so that it does not even have an air-raid shelter. The city itself, and particularly the older quarters where the station is situated, is neither a strategic nor an industrial objective. In consequence, no sizable shelters have been built here like those in Mainz, Stuttgart, Frankfurt, or Berlin. There is also Neu Ulm. Although not officially declared a hospital city, it is thought of as such because of its total lack of industry and its many hospitals. The latter fly huge Red Cross flags, and the Geneva symbol is also painted across the full breadth of its main intersections.

Jean is waiting for the twelve-ten train to Friedrichshafen. There is no problem finding a seat on it. At exactly noon, when the passengers have all taken their places, the alert sounds. The trains are evacuated. Since there are no shelters, the passengers are directed to the cellars of neighboring houses.

The raid is one of exceptional violence. The station is demolished, and the entire quarter as well. It consists chiefly of old houses, not one of whose shelters holds up. Of the hundreds upon hundreds of dead dug out of the houses on the station square, all of them travelers, two hundred and fifty cannot be identified. For the town, the count is in the thousands. Other thousands of injured have been hurriedly packed into the hospitals of Neu Ulm.

On March 3, the fires have still not died out and the shelters are not entirely cleared. Once again the alert sounds. This time Neu Ulm is to be the objective.

Not one hospital is left standing. On that day, the unfortunates who have survived the first bombing are blown to pieces and burned, together with those who rescued and took care of them.

In search of a clue, since Jean has not been identified, it is necessary to sift through bloody piles of identity cards, wallets, bags, smaller effects, and ragged bits of clothing: nothing the least bit certain is found.

Between February 24 and March 3, somewhere between Constance and Wiesbaden, Jean—my little Jean—has vanished: become part of the German soil, one among the several million victims of the Third Reich.

GRAND FINALE

April '45: the collaborators are swarming from the hulk called Germany. Each man jumps aboard the first car or truck that comes along, or waits for the miracle train that will carry him to Italy, Switzerland, or any refuge far from the Allies.

Albert has disbanded the small FPP groups for which he was still responsible. He finds himself alone in Bregenz on the Austrian frontier, without papers and without a car. In this panic-ridden, last-ditch rendezvous of supporters of Vichy and other Frenchmen in a hurry, he is supposed to meet a comrade in possession of a party car in which they can join the caravan of fugitives. He waits in vain for car and driver.

This stinging betrayal destroys his last illusions about the party. In a brooding rage, resolved to take whatever train next passes through, he is pacing the station platform when he hears his name being called. Emerging from his gloomy reverie, he turns around and sees a group of men from the FPP. They look as lost as he is, but they are weighed down with a huge quantity of luggage. Albert asks to be enlightened.

Three of the men had been in charge of a radio unit set up by Doriot in Neustadt. The day after the chief's death, they had left with their equipment on a "secret mission." A mysterious German—a double agent, in their opinion—induced them to join him in a hazardous new enterprise: helping the Allied armies. For nearly two months these men had been in touch with the American intelligence services. Then, as the hour of final collapse was sounding, the double agent left them in the lurch, equipment and all, without any explanations.

At this point, Albert suffers an attack of anti-Nazism: the fruit, no doubt, of thoughts that had been tormenting him since Doriot's death. He later analyzed his motives in his diary:

This time I was through with the FPP for good; and I no longer had any scruples concerning the Wehrmacht, to which the anti-Bolshevist struggle had linked me for a while. Wasn't it giving up ground on every front? It no longer afforded any sort of obstacle to Bolshevism. The "German stronghold" being established in the Tyrol was not intended to make a stand against the Reds but to provide a final National Socialist refuge for the retreating SS. My eight months of exile had taught me—dismayingly late—that National Socialism was as great a danger as Bolshevism. Then why not aid the Americans in the destruction of this Nazi bastion that eventually had to disappear, since the anti-Bolshevist fight was about to be taken up by them? I had no plan of action, but this meeting with my bewildered comrades might open the way to new undertakings.

"What equipment are you carrying?"

"A transmitter, batteries, an antenna, weapons, food—"

"Can you re-establish contact with the Americans?"

"We only need to set up the antenna in a safe place."

"Fine. Do you have any plans?"

"No. We've been waiting for a sign to point the way—"

"You're about to get one. We're going to fight the Germans. How does that sound to you?"

Enthusiasm sweeps the FPP ranks—seven lost sheep.

Albert takes command of the troop.

A train stops. Men and baggage are installed: destination Feldkirch. There Albert expects to find Count K., who has offered, as a last resort, to go into hiding with him in Liechtenstein. Now that his plans have changed, Albert hopes that the Count will furnish the papers needed to cover his new activities.

After a night spent on the crowded station platform, he goes to the Hotel Löwen, their hypothetical meeting place. He passes Laval and his entourage, ready to cross the first available border. The hotel is jammed. People from Vichy are sleeping in the corridors wherever they can find a chair. But no Count K. Should Albert wait for him? Amid alarming reports of the progress of the Allied armies, the atmosphere is one of flight.

Unsure of the merits of his undertaking, Albert returns to the station: and there runs into Novak, Doriot's former liaison chief at Mainau. He had been in a particular hurry to leave the enchanted island, obsessed as he was by the idea of going into hiding. (He was not the only one, in that time of every-man-for-himself.) Albert attacks and insults him, taking revenge on him for all the disillusion accumulated during the past weeks. He demands identification papers, passports, documents for his secret expedition—he knows that Novak has all the RSHA's seals in his possession. The latter has to be asked more than once, but he finally agrees, at gunpoint. After all, he says, considering the situation . . .

And so Albert receives orders from the Gestapo for a secret mission that will allow him to enter the Tyrol without attracting the SS's attention. In Feldkirch his honor the *Landrat* receives the agents Novak is obliged to introduce to him. He advises them to proceed to Schlins, a village between Feldkirch and Bludenz, where the mayor (a National Socialist, who will be warned) will help them find a hide-out in the mountains. They arrive there without incident on April 24.

The Austrian mayor is somewhat surprised at having to welcome eight French special agents from the Gestapo. But their orders—covered with official stamps and bearing a high-level signature—are ultra-secret. In fact, they do not even show them to him: only superior officers have the right to see them.

Albert gives his instructions: "We are asking you to help us with a very specific problem. We are looking for an isolated place at high altitude with access to electricity. Once this is taken care of, please be so kind as to forget us. Do not try to communicate with us. For you, as for the rest of the population, we shall be French workers who have fled the war zone and sought asylum in the mountains to look for work as farm hands."

The mayor suggests a chalet at nine thousand feet that is used as a refuge by chamois hunters. It offers an incomparable view, which (thinks Albert, focusing his binoculars on the spot indicated) will enable them to follow every German and Allied troop movement.

The mayor who is evidently a Francophile, timidly asks, "Forgive me, but won't your activities entail a risk of bombings?"

Enigmatically, Albert reassures him, "As long as we are here, you have nothing to fear." The perhaps imprudent words have been spoken.

The mayor's courage picks up. "Would you be willing to do the inhabitants a favor by warning me of the Allies' arrival?" Seeing Albert hesitate, he adds, "We're Austrians, you know, and for us this war—" His hand flutters eloquently above his head.

Albert promises to do so. He asks the mayor, in case any information is forthcoming, to respect the secrecy of his sources. It occurs to him that the National Socialists in Schlins are less Nazi than they seem.

They needed to start sending out signals and make contact that same night at midnight. They moved into the chalet after dark and set up a provisional antenna. The batteries had been charged. A first coded message went on its way: "Occupying exceptional position in zone of probable German last stand. Need resume contact today noon."

They found the right frequency. Ten anxious minutes; then the reply, "OK for tomorrow."

This was the first of Albert's ten American days, his last, wildest, briefest adventure. From one day to the next—no taking time into account. So let's make it up as we go along. It's like a game. And what a crazy way to join the Resistance!

April 25

The chalet is a magnificent lookout. It dominates three valleys. With binoculars you can keep the railway line and the roads that converge toward the entrance to the Vorarlberg under observation. The antenna has been installed on the trunk of a tall spruce that functions as its pole.

At noon contact is re-established with the services of the American Third Army: Indicating exact positions, request instructions.

That evening: Answer received. Immediate mission: observation and surveillance of general staff, services, troops, equipment, operating in zone bounded by Dornbirn, Feldkirch, Bludenz, Landeck. Next: organize mobile sabotage groups able to attack bridges and lines of communication. Finally: search for terrain for drops of men and equipment.

April 26

We explore the mountain behind us. We discover an abandoned, completely isolated hut that we decide to organize as a possible fallback position, concealing in it part of our equipment, food, and weapons. A mile above it, there is a meadow surrounded by forest, suitable for parachute drops.

April 29

We have marked our terrain with sheets spread on the grass. It has already been reconnoitered from the air.

The Third Army is asking for three radio contacts daily. This is giving us problems with our power. We have six batteries, and each transmission discharges one of them. Every evening we go down to Düntz with the batteries in our rucksacks. We leave them to be recharged overnight at a farm, with peasants with whom we had very quickly become friendly. We have given them a receiving set, and we listen to the news together, drinking schnapps. We were about to leave one evening when one of them stopped me and said, "Please forgive me. Your mission is secret, and you say you're working with the Nazis. But you have a lot to learn before you act like them! We know your equipment is American. For us, you're above all Frenchmen and Catholics. We're prepared to help you."

I'm perplexed. I don't want to give myself away. But I decide to trust him. I ask him to recruit—unobtrusively—a few men for dangerous missions. He then tells me that he is hiding three deserters in his cellar.

April 30

Dawn. We are still in bed. A car draws up in front of the chalet. Violent knocking on the door.

"Polizei!"

I'm on my feet at once, submachine gun in hand. I half open the door, which a comrade blocks with his foot, and point my gun at the civilian outside. He drops his pistol in surprise. Another comrade mutters in my ear that about ten men have surrounded the chalet.

I loudly order, making sure he hears, "Take the machine guns and the grenades. Get in position by the windows. Shoot when I tell you to."

The man is very pale.

"Do you speak French?" I ask.

"*Ja. Ein wenig.*"

"Who's in charge?"

"I am."

"What do you want?"

"I would like to see your papers and inspect the chalet."

"Who sent you?"

"Security police."

"How many are there of you?"

"Ten."

The assault is not to be taken seriously. I don't want any damage done. While my comrade covers him, I fetch my orders and fold them so that he sees the heading: RSHA. ULTRA-SECRET MISSION.

"You have no right to see this, much less come in. If you want to know why we're here, send somebody who's qualified. Now get out."

He shouts an order, and his men go back to their cars. They drive off.

I feel that we are getting too much attention. I start planning for our withdrawal up the mountain.

May 1

It has snowed all night. This will jeopardize the drops scheduled for May 2 and 3, as well as our departure from the chalet. We are afraid of leaving tracks.

May 3

We notice considerable troop movement on all the roads visible from the chalet. Several convoys stop at Schlins. One of our peasants informs us that they belong to a Waffen SS division whose staff is at Düntz. We immediately report this to the Americans.

That evening, at the time when we generally go down with the batteries, two of our friends suddenly appear, out of breath, and tell us that it is imperative for us to remain where we are. The roads are overrun with cars, trucks, and black uniforms. They offer to take care of the batteries, using secret shortcuts. They curse the SS and the occupation of the valley, and describe the villagers' panic at the prospect of the battle they feel is imminent.

Taking advantage of their confusion, I imperturbably promise that there will be no bombings if by tomorrow morning at ten I am fully and exactly informed about the positioning of the division. They agree to provide the information.

I am somewhat reluctant to exploit their trust, but there is little else I can do. The division must be attacked, and for this to happen, the Americans must be apprised of its positions as soon as possible.

May 3

We send a final message at dawn. Then—is it intuition?—I decide to leave a man on watch at the chalet and go with the others up the mountain to a better vantage point. We have meanwhile concealed our weapons and equipment in various places in the chalet.

It was a lucky move. Two hours later, I train my binoculars on the chalet: several cars and a sizable troop in black uniforms have surrounded it. It's nine-thirty. I send one of my comrades, unarmed, to meet the peasant who is bringing us the information at ten. He meets him by chance while he is making a detour over the mountain behind the chalet. He has noticed the unusual activity there.

By eleven o'clock I have all the information in hand. I draft a long message. Nice work, but how can we deliver it? The next transmission is at noon, and the transmitter is in the chalet in the midst of Germans.

I decide to go down, as relaxed as can be, my submachine gun slung on my shoulder, without the message. I instruct a comrade to watch me through the binoculars and join me at a prearranged signal.

The first Germans to see me are surprised but not hostile. While I proffer broad smiles and friendly greetings, they let me through to the chalet door. There I find a second lieutenant, whom I salute Hitler-fashion. He returns my salute. Then: am I in charge? Yes. Pointing to my American machine gun: Whom do you plan to shoot with that? Why, chamois and roebucks, naturally. *Ach so!* I ask my comrade, who is relieved to see me, why he hasn't broken out the schnapps.

The officer speaks French. "Now, our staff finds this chalet advantageously situated. They would like to take it over. Your presence here may not be perfectly correct as far as the police are concerned, but"—he smiles—"that is no business of mine. The only thing I must ask of you is that you come with me, together with your men and your materiel: the chalet must be vacated by evening."

"Are you planning to stay here?" (I act very unconcerned.)

"A few officers, as observers, yes."

"I mean, your division."

"Oh, yes." He smiles. "We've done enough walking. We're going to fight for a while."

It's almost noon—time for the message—and I take the plunge.

"In that case," I say, using my "officer" voice, "it will be necessary for me to tell you who we are. Be good enough to send your men outside."

Suddenly interested: "Is it that serious?"

"Very serious. I should keep the matter secret, but there is so little time. I am here as an agent of the RSHA." He smartly dismisses his men. "Allow me. I am not supposed to show you this document, but time is short. Read it."

His deferential perusal of the orders is punctuated with "*So . . . so.*" I excuse myself, step to the door, and give the prearranged signal.

"Have you finished? Here is my passport with my photograph."

"That's quite all right." He is impressed.

"I shall follow you in a moment to headquarters. Right now, I must attend to urgent business, if you will permit me. No, no, you can stay." I'll stop at nothing now.

Without hesitating I summon my radio operator, who comes in with his transmitter. I ask him to try to make contact. My comrade also arrives with the message, which I set about coding, while the lieutenant, who no doubt has never seen American code books before, starts following the radio man's activity with interest. Contact. Under the officer's nose, I hand the sheets to the operator and toss the clear text into the blazing stove.

At the end of no less than an hour, the radioman switches off the current and removes his earphones.

The officer asks, "This is American equipment you're using?"

"I don't know of any that's better."

"If I'm not being indiscreet—whom are you in touch with?"

"Why, with the Americans, of course." He is open- mouthed. "Don't try to understand. You saw my orders. They authorize me to communicate with the enemy. Still—since I've already confided in you, here's the story. I *am* giving information to the Americans. False information, courtesy of RSHA."

"Aha!" He is reassured. "You are also in contact with the RSHA?"

Silence. Keeping up our casual tone, I ask: "Do you expect to stay long in the area?"

Very vague: "I suppose so."

"And then? Will you let yourself be made prisoner?"

Indignant: "Of course not! We're going to fight."

"Will you have time?" Offhandedly, to a comrade: "Bring me the maps of the region. Here. Let's see how things stand. You're pretty much established in this sector." (I'm careful not to appear too well informed; he corrects the position). "You see, you're about to be trapped in a pincer movement. American armor is closing in on both sides."

Dismayed: "Are you certain?"

"Certain. But you will be informed of this at any moment now. I've told RSHA."

The credulous lieutenant dashed off to find a superior officer, to whom I repeated these lies, and who believed them. The black uniforms hurried away toward the valley, while we began preparing to evacuate the chalet.

At eight in the evening, the peasants arrived in a state of great excitement. They've gone, they've gone! Who? What's happening?

The SS! There was not one SS soldier remaining in Düntz, Schlins, and environs. The road lay open to the Liberators.

May 4

At midnight we inform the Americans of the division's withdrawal. I send someone to tell the mayor of Schlins that for him and his constituents the war is over. The Allies are on their way.

During the morning, I learn that the bridge at Feldkirch was blown up the night before. The SS retreat is done for.

May 5

We are on the lookout at dawn. The night's message announced the arrival of Allied troops and recommended we keep out of sight. The weather is marvelous. Through our binoculars, we can make out red-and-white flags flying from the tops of buildings in the direction of Feldkirch: the Austrian colors. In an hour the entire valley is covered with white and red-and-white flags.

At ten o'clock, there are a few explosions; then tanks in close order; and soon after, trucks. On their sides we recognize the *French* flag. We are in the sector of the French First Army!

At noon, the Americans let us know that the Germans' "last stand" plan will never happen: Germany is in its death throes. The American Seventh Army is advised of our position and will pick us up.

May 6

We thought that for the first few days the French would keep close to the main lines of communication, but we have watched them spread out over the whole valley. A sizable contingent seems to have settled in Düntz.

Our situation is getting risky. There is no question of our explaining our position to them. We've heard about the "cleanup" in France. Should we hide out? No, the Americans say, that would make us suspect: just refuse to explain anything. That's easy to say.

Still doubtful, four of us nonetheless decide, after raising an improvised tricolor flag over the chalet, to go down to Düntz and meet our compatriots. We come across a group of forty very young men who have set up their mess at the inn. They cheerfully invite us to join them: Fill up, friends, you guys must have had a rough time here! They're very lively and talkative. These budding resistance fighters had enlisted when the Allied advance reached them, and they have been subsequently regrouped into a "special liberation commando." It is, in fact, very special. Their "battle train" consists of a few regulation jeeps together with "requisitioned vehicles" of the most varied description, into which have been packed (as they proudly show us) cases of brandy, silver, suitcases full of linen, jewelry, curios, cameras, and so forth.

"We've been having a great time," they explain. "We had all the Gretchens we wanted, If one made a fuss, pow, right between the eyes. Here in Austria, it's not so much fun. They told us to behave. That's why the officers are taking a little trip to Germany, the lucky bums."

We understand. We return to the chalet with our very French meal sticking in our craws. We now know all we need to know about the French First Army; and we are worried about our future.

May 7

Be patient, you're under our protection, the Americans answer when we say that we are in a hurry to leave the area. Especially since we were paid a visit by twelve armed Frenchmen who "just thought they'd drop in." They left unconvinced by the very vague account we gave of ourselves. They'll be back.

May 8

Germany has accepted unconditional surrender. Hitler is dead, and the country that has just capitulated now has Admiral Doenitz at its head.

Time is running out. We are starting to feel anything but safe. Leaving the chalet, we spread out over the mountainside. One comrade stays behind as sentinel.

May 9

We have spent the day in the woods, with no cause for alarm.

In the late afternoon, see a jeep drawn up outside the chalet. The letters USA stand out clearly on its side. We hurry down, and Captain Charlie, a tall, friendly character, welcomes us with a smile and an armful of cigarettes and canned corned beef. He belongs to Seventh Army intelligence. He knows nothing of our activity but has been ordered to bring us to the American zone "to receive compensation for important services rendered."

As soon as he was safe on American territory, Albert was warmly thanked. They knew who he was. They explained to him in detail the risks he would run if he went back to France, as he said he wanted to. It would be madness. They kept him at Seventh Army headquarters, and there, for the first time since the previous summer, he was able to communicate with his family and announce Jean's disappearance to Pierre, silent at the other end of the line. They pampered him for a week to give him time to think. They proposed sending him to the USA a free man. He would be given a place to live, work to do, and a brand-new sense of dignity. They would send him his family at the first opportunity.

He refused. He was a good Frenchman, a stubborn peasant who missed his home, a prodigal son convinced that his own people would be capable of understanding him. The Americans gave up trying to fathom this eccentric. They had done what they could. But they forced him to wait nine long months under their protection, in a camp where the cream of the first war criminals had been herded while awaiting trial.

Recovered by the French security police, brought home through official channels in the spring of '46, and put behind bars forthwith—without even a moment's stop-off at Suresnes—he was thus saved from summary liquidation.

It would scarcely be an exaggeration to say that the courts of justice received him with open arms. This was by no means their first case since the end of the war, but the FPP was thinly represented in Paris jails. With Doriot dead, and the majority of the party's leaders at large, Albert became an interesting quarry.

II

HOPSCOTCH

One spring day when I was four, I had to put on my plaid dress with the white collar, solemnly wash my hands, comb my hair more carefully than usual, and abandon my games and the garden in Suresnes. One two three down Rue du Bel Air to the station, four five six hop on the train. Don't ask questions, give me your hand. Seven eight nine Gare Saint-Lazare, hurry up, we're late.

At Rue des Saussaies, I had to climb three flights of stairs. I'm tired, don't squeeze my hand so hard. Maman, why are you shivering? Ten eleven twelve open the door.

A corridor. A waiting room. A large office.

In the years to follow, hanging on to my mother's sure hand like a little shadow, I became familiar with so many corridors, so many waiting rooms, so many offices. They would all have the same smell of stale tobacco, dampness, and stacked papers, the same brownish, yellowing, mildewed walls, and the same enchantment of not being alone, of being able to go there and leave with her. She took me with her everywhere. She sat me on wobbly wooden chairs. (Wait here for me, I'll be back, draw me a baby rabbit in the forest.) She settled me on Persian rugs in vast sitting rooms that smelled of floor wax. (Now be very good, I have to talk to this gentleman.) She buried me in the depths of velvet armchairs, in whose dusty odor I counted and recounted their gilded studs. With her, life was never less than beautiful.

In the office on Rue des Saussaies there is a large table covered with ink spots and cigarette burns. In a swivel chair behind it sits someone rather dreary and rather polite, who says to us, Wait, I'll send for him. He picks up the telephone and says, Madame B. is here with her little daughter. I think he's calling the doctor. I don't much like the idea but I tell myself I'll open my mouth cough cough cough then a little pat on the back of my head and bye-bye, back to my games.

The door opens. There are three of them. In the middle is someone rather dreary and rather nice. He comes toward us. Mother hasn't moved. I clutch her sleeve. I don't back away. He is very close to us. His eyes are moist, he is wearing a black tie and smells of lavender. Mother throws herself at him with a cry that is new to me. Even her weeping at night doesn't produce that sound. She draws back from him, her face beaming with the light of a broad, unsteady smile.

"Aren't you going to say hello?"

To please her, I hold out my hand and say, "How do you do, sir?"

My father picks me up in his arms and weeps quietly into my neck.

So it's you. I hadn't imagined you with those soft eyes. I thought you had a beard and a kepi, like the photograph from Aleppo in the green leather frame on the night table. You aren't scary, with that little smile. Next time I'll give you a kiss.

I touch his forehead. "You don't have much hair."

He laughs. "From now on, we'll see each other more often."

I ask where he will sleep in our two tiny rooms. No, no, there's no question of that. Oh.

One man is swiveling in the chair behind the desk, his nose buried in a filing folder. The two others are conversing in low voices without looking at us. He and she are smiling at each other. They whisper sweet words, touch, and look at me together: smiling, crying.

Then we have to leave. It's time for parting and no longer seeing each other or touching each other for years to come. I keep waving good-bye all the way down the corridor. My father is standing in the doorway between his two guards, blowing me kisses. Mother walks faster and faster, one two three down the stairs and quickly into the street, the air, the sun.

At the first pastry shop, she abruptly makes me go in. Without a word, we gorge ourselves on cake.

In the waiting room at Gare Saint-Lazare, Mother drops a coin into an American chewing-gum dispenser. Five little colored balls fall clicking into her hand, and she passes them to me.

Seated by the corner window of our third-class compartment, she speaks to me softly.

"Didn't you recognize your father?"

"I'd never seen him."

"I've shown you pictures."

"I thought he was younger."

"You won't call him 'sir' any more, will you?"

"When are we going to see him next?"

"Soon. We'll all go back together."

"And is *he* going to come and see us?"

"No. Not for a long time. Your father is a prisoner. That means he isn't allowed to live with us. But we'll wait! We have to love him very much and pray very hard for him to come back. Before you're grown up."

"And drink my soup and go to Mass and wash my hands and love you too?"

She smiles. "Yes, those things too."

In sparkling April sunlight, we start up from the station on Rue du Bel Air, catch our breath, then Rue de Bellevue, and we're home.

The great gray cube of the Suresnes house sits under its terraced roof on the side of Mont Valérien above catch-your-breath corner.

It is in the upper part of Suresnes, which is very different from the lower. The upper people have gardens, as well as their own shops, market, and church. They live high above the station and Hôpital Foch, and they have the privilege of buying their milk every evening at the farm near the top of the hill, just below the fort.

The ground floor of the house consists of garages and our small apartment. Upstairs live Pierre and Mathilde with their cats and two children.

The floors are connected by a dim flight of stone stairs, where the carpeting smells of tomcat and the brass rods holding down the carpet make a dull clink when you strike them with your foot. Halfway up the back wall between floors, a medium-sized square window fitted with bars looks out on dense, wild vegetation. Later, I will spend long hours at the foot of this window, trying to imagine a life passed behind bars in all weathers, trying to imagine the changing sky, the birds, the leaves, and the outside that belongs to other people.

In front of the garage doors there is a courtyard covered with clinkers; and surrounding the entire house, the garden.

It's among garnet-leaved cherry, unkempt elder, beds of violet iris, and ranks of Alpine fir saplings that I learn how to walk, how to keep my eyes open, how to name grasses, how to fashion skirts out of linden leaves sewn together with pliant twigs. I pirouette by the dwarf roses. I go shivering down the steps of the grotto (the relic of a former pleasure garden). I pluck geranium petals to give myself geisha lips. I learn how to climb trees, my heart beating fast, how to make animals out of smooth fresh chestnuts, how to stare unflinching into Pierre's bonfires, with tears running down either side of my laughing mouth.

The first memories of life—bubbles of dew threaded on a strand of gossamer—hang suspended between a pink horse chestnut and a privet hedge.

There is a garden in every childhood. The older children pursued theirs, through the well-kempt park of Tassin-la-Demi-Lune, in search of a roving father. I shall bury my childhood deep among the branches of Suresnes, in flight from this unknown father who has come back too late from his travels.

A thin, dull-complexioned girl is crossing a garden playing hopscotch. As events follow one another, she stops hopping (first on one foot, then on both) to consider and evaluate the changes they will make in her wondering-child's life. The straight brown bangs rise and fall across her forehead as she lands or jumps. They call her, and she answers. Time for supper, time to go to sleep. Get dressed now, you're going to school. Give me your hand, we're going to see Father. She goes, she returns, then back to her hopscotch; on one foot, then both, she makes a thousand round trips between "home" and "rest."

The postwar years bring their particular flavor, their uncertainty and monotony, and the little girl sings to herself as she hops. Hers is a closed world, marked out and hemmed in for years to come. She moves through it obediently, trotting along behind the grownups.

She is four years old with the cat and the fiddle, four years old as she rows her boat and runs after the farmer's wife. She is four years old in the name of the Father and of the Son, O lamb of God and who's afraid of the big bad wolf? She is four years old, and who killed Cock Robin, Jack fell down and broke his crown but the cow jumped over the moon, thirteen fourteen, maids a-courting, and you *will* come back. Four years old: and we'll all feel gay when Albert comes home; but it won't be all that soon.

Come rain or shine, I never stopped playing hopscotch.

Mother had never been a sanctimonious sort of Catholic. As a romantically minded girl, she had liked to spend time inside churches: their cool, dark mystery made her shiver. She had looked beautiful at her first communion, with lowered eyelids and white kid gloves tightly covering her wrists. Before religion could fill up her dreams, she fell in love, and it was to love that she dedicated all the piety of which her imaginative soul was capable. She made a gentle bride. Religion accompanied her throughout her life, along with other faithfully observed rituals. You baptized your children and went to Mass: that's what is done in provincial towns.

But in the uneasy period after the war, there blew through the family a gust of piety from which she had a hard time recovering. Alice in Sorrowland was fertile ground, and she was looked after: God stretched forth His hand to her, the Church extended its charitable arms, and for a while it became her refuge. The two years before the trial provided a foretaste of the mystical inveiglement that was to follow. No one expected a miracle, and living under the shadow of a verdict, without knowing how many years of penitence were in store for you, was a painful ordeal. In this atmosphere of contrition and hopelessness the family religion set its roots, from which sprang the jungle that later engulfed us.

For a long time Alice went to Mass every morning. If her devotion eventually weakened, it was through no wavering of faith but because Juliette, as the period of atonement went endlessly on, rebelled and stopped her getting up so early. On an empty stomach, Madame, in every kind of weather and going to work afterward, all that effort, no, you won't be able to stand it. She brusquely pointed out that even little Jesus, the Good Lord Himself, was not likely to count up her Masses and deduct them from the prison term.

People were very pious in our part of Suresnes, and they spread the mantle of their charity over us. On Sundays we would gather after Mass around the vendors of *Catholic Life*; and we could have done a lot worse. The Catholic Scouts were then very popular. Paul and Anne joined them and found a refuge of sorts. They naturally felt somewhat apart, afflicted as they were with a wound no amount of Christian balm could heal. But the others all "knew" and kept their peace.

Once the gossiping was over, and Juliette had satisfied momentary curiosity by telling everybody in plain language exactly what had happened (That way, Madame, they won't ask any more questions), the community very quickly took us under its wing.

In the Bellevue-Bel Air district of Suresnes, no one ever referred to us as "quisling kids."

Where could I have been not to have heard her screaming on the spring day when she received the message from a far-off camp in Germany? No doubt I was running behind Pierre down the untended pathways of Mont Valérien, along the edge of the cliff that surrounds the fort. No doubt I was laughing, gasping for breath, falling down in the daisies—he had never made such funny faces to keep me laughing, far away from the house, far away from a mother's screams. I was no doubt spinning on the merry-go-round in lower Suresnes—faster! faster!—astride my pink pig, clutching its worn papier-mâché ear in one hand, stretching the other toward the tassel ring that swung beneath the pastel corolla of the old carousel. If you catch it, you win a ride (just one more! just one more!), while Juliette's bright gaze follows you around. Enjoy yourself, we have plenty of time, enjoy yourself, far away from the house, far away from a screaming mother.

Jean. My little Jean. Gone. Flown up into the clouds on the wings of a burning merry-go-round. —And the whole gray house resounded with the horrible refrain of her cries, from the core of the dim stairway to the quivering tips of the horse chestnuts. She hadn't, she hadn't want him to leave; had said nothing; did not fall down. Now screams. Paul would hold her hand: Mother, you aren't alone. Mother, make the tears come, you have to empty this grief that's howling through you. Mother, I'm here, stop frightening me.

She had calmed down. The sobbing of the storm broke up into rivulets, which year after year drained into her deepest glades.

She fell silent, but she sought him everywhere: among the tapers of memorial chapels, in the scent of damp earth, in the wind among the cypress trees, along the roadsides of France and Germany whenever she came across a white and green cemetery. She would walk through it, laden with flowers, stopping at the crosses marked *Unbekannt,* "unknown," coolly depositing a flower and proceeding on her pilgrimage of the absurd. Disappeared. Dispersed. Why here rather than there?

All the *Unbekannten* of the earth were my brothers.

I was fascinated by the American cemetery on Mont Valérien. Our sunny Sunday walks often took us there. I would run between the rows of white crosses, whose straight lines were laid out across gently sloping lawns. From one Sunday to the next, I would stop in front of all the crosses in one row, and then another, until I knew them by heart, in the innocent and renewed hope of reading his name, which would at last glitter through my tears and set me running down the grassy slope to throw myself into my mother's arms and whisper in her ear, I've found him, he's up there, stop looking for him, let him sleep and stop haunting my dreams.

Because for months on end, when I said my prayers, she made me repeat with clasped hands, O God, make Jean come back. I didn't want him to come back, that boy with the worried look and vague smile out of the poor snapshots of his last weeks in France. I knew nothing of his body, his arms, his embrace, or his breath in my hair. I knew nothing tangible. I no longer knew how he had loved me and rocked me and kissed me as she kept endlessly telling us so that we wouldn't forget him. Make Jean not come back, answered the voice in my breast, make him go on being a snapshot, a few scattered letters in that irregular, clumsy handwriting, a frailness, the handful of things moldering inside a carton fastened with tenderness, clothes kept in mothballs. Make him stay inside the closet, snug among his blue baby's ribbons.

He never came back. But at night, I was afraid that a young ghost would open my bedroom door, afloat on a cloud of incense, gather me in his arms, and take me up the hill to the shadow of his white cross. By dint of staring at his photograph—as in a ritual to ward off witches, I used to hide it under my pillow (fearfully)—I would see his lips move and his eyes come to life, and I would die of fright. I would command him to disappear forever into his starry night. Then I would be overcome with remorse, call him back, and imagine I heard his voice singing me "Stille Nacht." In the morning I would wake up reassured to see the shadows on the wall dispelled by daylight, to find Mother smilingly bending over the bars of my crib, have her pick me up, carry me into the warm kitchen, and set me down, limp, in front of my cup of Ovaltine. She would not speak about him again until that evening.

There was a mute shriek that issued from her smile, from her serenity, from the bosom in which I buried myself each evening to say my prayer. It was this shriek stifled in her heart that prevented my young brother from dying and made me keep the taste of him in my mouth, like the wafer at Sunday communion that I used to swallow with nausea—a bitter medicine that makes you shed tears of disgust; but swallow it, it's to make you get well.

For a long time, Alice would not believe that her son was dead. She made every possible inquiry, without telling Albert. His proofs were not hers, and in any case they could not talk about Jean together, they could not do it. For a long time, she expected a letter, a message, the return of an amnesiac, a door opening to reveal him standing there, clothed in rays of light like the illustration of the Sacred Heart in my missal. She said nothing; but every once in a while she would stop still, no matter where she was, in the street, on the train, at dinner, and her eyes would overflow. *I* knew what that meant—here we go again, he's back—and I would loathe this young *unbekannt* brother.

Little by little, the chances vanished of finding the least particle of her disintegrated son somewhere under an eastern wind. There remained the terrible certainty, the only acceptable one, of his definitive and absolute disappearance; and so the evening prayer changed its tune. "Our little brother who art in heaven, make Father come back." The prayer took on meaning, and it held its course until it was granted.

Since the end of the war—since the time he laid his wife Marie to rest, in the shade of the gray steeple on the hillside at Saint-Eusèbe—Grandfather Louis has not left his lair. In the aftermath of dubious investments whose failure was hastened by the war, he has sold his farms to raise money. He has retired to his estate. He sees no one. He writes, counts, meditates in his little green office, and only drives his Citroën 15 to the bank or to the office of the lawyer who handles his lands.

He drives through the forest at eighty miles an hour, as if to avoid hearing what the trees are murmuring as he passes. He traverses the gloomy town of Champagne-sur-Seine, avoids the eyes of others, does not acknowledge the greetings of a few rash, persistent acquaintances, and imagines that gibes and insults accumulate in his wake.

He is contemptuous of the poor folk who gleefully mock his shame-ridden fate. They draw up at his gate on Sundays and point at his house with open mouths and nodding heads, as if they imagined it to have been a Nazi hunting lodge or one of the Wehrmacht's brothels.

They even came to demand an explanation of the tunnel dug under his garden: he might have hidden Germans in it. Louis said, Why, of course, come and see for yourself. He led them behind the house up to the chicken coop. There is indeed a tunnel. It was an idea he had had to let his hens go peck in the upper orchard, which is separated from the garden by a lane. I don't advise using it, you might get dirty. It's ten years the little pests have been messing it up. You understand. —The others went away laughing.

As the weeks passed, they harassed the old man less. They let him live in peace in his Thistles; they would only turn to look at him when he went by in his gray hat and yellow leather gloves, at the wheel of his black car.

He has learned without flinching of Jean's disappearance and of his son's return and imprisonment. Shut inside his château, walled in by impenetrable silence, he seems to have lost interest in a family that has disintegrated when it was on the point of succeeding him. He had erected a setting appropriate to its prosperity, not its collapse.

Alice is weary of being frustrated by his absence and by his refusal to visit the children in Suresnes. (And what about his son in prison? He has not deigned to reply.) On the threshold of her first winter as the wife of a political prisoner, she decides to break the rule of silence, to confront the bear in his solitude and force her way into the icy house.

One snowy evening before Christmas, she takes a train from Gare de Lyon and arrives during the night on foot. The dog barks, and a light is turned on over the front steps. Germaine comes to open the door for her, welcoming her with her nasal twang and carrying her big bunch of keys. Louis receives her dressed in indoor attire—a dark red jacket of heavy wool with a cord tied around the waist and a nightcap pulled down to his eyebrows.

"Alice, you shouldn't have gone to so much trouble."

"I wanted to see you before Christmas, Father. And bring you a little present."

As she enters the vestibule, she is submerged in a winter worse than the one outside.

"How can you live in such cold?"

"It's nice in here! Touch the radiators."

She declines, shivers, and hands him a package.

"It's not much. Wool gloves. Juliette knitted one and I made the other."

"How nice! Come into the kitchen and warm up. There's some soup Germaine has been keeping hot."

The vast kitchen is agreeable and warm. A pleasant smell of leeks rises toward the opaline lamp. Germaine is merrily emptying huge ladles of vegetable soup into a bowl. Hunched over, Alice presses her two hands, blue with cold, against her breast. She closes her eyes in the comforting fragrance. Then she looks across the table at Louis. She slowly pushes her purple knitted toque onto the back of her head, shakes her hair loose, and smiles.

"It's been a long time, Father."

"Yes, a long time."

(Father not mine, how I wish you would understand me! Just one tender gesture, one glance. How strong you are in your solitude! In what country, under what stars have you known love?)

The scalding liquid makes her shiver. The dog lying under the table heaves a long sigh. Louis is turning a salt-free rusk in his fingers.

"How are you, Father?"

"Fine, just fine."

(You don't want to talk to me. You'll tell me nothing. You're like a snowman: a stiff lump in starlight. What spring will thaw you out? A dull weariness descends through all her limbs. To sleep in this milky light, sleep without dreaming, sleep for days and nights in a snowy stillness, with no images leaving their deposit of indelible migraines at the back of her eyes. How many more winters must be spent huddling in a void? He is alone, too, behind his walls, doors, and locks. He's cold. He is watching his cell walls crack and ooze from the cold outside.)

"Father, he needs you."

"There's nothing I can do for him. You're his wife. Be a wife to him. He has lawyers. He has his conscience. He doesn't need a father."

"But he's your son!"

"I had two sons. One of them died. I lost the other. That's all there is to it. I don't ask anything of anyone. Except to be left in peace."

The water is singing in the kettle. Germaine is preparing the hot-water bottles.

(Soon I'll sink into sleep in an ice-cold room. In the early morning the kitchen will be warm, my coffee will be ready, and Germaine will butter my pieces of toast. She will squeeze my hands and tell me how many rosaries she says each day to save the world. And you will watch me as I leave, slipping on patches of ice. "All there is to it"—how true! I wanted to tell you about our cramped life. How at school the children suffer from being different, from never being able to speak out. About the jewels I've sold, and the money that will soon be gone. How mixed up I am. And the questions he asks me about you. Fearful father not mine, I accept the role of orphan. I'll never ask you for anything again.)

She left in the morning, feeling ice-cold within. Louis kissed her good-bye and told her not to be discouraged.

"Since the roads are frozen, I'm not taking the car. Germaine will go with you. Phone me. Let me know the date of the trial. I'll be there."

She turned away. He might have said, just as calmly: Let me know the date of the execution. I'll be there.

Months passed, and the preliminary judicial examination dragged on. I wasn't yet going to school: in the afternoon, a woman from our neighborhood used to teach me how to count and read. It was ages since the last of our savings had been spent, and we were now dipping into Mother's jewels. She used to take them secretly to Paris and sell them in dark, out-of-the-way places where, naturally, they robbed her.

I saw less and less of her during the day. She made the rounds of lawyers' offices, police stations, prisons, and Lord knows where else. I used to wait for her patiently, playing hopscotch on the gravel, stopping every two minutes to ask Juliette the time. At the approach of evening I was given my signal: she won't be long now, off you go.

I would rush out to my lookout station and perch on a rough concrete boundary stone under the branches of the big catalpa, above the corner of Rue du Bel Air. While I waited for her, I hummed the songs Juliette had been singing to herself since morning. Suddenly she would be there: a weary silhouette at the lower end of the stony street. She was an apparition more miraculous than any in sacred story, from Archangel Gabriel to the Holy Ghost. With a laugh I'd run off, swinging my outspread arms back and forth until, at the end of the path, I wrapped them violently around her neck.

We had a passionate, loving relationship. I found her mysteriously beautiful and strong—someone watched over by fairies. In spite of all the tears and shocks that filled her life, I used to think that nothing awful could ever, ever befall her. Every morning I would go on opening my eyes to her smile. Every evening I would wait for her at the intersection and jump into her arms to breathe in her perfume and nuzzle her neck; and make her laugh, taking her weariness by the hand and tugging it toward the top of the slope.

Months passed, and every night, once the door had been shut on my haunted sleep, the two women held counsel. They stayed together for hours, until very late at night, whispering beneath the red lampshades of the chandelier in a flurry of knitting needles. (To make a little money, they knitted pullovers commissioned by a woman friend who resold them to dress shops. Jacquard patterns were then the fashion. They made intricate, variegated miles of them, drooping with sleep, to which they finally yielded with their heads full of zigzags.)

Because Juliette was still there. It was now ten years that she had been moored to our ship. She was from a poor peasant family, one of four sisters. Two had married early, the other two had gone to work "in service" because there was no more bread at home. Beautiful as she was, after one disappointment she had never again tried to marry. "My pet," she would say, "I'm through with men. I'd rather grow old alone than look after some old man who has rheumatism and who'd spend all my savings and run after trollops. Or worse. Look at your poor mother!" Juliette hadn't had a man, never mind, she'd still had a family. We were the sole beneficiaries of her youth, her laughter, and her unbelievable vitality. She was the panacea of those dark years. On our prison ship, she was a voluntary member: our misfortunes were no concern of hers, and she could have shut her ears and fled. She stayed on, took the helm, and assured the survival of the entire crew.

There had been other maids in our household, but when I looked at Juliette, I used to tell myself that the others, whose quips or blunders were sometimes mentioned, must belong to a vanished species. Martha, Marie, and Adèle had been in Mother's service in some long lost epoch. They were anecdotes. They belonged in Madame Tussaud's. But we had Juliette. On the day I was born, she was still a maid; then, very quickly, I became her daughter. I had no father; but she was a second mother.

Chocolate cake, mustard plasters, homework (I-don't-know-what-it-means-but-hurry-up-and-finish-it—you can count faster than I can): Juliette. Nose drops (no, Mother, not you), bread and butter with apricot jam on the train to Mâcon, holidays in the country (the children look so peaked, I'll take them to my mother's, we'll all squeeze in), cows in the meadows: Juliette. Packages for prison; you'll have to leave, Juliette, I can't pay your wages, but Madame, you're crazy, who'll raise the children? and the waiting in the evenings, the smiles and chapped hands: Juliette. Doing the errands in town, come on, we'll go meet Mother at the station (the train was pulling out, she wasn't there), ta-rom-pa-pom-pom: Juliette.

She never asked for anything. She glued our family together again and placed a roof on our ruined house. She stayed on. It was as simple as that.

One morning they came for her. She asked, Will it take long? They weren't nasty, they didn't rush her. They said, We have to ask you some questions. Mother did not want to let her go. Why her? What do they want of her? We have orders. She won't be harmed in any way.

As if she had been doing it all her life, she untied her apron, took a blanket on her arm, and kissed me good-bye. Don't worry. I'm too smart for them. Go play in the garden. I'll be back tomorrow in time for your afternoon snack.

I waited for her with my nose glued to the windowpane. Pierre consoled Mother: "Don't be upset. It's standard procedure. They're only doing their job. Servants talk a lot, and a little fooling around in the pantry here and there—it livens up the indictment. With Juliette, they're in for a disappointment."

She returned two days later, with her hair a little mussed, her cheeks aflame, her eyes sharp, very proud of herself. She put the blanket away, stroked the cat, tied on her apron, and sat down at the kitchen table.

"Well?"

"Don't give it a thought, Madame. I had nothing to tell them. The bother was all theirs. Good heavens, what do they expect! So servants hear a lot of things, and you know—now they're going to kick you out, and who came to see them and did they speak German, did they mistreat you, and where did they get their money, and did he ever take any interest in the children, and did he travel a lot, and what about his wife, was he unfaithful, and what about phone calls and so forth and so on. I said no, a fine father, a fine husband, and anyway, I don't eavesdrop, I just waited on their guests at table, when people are pleased they say so, I don't have any idea what they talked about. And Monsieur B.'s work—what do I know, I'm not educated enough. I'm paid well, I'm treated well, I'm lodged, I'm fed, and I've nothing to say! There!"

As she started to laugh, she wiped away a tear that was making a detour around her cheekbone, and Mother rushed across the room and embraced her.

Alice had been asked questions, too. When she went to see them, she would be made up, inaccessible, dressed in her most stylish suit. She would take out her cigarette holder, raise a finely drawn eyebrow, and cross her silken legs in such a manner that they would never have dared push her. They were always very discreet with her. They even offered to make everything easy for her in case she wanted a quick, clean divorce.

Atop her high wooden heels, her hand gripping the bag that hung from her shoulder, she had left the room without answering.

THE KING AT COURT

January 1948

Letter to a friend from the Fresnes prison; or, a collaborator's backward glance on the eve of his trial.

So this is the point I have reached. My preliminary examination ended two months ago. It went without difficulty, because I had nothing to conceal. I hardly need tell you that my file contains no hint of criminal denunciations or actions of any kind whatsoever. It does nevertheless include two murders for which I bear a share of responsibility—one because I authorized it, the other because I transmitted an order that Doriot had given me. The victims were two FPP members who were executed as examples. They were guilty of looting and informing on behalf of the Gestapo. The prosecution has acknowledged this.

I may be blamed for having organized a secret service, but aside from the training of new cadres, its real purpose was to combat the Russian spy network (NKVD). I may be blamed for having been named Commissar in Normandy, but that plan was never even initiated. Lastly, I may be blamed for the party's schools, but there again they led to no actions—none of my trainees was ever dropped by parachute. Obviously I was a member of the governing council of the FPP, but, in this domain, nothing can have been held against me since my activity was social and corporatist before everything else. Otherwise, I was constantly hostile to all the disreputable and dishonorable activities that were carried out under the shelter of our flag for the material benefit of a few people.

If everyone accepted their responsibilities, my defense would present no insurmountable difficulties. But this is not the case. Furthermore, Ambassador Otto Abetz has declared that "he did not remember knowing me, but that he had always heard me referred to as Doriot's chief lieutenant." Since this stupid statement cannot help but impress the jury, I have a hard row to hoe.

What will be my attitude in court? You can guess the answer. I shall go in with my head held high and explain my conduct in straightforward fashion. I hope I make myself heard. It was the imperative desire to combat bolshevism that led me to actively enter politics. Again, it was anticommunism (I accept the possibility of its having been overly exclusive and narrow) that impelled me toward "collaboration."

But I utterly repudiate the tendencies that made me strive to achieve "personal power" for the chief I had decided to follow (or for any other). My experience in the FPP first of all, and later observations during my internment with Nazi leaders, have shown me the folly of such a system. What's more, I no longer believe in "politics." I have seen too many dirty tricks, too much degradation (whatever the party concerned), and I have come to the conclusion that in order to be honest and beneficial, politics must be conducted by saints. Since this is not possible, I can only see it as a field for profit and personal ambition, and I have only one wish: to keep clear of it forever.

There remains the question of my attachment to Doriot. I believed in him. He had seemed to me an extraordinary political animal, and it's to him that I owe my improved understanding of social problems. Because of the clarity of his views in this domain, I continued to follow him, even when the closer contact I had with him, after '42, showed me that he was far from possessing all the virtues I might have wished for in the party leader I had imagined.

Unfortunately, I am obliged to admit that he was terribly mistaken, and that he committed unforgivable errors in allowing his party's flag to provide refuge for adventurers and criminals.

I am now convinced that I was not cut out for such activity. I wanted to devote all my faith and all my strength to an ideal that today I see was pure illusion. That is where my great error lay. I am ill suited to any activity that cannot be pursued unabashedly and wholeheartedly. It's a little late, unfortunately, to realize this. In a word, I regret—the expression does not frighten me—I bitterly regret giving nine years of my life to an unworthy cause.

Today, what will the result be, with Doriot gone? I have no illusions. I shall be condemned to death. This conviction will dictate my attitude in court. The question will not be to what punishment I may be sentenced, but how.

What concerns me above all is proving that my conscience is free of blame and that—no matter what happens—my children can always be proud of the name they bear. The rest no longer matters.

This evening, when I pray, she hugs me harder than usual. And she repeats over and over you have to pray you have to pray my beloved sleep tight pray tomorrow think about Father very hard he needs God you have to think of Jean he's alone you have to pray. Gently I draw back my forehead from her neck and look at her. She resembles someone who has just awakened bolt upright from a nightmare. She gets up from the creaky chair keeps me in her arms I cling to her neck in silence voices whispering behind the half-open door she lays me down in my bed my arms do not let go her smile is frozen, a tear falls into my ear.

She disengages herself a small high sob sticks in her throat. Mother don't close the door she turns out the light behind her disappears into the yellow light of the corridor, for one second her profile bent and my eyes wide open stare at the bright frame hovering around the door. Outside, winter.

A bitter aroma of black coffee comes from the kitchen. I hear the water gurgling through the filter in the coffee pot. Juliette's foot-steps—she must be setting a tray down on the dining room table. Coffee glasses being filled. Something's happening. Sighs. Silence. Voices. Anne feels her way into the bedroom and starts undressing.

"Anne—"

"Aren't you asleep?"

"No."

"Shut your eyes, right away. You have to go to school tomorrow."

"So do you."

"Not me. Not tomorrow. Neither does Paul. We're going with Mother to court."

"I want to go too."

"You're too little."

"Is it a beautiful court?"

"I'll tell you about it if you're good. You've got to be very nice. It's going to be a hard week. Mother is upset."

I bury my nose in my pillow. All at once, I'm very tall. But only my legs have grown, like stems. I am walking through the snow on my stiltlike legs. For a long time I glide between two rows of firs. At my passage, the light snow rises like iridescent stars from the branches. When I reach the Court and start up the palace steps, frost has set a fine crown on my hair, which is dragging along the ground, like a long cape. I am about to knock at the lofty sculpted portal when, with a hushed sound, its two doors swing open, and I enter a wonderful château. The ceiling is made of violet glass, and the walls are hung with bird feathers and butterfly wings. At the far end of a long hall, its floor of blue mother-of-pearl, my father is seated on his throne, smiling. He says to me, Come nearer, do not be afraid. He offers me a tray laden with sweets. He says to me, I know you are a good child; so you may stay in my Court, at my side, until the end of time. He claps his hands, which are covered with glittering rings. A very beautiful girl comes toward him, half reclining in a little barque drawn by two white swans. Her long hair is curly and blonde, her violet eyes are very large, but they have forgotten to draw her mouth. My father rises, offers her his hand, and says to me, Allow me to introduce Princess Justice! Thousands of bells start pealing. It's six o'clock, the alarm clock falls under Mother's bed and she can't turn it off, Anne is grumbling and already saying, Juliette, open the door! In the kitchen, the kettle is singing.

Monday, January 12, 1948

At seven o'clock sharp, a car comes to a halt on the gravel. Its door slams shut in the navy-blue morning. Grandfather rings. He is very formally dressed. He is close-shaven. The sides of his nose are slightly blotchy.

"Sit down, Monsieur. You'll have a cup of coffee, won't you?"

"With pleasure, Juliette. But let's not linger."

He does not sit down or take off his dark gray coat with the beaver collar, and he holds on to his hat and gloves. He stares down at his black shoes and then asks for a brush. Sitting down at last, with his coat bunched about him, he starts working away at three specks of mud on the edge of one of his soles.

Mother is very pale: powdered face, black suit. In the bathroom's harsh light, she bends her face toward the mirror and rubs her cheeks with her fingertips. She reddens her lips and pulls a fur toque down over her hair. Juliette helps her into her Persian lamb jacket. Watching her, Grandfather nods his head as if to say, you're looking splendid. They're about to leave. I run from hug to hug. Juliette sniffles, it'll be all right, Madame. There is a knock at the door. It's Pierre, smiling: I'm coming with you. He pinches my cheek. Why are they still waiting around?

Lifting the curtain from the frost-whitened pane, Juliette and I watch the car drive off into the bluish glow of the street.

"Come and drink your hot chocolate. How many slices of bread this morning?"

That evening, we listen for the sound of a car. Juliette has set the table in the dining room. Grandfather will be dining with us. This worries me.

"What bed is he going to sleep in?"

"He's staying at the hotel down the hill in Suresnes."

Truly unusual! These are very special days in our lives.

"Tell me, what do they do in this court?"

"My poor darling, it's your father's trial. It's too complicated for you. Listen, at the end of this week, we'll know if he's all right, or if—what can I say?—he isn't all right."

"So Grandfather's come to pick him up and bring him home?"

"You can count on that like snow in July. We just want him to get out of it alive. If we were only sure of that . . ."

She turns away and addresses the faucet. I think, it's like Jean. He's going to die, and Mother will cry twice as much.

Here they are. No one speaks. Mother smiles at me—so sad-ly—as she removes her toque. Grandfather is very red.

The soup is already steaming on the table. Everybody sits down. Everyone sighs. You hear only the clatter of spoon on dish and the gurgle of soup being swallowed. I've been good long enough. I finish my soup, I put down my spoon, and I shout:

"So, who is the king in this court?"

Spoons stop in mid air. They glance at one another and burst out laughing. Soon, paying no more attention to me, they all start talking.

Having six FPPs in the dock is no good for Albert. . . . The indictment was very hard . . . The defense will have a hard time . . . Look at how he took it today . . . He'll never manage to stay calm till the very end . . . I thought Father looked very handsome in his glasses . . . He's grown thinner . . . He won't get through it . . . What a lot of people . . . It's scary . . . They're going to blame him for every collaborationist crime in the book . . . Just wait till you see the morning papers . . .

Maman hides her face in her hands. That's enough. We're talking too much in front of the little girl.

Grandfather stands up with great dignity. No, thank you, no coffee. I'm going to bed. I'll pick you up tomorrow at seven.

From the defendant's diary

After the indictment had been read, business began with my interrogation. For twenty minutes I was allowed to justify my conduct the way I wanted to. At that moment I truly believed that the presiding judge would keep his promise as a man of honor and let me have all the time I needed to express my views.

But when I came to Oran and underlined how that tragic event had radically changed my attitude, the judge interrupted me and said, "Now listen, B. You're a man who has won praise wherever you've gone—at the university, in the army, in business. You're a man of your word. You were a brilliant officer. You have submitted statements that I found compelling and sincere. I'm sure that a man like you will now be able to tell the Court, with the same sincerity, how this could have happened to you: how—and by whom—you were persuaded to betray your own country."

That made things clear. I was to humble myself, beat my breast, and accuse Doriot, that traitor, of having lured me into treason. I would then become the well-behaved little boy who has gone astray and to whom the Court could show leniency. At the same time, thanks to my "sensational revelations" about Doriot's infamous behavior, the newspapers could blacken and tear to shreds this man who, with all his faults, was still a giant compared to the midgets of the Fourth Republic. No thank you. That is not my way.

So it was with my usual intensity that I shouted my reply at the bench, leaving them in no doubt as to the humility they could expect from the defense.

From then on, it was a free-for-all. I was faced with a presiding judge who was furious at having failed in a maneuver in which he thought I would join, and who now resolved to get rid of me as soon as possible by using every means to cut my explanations short. It was an exhausting five-hour struggle.

Tuesday, January 13, 1948

On her way with me to the School of Our Lady in lower Suresnes, Juliette stops at the newspaper store to ask for *Le Figaro* and *L'Humanité*. The little lady looks at us pointedly. She is about to say something to us: the wart under her chin, with its sprouts of hair, is trembling. Juliette's hand is already on the door handle, but we are not to escape that nasal voice.

"So this is the week?"

"I see you've been reading the papers."

"Not exactly reading them—it was on the front page of *L'Humanité*, it caught my eye."

"On the front page! They're laying it on. At least there's no picture, that's something."

Madame Rosette forces a smile in my direction, nodding her head and probably feeling very righteous.

"It's not the children's fault."

"You leave the children out of it!"

"Well, just the same, if he gets out of this, he's a lucky man!"

Juliette grabs me by the sleeve and slams the door. We walk fast. The cold is stinging my skin, and I pull my scarf up over my nose. I hear Juliette muttering incomprehensibly. I look up at her—Your nose is dripping!—and she wipes it with her woolen glove. We pass people hurrying to catch the train and women in headscarves with shopping baskets. At the school entrance, she kisses me good-bye without a word and leaves me in the courtyard. With my schoolbag strapped to my back, my clogs tapping on the cobblestones, I join the dance.

ABWEHR SPY AND DORIOT HENCHMAN:
ALBERT B. DESERVES THE DEATH PENALTY

Albert B., the former national secretary of the FPP, of which he was a charter member, appeared in court yesterday with four FPP accomplices. They included Yves D., editor-in-chief of *Le Petit Parisien*.

B. was a member of the Abwehr and was Doriot's right-hand man. With the help of an annual German subsidy of 150,000 francs, he created with Doriot a "counterespionage service" on behalf of the Nazis.

B. is eloquent and arrogant. But in spite of all his bad faith, he was unable to deny his treasonable acts. In particular, he admitted that in Germany after the Liberation he established special schools for spying and sabotage that were truly seedbeds of treason.

The trial, which promises to be highly instructive, will last through the week.

(*L'Humanité*)

A light, dry wind is snapping the branches in the overarching ink-blue night. Sitting next to the furnace, Juliette is holding me on her lap and telling me the story of the little match girl for the tenth time. She says that's enough for today. Then sing! But the visitors at court are back.

Paul is white. Grandfather is unchanged. Mother collapses sobbing in a chair. Juliette brings over a bottle of port and fills a glass: drink it, it'll warm you up.

Alice grasps her wrist and holds it tight.

"You understand, Juliette, you do understand."

"I understand, Madame."

". . . seeing him there so tense, in that horrible courtroom, listening to them go after him as if he were a criminal . . ."

"I understand, Madame. Try to calm down."

". . . seeing him there a few feet away and not being able to touch him or talk to him."

"It may still work out, Madame."

"But they're doing it deliberately. They're out to kill him."

"My dear Alice, be reasonable. You surely didn't expect them to welcome him with flowers. Everything depends on the way he acts. He's very nervous. I'm afraid he's capable of saying anything."

"He trusted them too much. When I think that he wouldn't allow the work he did for the Americans to be used in his defense—he's insane!"

"The boy suffers from pride. It's congenital—"

"And hereditary, Father!"

"Really!—But we're not in '46 any more. Other FPP officials have been given relatively mild sentences."

"Oh, of course! They repudiated Doriot. They claim they 're-sisted' the majority in the political committee. Ask Albert, who knows what really happened. But *he* didn't abandon Doriot. He went right down the line with him. Loyal friends! But the worst—and you know it's just a maneuver—the worst is that the Albert B. affair and the M. affair are being judged at the same trial. One has to do with politics and the other with murder. They've done it to confuse the issues—to make him look like the boss of a gang of killers. That way there will be bloodshed involved in his trial."

"Albert has accepted his responsibilities. He will have to justify what he did."

"You saw very well that they won't let him speak!"

ALBERT B., FORMER FPP LEADER,
TRIED FOR WARTIME ACTIVITIES

Otto Abetz has declared that Albert B. was Jacques Doriot's "Number One" subordinate. But in the courtroom yesterday, the defendant cast himself in a minor role. . . . He is vainly attempting to minimize the part he played by insisting that he only informed the enemy in matters of "public opinion." It is clear that he remained in constant touch with the officers in the Hotel Lutetia, where he was registered under the number 30,018.

(*Le Figaro*)

THREE FPP LEADERS WERE SPIES

The court today was concerned with another important member of the FPP, Albert B. . . . Successively regional delegate for Lyons and member of the political committee, he was named by Doriot in June, 1941, as head of a secret espionage service that operated in conjunction with the OKW. After the Normandy landings, he turned his energies to the creation of commando squads to harass the Allied rear lines. In Germany, he organized and directed a number of schools specializing in sabotage.

(*Le Monde*)

Anne is not going to Court tomorrow. She will stay home; and *I* won't go to school. If the weather is nice, we'll go walking on the hill by the fort.

The second day of the trial was taken up with the interrogation of my comrades, which was quickly dispatched. But the presiding judge took evident pleasure in prolonging the examination of the three men involved in the M. affair. Whereas everything that touched on the very substance of the trial—all the issues of politics and collaboration—were quickly set aside, when the question of the executions in Normandy and Germany arose, why, then the judge had all the time in the world.

How patient he became in spite of the late hour, and how scrupulously methodical! The three men had acknowledged the facts. They themselves were the source of the accusations leveled against them. There was nothing to argue about. Nevertheless, the judge turned the question over and over again, so that the jury would be in no doubt that everything else was of no importance, and that all our activities were drenched in blood.

This procedure is among the more flagrant outrages of the trial. But all that effort went unrewarded, for there was ultimately no way of avoiding a ruling of incompetency.

Wednesday, January 14, 1948

It's very cold. I didn't hear them leave this morning. I'm lying in bed under a pile of Babar books that I know by heart. Anne is also spending the morning in bed. She's brought me my hot chocolate.

Mathilde enters in her bathrobe and slippers, with our little cousin hanging on her hand behind her. She offers Juliette the newspapers.

"Did you see the papers this morning: Juliette, it's awful. My poor sister! I'm afraid that this time he's done for."

The examination of B.'s five co-defendants, all influential members of the FPP, only confirms what was evident during B.'s testimony the day before. From the beginning, the FPP indulged in the most abject forms of treason. The entire day was devoted to vileness and bloodshed. All five belonged to Action Groups whose mission was to spy on behalf of the Nazis in Paris, Tunisia, and Normandy. . . .

(L'Humanité)

Anne closes the bedroom door. She sits cross-legged on the double bed and leafs through the newspapers, rocking back and forth, her lips drawn as she repeats it's not true, it's not true.

"Read the story you're reading out loud!"

"It's not a story for you. You wouldn't understand it."

"You promised to tell me about the court."

"Yes, my baby. As soon as I know how it ends."

A misty evening falls. When Juliette opened the windows to draw the shutters, a damp smell of cold smoke entered the kitchen. The three of us are sitting around the flowered oilcloth. We are playing Memory. The ticking of the old alarm clock fills the silence. I'm annoyed with them for playing so apathetically, and for a change I suggest a game of War. Anne pouts. Juliette says, I have to strain the soup. She stands up armed with her ladle and sets about her task. It is soon interrupted by the rattling of a key in the lock. We jump up.

Alice falls into outstretched arms. She closes her eyes and leans her head against Juliette's shoulder; opens her eyes, which meet mine; in a choked voice enunciates her words, "They want the death penalty."

From the defendant's diary

How can I describe the summing up for the prosecution? A long scream of hatred punctuated by the hysterical gesticulation of a sadist. Talent? None. Dignity or vision? Not a trace. For more than two hours this lunatic kept at it. He was out for blood. The Communist Party—his party—required it of him. So he threw himself into it body and soul. He piled up what he must have thought were elegant rhetorical effects in a speech that was nothing more than a misreading of the indictment. In order to underline the enormity of my crime, he did not omit the classic stratagem of showering me with praise: I had talent, even genius, and all the virtues that make up a great Frenchman (*sic*).

He wanted our heads—all six of them; but he asked for mine a thousand times over. No doubt he hoped that his relentlessness would earn him not only the gratitude of the Communist Party but the sympathies of the jury, which would grant him one head as a consolation prize.

He gesticulated, he shouted, he wept and begged. I can say without boasting that hearing this clown clamor for my death had no effect on me at all.

Thursday, January 15, 1948

Bundled up in our woolen scarves, clumsily holding hands through our mittens, my cousin Serge and I are scampering on our way down to the fair, risking perilous slides along the frozen gutters. Come on, run! And then let's fly away—you in the plane and me on the white horse. Faster and louder, to the tune of "*Sur le Pont d'Avignon*." The man turning the crank has red chapped hands. He smiles at our crinkled faces and the pompoms on our bonnets that bobble in the searing cold. Giddy up, horse! Take me away to the country where people don't cry and where they don't count out the hours and the days! One last ride in the cavalcade, still feeling faint in the wind, still flying far away from Suresnes, far away from January and its voices.

We are dizzy with cold. Mathilde drags us over to a stand and shoves burning-hot waffles into our hands. But look at the chestnuts, so hot so hot, yes, afterward, eat this for a start. Hopping from one foot to the other, we stand in line outside the Punch and Judy show.

The children giggle with pleasure or scream with fright whenever Punch does something silly. The big idiot knocks a policeman on the head and vanishes into his cloth jail, complaining loudly. They follow open-mouthed every move he makes and applaud and say what a silly story and wander off skipping and get the tips of their noses and woolly fingers sticky as they bite into their cotton candy. And they forget about winter as they climb the steep slope of Mont Valérien and with apple-red cheeks and collapse tired and happy on the living room rug and shut their eyes, crunching the last holiday sweets between their teeth. What a wonderful day!

My aunt says, "You can go downstairs. I see the car. They're back."

(Wake up, Marie. Climb off your papier-mâché horse. Run in your fallen kneesocks down the two flights of worn carpeting, turn the lock, and don't look at her, just throw your arms around her neck. It's been a hard week.)

"It's not over yet?" Juliette asks, offering a cup of coffee to Maman, who is lying down and burying her migraine in the depths of a blue pillow.

"The verdict is tomorrow. The lawyers were good, really good. The foreman of the jury is a young woman. I tried to catch her eye. I wanted so much to talk to her. So very much."

"You need to rest."

She raises herself on one elbow and notices me: a wan smile.

"Juliette, come with Marie to court tomorrow at five. To the door of the courtroom. Ask at the main entrance, they'll show you the way. At the end of the session they let the family in to kiss the condemned man good-bye."

A thin, faint laugh escapes her lips.

"The children have to say good-bye to their father, don't they?"

She shuts her eyes and falls asleep.

From the defendant's diary

Today, the summing-up for the defense. My lawyer spoke for two full hours in a courtroom where you could hear a pin drop. He stuck to our agreement and resumed the arguments I had tried to set forth on the day of my interrogation. He deserves thanks for having raised this trial to a level of dignity it had not known before. But it is undoubtedly too late. I can't wait for this sideshow to end, whatever the outcome.

Friday, January 16, 1948

At noon, she brought me home from school. We ate our lunch feverishly. I'm going to see him, I'm going to see him at his court. Juliette said, not *adieu*, just *au revoir*.

We catch the three-ten train. Gare Saint-Lazare: we plunge into the subway entrance. Juliette keeps a tight hold on my hand. "Portes des Lilas," she says, consulting a large map on the tiled wall. We change at Réaumur-Sébastopol. At the intersection of several corridors, a fat lady is selling anemones from a pile in a carton. My sweet, take your pick. I choose the purplest and least battered. He'll be pleased.

We get out at Cité. Juliette tells me that we are deep beneath the Seine. We are about to emerge on the island—the court is next to Notre-Dame. So soon?

We're a little early. Let's go for a walk.

A barge floats down the milky-green Seine. A light wind freezes our thighs. I hold the anemones tight beneath my chin.

Come on, let's cross over. We'll ask where the entrance is. *That's* where your court is? So dirty and dismal? Where do you think you are, Cinderella? This is Paris-on-Seine. There'll be no Prince Charming on the steps of this court, just cops. Life is no fairy tale—and don't make that face! Juliette, you're mean. But she doesn't hear and asks a guard the way.

We walk and walk, it's never the right door, if only we could never find it and run away down subway corridors, buy all the anemones and fling them against the Lilac Gate . . .

We're there. I hang back. Come on, in we go. We climb the steps, I shut my eyes and trip on the top one. Don't be such a baby! Her voice is trembling slightly. The anemones dangle head down from my limp hand. Uniforms, overcoats, and black robes brush against me in a long tunnel filled with voices. The stifling air smells of steam heat, cigarette butts, and sweat. Doors are slamming, people are walking about, steps echo heavily, clusters of people are waiting in front of other doors. I'm too hot. Keep your coat on, it's drafty inside. Will we be there soon?

At the end of a corridor, a double door opens and noisily releases a long, damp, blurred-gray flood of hats-coats-ties. It must be there, says Juliette, don't let go of my hand or I'll lose you. Clutching her arm, I fight against the rush. She sets me against a wall, stands on tiptoe, lifts her face toward the door, and suddenly picks me up in her arms. My anemones! My anemones are trampled underfoot, I'm on the verge of tears but she is cutting through the crowd like a cyclone and not knowing what is happening I bury my face in Mother's hair scent neck warmth and we're dancing on the waxed floor among people turning away with vacant faces we're spinning we're waltzing she wipes her tears on my grin and chants breathlessly in my ear "life life he's saved life" and we whirl beneath the blue mother-of-pearl ceiling the sun hums in the great court, and we waltz to the tune of hard labor for life.

My feet bump against the brown floor. The butterflies and birds fly up through a purplish hubbub into the contracting sky. They're all here. Paul and Anne each take me by the hand, Juliette is exuberant, Grandfather imperturbable, and Mother is combing her hair. They are weeping and laughing, and handkerchiefs are fluttering.

We are led Indian file through the corridors to a low, light brown door. We go in, with Juliette right behind us. A uniform stops her. But I'm his sister! Identification? Oh, all right, forget it, I'm the maid, she shouts, I'm Monsieur B.'s maid, and she hides her face in her handkerchief in front of the slamming door.

The little room is dark and bare, with walls of dirty wood, without table or chair. No need for furniture—here people only pass through. A kind of sacristy. In the darkness of the far wall, there is another door. A bunch of keys is banging against it. It opens.

He comes in, a guard leading him by the wrist. A metallic rattle frees him. He stretches his arms in my direction, Mother presses me toward him. He bends down. His cheek is rough, and he smells of lavender and tobacco. Mother gently approaches him, and I wrap their two necks in my arms. Forehead to forehead, they shut their eyes. For a long time they do not stir. I breathe in their mingled breath and scent. To hold them, once, both of them, together, just once.

I slide down his body and take his hand in both of mine. It is white, a little square, the nails neatly trimmed, the thumb and forefinger very yellow. He kisses Paul, stiff as a board; and Anne, who is sobbing; then takes three steps toward his father and stands with his forehead resting on his shoulder. I see his back quiver. Grandfather is quite gray. He clasps him by the arms, steps back, and says, Come, come, this is no time to falter. Everything's all right, Albert, everything's all right.

Hurry! The guard is looking at his watch. Yes, we'd better hurry. We could be late for hard labor. Life imprisonment can't be kept waiting. We'd better hurry. We're starting to get emotional.

The family leaves the court.

Above Notre-Dame, the evening is turning blue. A barge floats down the Seine. Paris has spread out and forgotten us.

ABSENCE

He runs everything from his cell in Fresnes, with indefatigable energy, as if nothing could ever break him. Each day she receives a letter adorned with the censor's stamp, often striped with broad, red, greasy strokes. He tells about his life between four walls with no complaints. He maintains the morale of his troop. He issues them their orders.

After the verdict of January 16, he fell fully dressed onto his straw mattress and sank into a sleep deep enough to blot out ten misleading years of his life. He is the kind of man who can wake up fresh and alert, ready to face life imprisonment relying on his own resources; a man who can relegate ten years of oppressive memories to a night that is dead and buried, to the level of old, lost dreams. A man who forgets and starts over.

You soon get used to being someone not condemned to death. The chains hang less heavily. The dungeon you strove to endure while hoping for clemency becomes a cell. With its little square of visible sky, it almost seems like a reward. For a while. Because after the euphoria of "I made it by the skin of my teeth, but they didn't get me," your unending life sentence imposes itself: by four seasons that you recognize by your damp, oozing, frozen, or stifling walls, or by the ray of gray, bluish, yellowing, or dull white light falling from the crossed bars. (Is there a word signifying the reverse of light to name the daylight that does not penetrate walls?)

But Albert won't let himself be discouraged. One January morning he has woken up in another world. It's up to him to adapt to it, to lift up his head in the icy air—after all, it's colder in Siberia—and think of this new life as an adventure, as a human experience from which, in one year or ten, he will certainly emerge stronger.

Like a monk in his monastery, he settles down to his retreat. He gets himself organized. He's not in the least resigned but ready to make use of each day as it comes. Bitter he may be, but not surprised. He accepts the fact that the Law has consigned him to the shadows. He is only dismayed that it has not understood him better.

He establishes his fiefdom very quickly. He imposes his character, his requirements, and his discipline on the prison personnel. The guards address him as "Monsieur." They knock before entering his cell and excuse themselves when they make their routine searches. With his experience in leading men, he has no difficulty subjugating these humble flunkies. They are only too happy to come and smoke the cigarettes which—politician that he is—he never fails to offer them. They are vaguely impressed by his broad shoulders and his booming voice. They tell him about their problems at home and keep him up to date on prison gossip. Albert is a lifer who behaves himself. He is a respected man.

The hair is receding on his forehead, but he is like an oak in his resistance to winter, chilblains, dripping walls, and insidious bronchitis. He smokes three packs of cigarettes a day. (They are smuggled in via the lawyer, the chaplain, or the guards, at whom Alice casts imploring glances on her way into the visitors' room.)

With the stub of a cigarette between his lips, the collar of his old sheepskin jacket turned up around his red ears, and his hands blue with cold in his pockets, he paces the freezing corridors. He is surviving. He's taking care of himself. He complains loudly. He wakes up bellowing his morning prayer: "Death to all assholes!" Then he schedules the coming day. Whatever the weather, it will include washing, shaving, the crossword puzzle on the john in the corner, coffee on the little methane hot plate (you also thaw out your numb fingers), a walk, reading, mealtime (with supplements sparingly allotted from the week's parcel), a siesta, reading, writing, meditation, and another walk. Everything is timed to the minute and carried out meticulously. He is a voracious reader and takes elaborate notes on every book. Lastly, he is writing his epic political work. On little ruled schoolbooks made of the gray paper of those postwar years, he tries to explain his actions. He slowly clarifies the contradictory, conflicting ideas that sprang from a series of events whose implications were all too often beyond one's grasp. But were they? Sitting on his unpainted wooden chair in front of a damp wall, he tells his tale, he philosophizes, and his solitude is no longer empty. As he unravels in the closely written lines of his tiny hand his years as activist, Doriotist, and anti-Bolshevist, does he emerge from his confusion? Does he tell himself, "I was wrong"?

It no longer matters to him. His life was what it was. It's a heavy page to turn over, but he turns it. He brusquely concludes from his adventures that he was "not cut out for politics" and completely loses interest in it, saving himself the trouble of drawing more penetrating conclusions, indifferent to the legacy of bewilderment he will bequeath us.

Only one thing matters now: getting out and starting over. Far away from politics and its snares.

Albert? Tough as nails.

The Dominican nuns of the Saint Pius X Day School in Saint-Cloud were very fond of us. Under their holy auspices, I started first grade, and Anne began Latin and Greek. The establishment, which had a good scholastic standing, was attended by girls from well-to-do Saint-Cloud families. It had been recommended to Alice after the trial, at a moment when she despaired of finding a private school where accusing fingers would not be pointed at us. We bore a name that had been given abundant coverage in the press. While waiting for time to pass and nourish the exasperated public opinion of the postwar period with other trials and other traitors, it was necessary to hide us for a while and let us disappear among the blue smocks of a schoolyard.

One morning, with beating heart and a daughter in each hand, Maman rang the bell of the day school's varnished door. We were led into a bright office that smelled of wax polish. Mother Marie-Dominique was very beautiful, with a face like one carved in stone. She received us warmly, listened attentively, and spoke a few sentences in gentle tones. She wanted to talk to Mother alone, and taking each of us by the shoulder, led us out into the corridor, where long cream-colored robes passed to the click of wooden rosaries. The air was warm in this calm and serene place, which hardly resembled a school when the shrill voices of its pupils were not ringing through it. After a moment, the two women came toward us smiling. We had found our home.

We stayed there seven years, pampered by the good sisters. In the beginning they had to overcome the objections of well-born parents, who, when they heard of the presence of the B. daughters in the school, took steps to have us expelled. When they failed, they instructed their own daughters, at least, not to associate with us. But faces that went blank and backs that turned away no longer made us cry. Soon feelings died down, and Jesus did the rest.

One day the Dominican sisters held a real celebration. We were told, "God is now dwelling here among us. Whenever you need to, you can prostrate yourselves before him. The bishop has given us permission to have our own chapel."

In a small, freshly painted room at the end of a corridor on the second floor of the large building, the altar was set up and draped in spotless lace. This was our oratory. Jesus was present as a small red lamp, an eye to witness our diligence in coming to pray for him. The shutters remained half closed. A heady scent of white flowers, floor wax, and Camay soap hovered in the air. Before opening the door on tiptoe, you had to cover your head with your handkerchief. Then you knelt down in the cool shadow and stayed there, hands clasped, for at least five minutes. (I counted out the seconds instead of repeating the Lord's Prayer.) At last you stood up, with the floor pattern stamped on the skin of your knees.

These rituals, dutifully performed, became a normal part of daily life, along with lessons, washing, catechism class, and hopscotch. We accepted it all calmly and dispassionately: it was like linden tea for a stomachache.

Anne, however, was very pious. Little Jesus even came close to turning her head. The kind Dominican ladies, the Catholic Scouts of France, and every sympathetic priest devoted themselves to the cultivation of a soul so astonishingly gifted in sacred matters. She was a true believer. The better she prayed, the sooner her father would come home. She went all the way to Rome on a group pilgrimage in quest of the miracle. Was God a little hard of hearing? The Church said not to be discouraged. We must shout louder and longer. We must prostrate ourselves. He will ultimately take pity on us poor sinners.

Alice was the high priestess of rituals whose observance became an obsession. Masses, prayers, visits to Fresnes, letters to the prisoner, Christmas trees, birthdays, graveyards—all were expressions of her personal creed, in which the sacred and the profane were equally represented. We followed this beloved witch in the vagaries of her superstitions and offerings. We were unquestioning disciples, putting our trust in the enchanted future that the return of the prodigal father would ensure us.

As for him, he was expected like the Messiah. He was present everywhere. His absence saturated our daily lives and transformed each of our acts into an exceptional event that would be related in detail in Alice's daily letter. She wrote it at night while we slept, downing cups of strong coffee so as not to keep from him the smallest detail of our life without him.

She did not merely pray: her energy made it impossible for her to confine herself to a role of passive waiting. One must also deal with reality. Everything, absolutely everything must be brought to bear to release him from the trap in which his manhood, his misspent strength, and his paternal authority were ensnared. Life imprisonment was an abstract term. It was a tactic used by men to destroy hope. She fought to reduce this indefinite eternity to a number of years you could count on your fingers.

She was determined to face and accelerate a reality that a part of her measured with all the coolness of a captain reckoning his chances with a sinking ship. (Time is passing, darling. With circles under our eyes and graying hair, will we still be able to love each other afterward?) In order to start the countdown of lost years, she attempted everything humanly possible. She went from ministry to ministry, knocked on every door, stood for hours in the reception rooms of prominent people—those who did or did not have influence, those who would or would not receive her, those who listened to her, or yawned, or eyed her legs.

As soon as some "important" person had promised to move our dossier to the top of his pile, we would live in dread of a change of government. Our hopes would collapse utterly when, after his third personal secretary had displayed a moment's compassion between two urgent appointments, the Lord Privy Seal (but why would anyone want to seal a privy?) changed occupancy or party.

Then everything would have to be done again, and the monotonous hours of waiting in the gilded rooms of the Ministry of Justice would resume.

The time came when Mother had to go to work. Debts were piling up, and the few things of value rescued from Avenue Rodin threatened to be swallowed up by pawnshops.

Grandfather didn't want to hear about it. Preoccupied with keeping the family wealth intact, he never stooped to helping out his little family. We were entitled to spend our vacations at The Thistles, where we had everything we needed; and he paid for our schooling and for our season tickets to the Comédie-Française. That was it.

There was also his good deed of the year. He used to arrive in Suresnes at lunchtime on Christmas day, in his gleaming Citroën 15. Before sitting down to his dozen snails, he would ceremoniously take out his black alligator wallet and distribute a thousand-franc bill to each of us. After coffee was served, he would leave, wishing Alice good luck and congratulating her on the children's good behavior. He never asked by what miracle we were able to make ends meet; but to those around him he spoke portentously about his daughter-in-law's courage.

Only once did she try to overcome his stinginess. That was when she was unable to pay the lawyers at the end of the first trial. After having been badgered incessantly for several weeks, he agreed to lend her the funds. The act was legally witnessed and registered. Alice emerged from the session so worn out that she swore never to ask him for anything again.

Since knitting brought in so little, she decided to get a regular job. Once again, Pierre came to our rescue. One of his brothers ran a small factory in nearby Levallois. He was looking for a telephone operator who could also do secretarial work. Mother accepted.

She starts work on a Thursday, a day when there is no school, so we all go to the factory with her. It is located in the middle of the Seine on Île de la Jatte, which you reach by a flight of steps from the Levallois bridge. Holding her purse and her lunch box in one hand, she resolutely waves good-bye to us with the other. She moves into her tiny office, a glass cubicle at the entrance to the factory's administrative wing. With her earphones perched on her head, she learns how to juggle filing cards, answer ingratiatingly while typing a letter, and breathe ammonia fumes when she has to draw plans in the back office.

She came back with her first paycheck as happy as a schoolgirl who is proud of her marks.

And so life in Suresnes found its cruising speed. Mother kept on the run, and we followed behind.

Each morning begins with setting-up exercises on the radio and a hurried cup of *café au lait*. We race down Rue du Bel Air to the station, where our two trains cross each other, Alice's on the way to Saint-Lazare and mine to Saint-Cloud. We talk to each other across the tracks. We blow each other kisses through the train doors. I watch her sit down and take her knitting out of her purse. She smiles at me and pronounces words I cannot hear. I press my nose to the glass and make faces at her. Then her head glides down the line of windows until it disappears.

She gets off at Bécon-les-Bruyeres. Hurry, hurry, there's a good half hour's walk through the suburbs before you reach Ile de la

Jatte. At the end of the bridge the wind buffets her. She closes her eyes and ties a silk scarf under her chin. She spins through the gusts on the stairway and plunges past the door. The lobby smells of leatherette and pencil sharpenings. Ping she clocks in. Ping the telephone. She runs a comb through her hair. Her earphones, her swivel chair—her mind a blank, rusty-fingered, she starts her day, with fatigue not far behind her.

For eight years, the robotlike gestures, the noise of the machines, and the dozens of faces that pass smiling in front of her glass enclosure helped her stay sane.

Every week, Mother pays a call on the famous lawyer Tixier-Vignancour. I like going with her, since she always seems revived when she emerges from the handsome building on Boulevard Raspail. Jean-Louis, as I have always heard him called, had been unable to assume Albert's defense. They were friends of long standing, but they had not seen each other since Vichy. As soon as he was imprisoned, Albert sent for Tixier, who came to his side at once and did not leave it during ten dark years.

Next to God in church, it was Jean-Louis whom Alice visited with the greatest diligence and trust. He was her connection with life behind the walls; he soothed her anxieties; and he made her laugh.

With muffled steps we climb the majestic stairway that leads to his door. Maman rings. Old Marie comes to let us in. Invariably clad in an apron of impeccable whiteness, she is short, slight, and all silver-gray, from her neat bun to the toes of her slender shoes. In a silence of carpeting and closed doors, she softly welcomes us, like a family come from afar that should be made snug by the fireplace. She gives Maman a furtive kiss before opening the door into the oval sitting room, whispers an encouraging word or two, and fusses over the arrangement of our chairs. With a roguish look, shaking her finger in front of her nose as if to say, I know a secret for nice little girls, she trots over to a console table, opens a drawer, and, her face wrinkled with smiles, offers me sweets and candied almonds. Then she nods her head, content to see us comfortably settled. Blinking her eyes as she looks at Alice, she declares in a churchlike voice, "I shall announce you. It won't be long."

The large armchair of quilted velvet engulfs me. I suck my sweets and leaf through old magazines. Maman takes out her knitting or her crocheting, and we talk softly to one another in the shelter of gilded moldings on the sky-blue ceiling. If we have to wait a long time, Marie looks in, gazes at us tenderly, and goes off again muttering some mysterious utterance: "Soon the truth will be told," or, "Time passes, but we do not forget." Through the half-open door, I see Rémi crossing the hall on his tricycle. I'd like to play with him but don't dare ask; and he pays no attention to me.

A little door opens abruptly, and Jean-Louis is holding out his arms to us. His gesture is ceremonious; his smile is warm. He embraces Maman tenderly and pats me on the head. I disappear into another armchair, like a good girl: white socks pulled up, a hand lying flat on each armrest.

Leaning forward in her chair, Maman asks: "Well?"

Maître Tixier does not have extraordinary news to tell her every week; but he always tells her something; and reassured by his solemn voice, she relaxes. Words pass between them whose sense escapes me. There is always talk of being patient, of new developments that never come to pass. Well, we'll see next week, says Maman bravely, looking at the toes of her shoes, while Jean-Louis gives me a wink. They exchange various papers. With innumerable admonitions, she gives him cigarettes and little parcels. He takes them all and puts them down at random—yes, yes, of course I'll give them to him.

He then takes us to the door. Turning around, I see Marie in the entrance to the pantry, blowing me a kiss and waving.

For years, Maître Tixier went to see Albert every Sunday afternoon. Madame Tixier waited for him in the car, knitting.

She is eight years old. Spring is bursting forth everywhere. Buds are poking their noses out of every branch. The horse chestnuts are putting forth first leaves like small, wrinkled hands. She runs through the damp morning grass looking for Easter daisies, and for violets under the fir trees. It's Easter vacation. She will be able to play and make bouquets along the waysides under the fort. She can climb in the elders and pull open the petals of geraniums to help them flower sooner.

In the house they are talking again about a trial. She doesn't want to listen to them. For two years now, time has smoothly revolved around Suresnes, Saint-Cloud, and Fresnes, like the length of yarn that she patiently winds and hooks on the pegs of her knitting-spool. For two years now, the days have passed by streaked with rain, snow, or sun, like the strand she pulls from the end of her spool: red, green, or yellow, depending on the wool. We were getting used to our life. It was regulated by an absence that for her was taking on the pastel tones of a routine.

And now it's starting all over again. They are talking about a trial; and early in the morning she eludes those voices. She hides in the moss-green depths of the grotto, talking to the white spiders, re-emerging into the light when the oppressive dampness penetrates her sweater. She takes refuge behind the house in the topmost branches of the big mulberry tree, breaking her nails on its bark, not answering when they call her. She doesn't hear—she's on the banks of the Amazon.

Just not to see their frowning faces! Anne trying to act like a grownup; Paul smoking tiny cigarette butts and no longer smiling; and the old curate with his cassock full of spots—he takes Alice's hands in his (yellow, their nails broader than they are long) and recites the gospel in a whiny voice. She hates them for speaking about another trial and harping on the same old stories, the same old prayers, when spring is erupting from every bush. Even Juliette infuriates her with her leek soup, her rice pudding, and her "There once was a young shepherdess." They can all go to hell!

The second trial began on March 27, before a circuit court. Albert is being tried as an accomplice to murder. The lower court had disqualified itself on this point two years earlier.

She asked, is it in the same court building? Juliette said yes. She asked, will it last long? Juliette said they'll get through it in two days. She asked, will it be in the papers? Juliette said she was afraid so. She asked, would they be going to the court again? Juliette said no.

She thought, that's good, I can go out and play.

The trial lasted two days. It concerned the M. affair. M. was accused of killing three men, all members of the FPP. Albert was an accomplice to two of these executions.

Headline in *Le Figaro,* March 28, 1950:

FPP KILLERS ACCUSED OF EXECUTING SUSPECTS

The men who entered the dock in Circuit Court yesterday have all previously been sentenced to hard labor. These men, who are former collaborators, etc. . . . . The following four men have been accused: B. and D., the leaders who ordered the execution of "black sheep whose behavior was harmful to the prestige of the party"; and at their side, M. and P., the killer and his helper. . . . The killer is at a hypocritical loss for words at this point to describe the anguish he endured after committing the murder. Later, the leaders state: "We were fighting for ideas. We could not afford to be weak."

Headline in *Le Figaro,* March 29:

FPP KILLERS CONDEMNED
M.: SENTENCED TO DEATH
B.: LIFE AT HARD LABOR

She thought,
Nothing has changed,
I can go on playing.

And so everything went back to normal—time flowing by, the seasons supplanting one another, nights wrapping the days in their indifference. It would last six more years: four plus six equals ten.

She didn't know this, the flat-chested little girl at her hop-scotch, indefatigably moving from "home" to "rest." She didn't know that one day she would have to hide her breasts beneath her crossed arms, and he would not have to bend down to brush her cheek with the kiss of freedom. She didn't know that on a cool September morning they would wait for him, lined up along the barbed wire of a camp in far-off Lorraine, where he had spent the last two years of his imprisonment teaching chemistry to young delinquents. She would say to herself, so that's the way he walks, as he advanced through the light but biting east wind, smiling, a cigarette between his lips, with his white cat under one arm and a small suitcase in the other. As they opened the heavy gate for him, she would say to herself, today's the day he's turning up in my life. She didn't know that this would happen. She wasn't expecting it. She didn't know that on a dry morning in Lorraine he would say to her, how big you've grown, you're really a young lady, and that at that moment everything would be brutally changed, spoiled, and lost, and that she would have nothing more to say to him.

He is still sitting on the terrace ledge. His legs dangle in empty space on a level with the third floor. The first time, Maman shouted, Paul, you're doing it on purpose to scare me. Then she got used to it. When she comes home at night, she can see him above the branches of the horse chestnuts from the corner of Rue du Bel Air. He waves to her from his high lookout post. She sighs, blows him a kiss, and says nothing. You don't wake up a somnam-bulist who is walking along a roof gutter. He stays there for hours, smoking, gazing at a horizon made up of roofs, the Seine, and, at the far end of clouds, the Eiffel Tower. He's like a cat crouching in a treetop. No one knows if he gets there over the roof or through his window. All at once you see him settled there, as though he had never come down.

I look up longingly from the garden.

"Can I go up with you someday?"

"You're *much* too little."

He is making fun of me. Sulkily I go clanking off on my old pedal scooter. He feels good up there. He's alone. It's a breathing space, a place to forget earth and sky, the way to Fresnes, Mother's eyes, Germany, the barbed wire, and the appeals for clemency. A place to forget Jean's smile, and the schools you enter and leave in a rage after still another fight. He can forget the names they call you: You're quislings, your father's a traitor!

Paul, come down off the ledge! It's time to get the milk at the farm.

There are about ten of them in the neighborhood—a young, peaceable, happily chattering gang that emerges from their cottages in the evening and climbs the hill to the Mont-Valérien farm. They care called Anne or Marie, Jean or Philippe, Jacques or Jean-Claude. They bang their milk cans, wander here and there, crack jokes, and remake the world under the walls of the fort, where not so long ago bursts of shooting echoed through the early morning.

On Sunday afternoons, they gather in one of their houses, assemble all their 78s, and dance to *"La Vie en Rose."* Paul doesn't dance, but he falls in love with New Orleans jazz. His melancholy is transfigured by Louis Armstrong, Sidney Bechet, and Mezz Mezzrow. He buys an old clarinet at the flea market. He has never studied music, but he has a good ear. To spare the household, he shuts himself deep in the cellar and tries to force sounds from the instrument. He spends days and nights in his lair, at first playing with records so as to learn a few pieces, producing an unbelievable din that Mathilde endures with sighs of resignation. Then, together with three friends, he starts a little band. It will later appear at gala evenings in Suresnes and perform at weddings, first communions, and holiday dinners.

Just as I had used watch him solder his miniature radios, I now go up to his room at the sound of his first notes. I admire him. He's a great musician—he makes so much noise! In a dusty corner, trying to be as inconspicuous as possible, I observe him lovingly. His right foot beats time. His fingers press hard against the black instrument, whose silver keys open and shut. Beneath his closed eyes, his cheeks puff out and stream with sweat. From time to time a high-pitched squeak escapes: he stops, out of breath, and looks at me, and we both burst out laughing.

But he still has his migraines: stabbing attacks that drive him crazy. No one can go near him. He roars, suffers, and threatens to jump off the terrace ledge if Mother so much as knocks at his door with a cup of broth in her hand. At last he emerges, pale and wobbly, and then cannot make up the time he has missed at school.

Prison corridors are now replaced by the waiting rooms of specialists. When they take his blood pressure, not one of them can help raising his eyebrows or giving him a fugitive look. Paul knows it's coming. He feels like biting them. Yes, my blood pressure is off the wall and my heart is beating its wild tattoo and I'm still on my feet. Just get rid of the migraines! We can't really tell—perhaps the consequence of a bad case of scarlet fever . . . Try taking this. If things don't improve, go and see so-and-so. Whatever you do, don't get tired. No strain. No athletics. Rest.

He buys a bicycle, tunes it up, takes loving care of it, and throws himself into bicycle racing. In summer he goes to Scout camp, preferably in the mountains, since high altitudes are forbidden to him. He writes us letters full of accounts of rock climbing. They end: You see, Mother, I'm still here. He defies life and the specialists. He plunges into ice-cold lakes and starts competing in swimming tournaments.

One day, they propose an operation. It's being done in the United States, Madame. There have been only a few attempts in France, but we could try it. She doesn't want to. They reassure her—science is making constant progress, one day or another someone will discover a treatment, who knows?

And time passes. Paul goes on living with his medicines (some taken, some thrown out), his athletic triumphs, and his irrepressible youth.

Saturday morning we get up early. Juliette hurries me through my breakfast. My eyes will hardly stay open over the steaming cup.

"You made it too hot again. And there's skin on the milk."

"No, little lady, I strained the milk. I know all your foibles. Skin on the milk, grains in the rice, and crumbs. What a fussbudget!"

This is a favorite word of hers. It is uttered with an affectionate scorn that wakes me up. I wait for her to add "just like your grandma," but this morning she forgets.

"You'd better hurry up if you want to do the shopping with me. Your mother left me a long list and not much cash. We'll have to work miracles again."

"Where's Mother?"

"At the hairdresser's. It's Saturday, you know that."

"Something smells good."

"You're finally waking up. There's a brioche in the oven."

"For lunch?"

"No, for the parcel."

I get dressed. Juliette keeps after me, handing me my clothes, tying my laces. Now: let's move, there, take this basket, you can make yourself useful.

We are laughing as we walk down the Avenue du Mont-Valérien all the way to the marketplace of lower Suresnes.

When we return, Mother is in the kitchen, her face powdered, her hair waved and curled. She has placed a carton by the scale on the table. The brioche is cooling at one end of the sideboard. There are already a few small packages in the bottom of the carton. Their contents and weight have been written down: coffee, sugar, rusks, condensed milk, tuna fish. I hop about the table, rummaging around and looking under papers.

"Where's my carton?"

Mother places a small box next to the big one. I set to work preparing a miniature parcel "for my dear husband." It contains mainly cookies and candy.

In the bedroom I have propped Lucius, my dirty-white, furless bear, behind the bars of the back of a chair. With my expression appropriately composed, parcel in hand, I go and stand in front of him and bring him up to date on the events of the week. From the doorway, Alice watches me acting out the afternoon visitors' room—my favorite game. Others play mothers and fathers. I've never learned how.

Anne and Paul arrive from school. The parcel is ready. Juliette weighs it: eleven pounds, not an ounce more. Before shutting it for good, Alice adds a tight, round bunch of violets. She cannot get used to the idea that in a little while, when the parcel is deposited, a guard with greasy hands is going to take the whole thing apart. When he pokes his fingers into the withered little flowers—never mind, she'll look the other way.

"Come and eat, children. Hurry. You'll miss your train."

Juliette keeps rushing us along. The coffee is already steaming on a corner of the stove. After the last mouthful has been swallowed—and while Alice sits down in an armchair, her legs crossed, with a coffee glass in one hand and her long cigarette holder in the other, enjoying a five-minute break—we fight over the bathroom. I step nimbly in front of Paul to wash my hands. He wets his comb in the running water and draws it through his thick black hair. Drops fall on my nose, and I complain. Paul laughs and shakes the comb harder over my head.

Mother is waiting for us. She has put on the suit she used to wear on Sundays, with her diamond brooch on the lapel. She smooths my bangs and attaches a starched white percale collar to my dress; she straightens Paul's tie (he steps away grumbling), picks up the parcel, and off we go.

Half an hour on the Paris local. I count the stops, announcing them before the conductor can shout them out as he leaps from the still-moving front carriage. I count traffic lights, signposts, footbridges, and the barges on the Seine as we cross it. I spell out Dubonnet, Peugeot, and Olida. In my pocket I hold tightly to our four tickets, which I shall present, standing at attention, to the ticket collector at Gare Saint-Lazare.

On Rue de Rome we jump on a bus. Paul rides on the open platform at the back. Serious and erect, he watches Paris go by to the bus's jerky rhythms, its stops and starts, the swinging handle of the conductor's bell. I try out all the empty seats. I like the one over the wheel best. It's higher and slightly warm. Paris: a stage in our journey. Forty minutes to Porte d'Orléans. When the bus turns into Place Denfert-Rochereau, I can't keep still. I kneel on my seat and twist around to get the best possible view of the Belfort lion. It's the most thrilling moment of the trip. The lion is my friend. From one week to the next I take passionate note of the changes in him. He's fatter. He's thinner. He's moved one paw. He isn't looking well. Maman gravely acquiesces. If the passengers around us take it into their minds to laugh, I wither them with a look, the poor idiots, and cast a terrible spell on them that will cause them, sooner or later, to be eaten by my lion.

Porte d'Orléans. Last stop, everybody out. We transfer to another bus. Women carrying large packages are waiting at the bus stop. They look at one another in sad recognition. There are no children. We climb on board for the last lap, a half-hour ride through the southern suburbs. Mother looks at her watch. We're all right. She takes out her compact and in its square mirror considers one eye, then the other. The pink puff for her nose, then the red lipstick: lips outlined, opened, shut. Pretty. Tired. Well-coiffed—but there *is* a telltale wrinkle! No, there isn't. Still lovely: the loveliest.

I'm first off the bus platform. The parcels—tall, long, or square, swinging in string bags or at the ends of handles that cut into the fingers—the parcels are crossing the avenue. The contingent of political visitors pushes forward and, after being cleared, passes through the entrance. It starts down the huge alley that seems to stretch in a straight, endless line between tall yellowish buildings, in whose sides are hundreds of small rectangular openings fitted with gratings. Between them runs a wide asphalt strip over which ambulances and police wagons drive. On either side of it there is a stretch of worn grass, then a path for pedestrians next to the wall. I go to the head of the troop, jogging, running—I dread being late, or having to wait, or arriving after the doors have shut. We pass in front of the women's building, into which men disappear. Farther on—keep running, there it is! The parcels are following through the low entrance and on to the gray stones of the yard.

A narrow glass door reinforced with mesh swings open. A whiskered man in navy blue counts those entering. In front of the guard, Maman catches up with me. She recovers her breath, looks up at the sky, lowers her head in the doorway, and as she passes through, catches my outstretched hand. There is a short corridor, then we reach the threshold of a square room. Here the parcels are handed over. There is a blur of hushed voices dominated by the sharper tones of the men in blue and the abrupt clang of weights on the scales. The room is divided into passageways by waist-high chains that are suspended from iron posts embedded in the floor.

One scale to a passageway, one guard to a scale, and the parcels step forward. They are weighed, opened, and turned inside out. Often, on their way out, women are tearfully carrying in their shopping bags items that the inspectors would not accept. That's the rule. You try, and if it gets through, you're in luck.

Mother is very tense when her turn comes. I feel her breath coming faster and see her heart beating under her jacket. She watches the guard's hand undo the parcel and rummage through all the little packages, then tries to catch her antagonist's eye. Her stare is as intense as that of a trainer bringing an animal to heel. The bleary-eyed beast holds up the packages, inspects them, and puts them back. The parcel will not close. He shrugs and reties the string too loosely. Mother shakes her head. What will it look like when it reaches him? Next.

I pull her by the hand past the cold chains. Come on, don't worry, he didn't make you take anything back, you're the prison Princess, you intimidate them, hurry, maybe I'll have time to play hopscotch in B Block.

The longest corridor stretches out in front of us: the one that leads to you. Dampness. A wet reverberation of footsteps on concrete. My hand twists in my mother's, until finally she relinquishes it. Taking a deep breath of bitter air, I get set and race away between walls blistered with moldy patches.

Run. Keep running. Fill the shut-up space with your shouts. I have a sneaking fear of turning around and no longer seeing them. But there she is, following at a steady pace, with Anne on one side and Paul on the other. Wait for us—you'll fall down!

Keep running. If I can get past the lady in blue before counting to twenty, Father will be in the third cell from the left. Now stop. Take a breath. Three steps on one foot, five on the other, ten with both feet together. Jump in the air and turn round. They're there. They're getting nearer. We're not late, but there will be a line on the stairs up to the visitors' room.

Our long gray path is crossed at regular intervals by other identical corridors. I add one corridor, skip three, and I'll be at Father's. At each intersection, slumped on an iron chair, a guard in dirty blue is dozing. I know the way, but I can't resist stopping in front of him and waking him up with a start:

"Which way to B Block, please?"

Beneath his dusty cap, he raises a sagging eyelid and mumbles vague directions. A polite "thank you" seems more appropriate than the curtsey Maman taught me on Avenue Rodin: everything in its proper place. Satisfied, I whirl around, wave to my family, and shout, "It's this way!"

Men and women glide past me in silence, looking at me with an absentminded and sometimes puzzled eye. Few children go skipping down these fetid hallways. We very frequently pass trolleys being trundled with an earsplitting racket along their rails, each bearing two huge greasy caldrons that emit a choking, nauseating stench of old soup.

We're coming to the visitors' room. A low door opens into a kind of waiting room, a high-ceilinged place with barely more light than a cellar. Down its walls runs greasy water that spreads in gleaming puddles over the uneven floor. Against the wall opposite the door, rough concrete stairs lead to a gallery from which one has access to the visitors' room proper. The banister is cold and sticky. Faceless grownups crowd the gallery and the full extent of the stairs.

Mother takes a small leather case from her purse and with quick fingers starts crocheting the lace that will adorn our nightgowns, my Peter Pan collars, or one of her innumerable, useless doilies. She hands me a pad of ruled paper and a purple pencil. I moisten it on the tip of my tongue and draw while we wait for the upper door to open.

Paul looks at his watch. It won't be long now. A lock resounds with a clang that reverberates from step to step. The voices fall silent. Punch makes his entrance. The lights are dimming, the fire curtain is going up, and Father is stepping into his cage.

From week to week, as soon as the Dust Man appears, I hear Mother murmur, "Nice," or, "Nasty." With the nice one she will exchange a word or two as she goes in and will slip two packages of Gauloises into his pocket, one for the prisoner and one for him. With the nasty one, we enter with bowed heads, very grateful simply to be allowed into his domain.

Punch straightens up and clears his throat. He proceeds to read the roll call in a hoarse, self-important voice. He deliberately reads it fast and carelessly. When their prisoner's name is shouted (or they think it is), each family elbows and knees its way forward, and a dreary wave of protest runs from step to step. Paul carries me in his arms so that I won't suffocate. Amid much pushing and shoving, we reach the visitors' room.

Another hallway—dark, stained, the color of rancid butter. To the right is a row of fifteen or twenty cubicles with gratings on their far sides. If we cram ourselves in like sardines, one can hold three of us, or four with the door open.

Women are shouting their prisoners' names and looking for them frantically from one cage to the next. In a pandemonium of creaking locks and banging doors—it's noisier than a chicken coop—I run ahead and sneak to the front so as to be the first to spot him. There he is. Hurry up! Hello Papa! I press against the grating. You can put your fingers through its little squares. Opposite, symmetrically facing ours, there is the same grating and cubicle where Papa is shut in. A door slams behind him, and there is the double click of a twice-turned lock.

No kisses through the grating, no chance of touching fingertips: between us runs a passageway a yard wide, lit with dirty, flickering light. A guard walks up and down it from one end to the other during the entire visit. No "I love you" through the grating, no danger of telling a secret. Try to forget the noise, the locks, and the hallways, try to keep silent and speak only with looks: that drab silhouette, that dismal witness, with the ears that walls are said to have, will loom up like a spasm of nausea. Nothing can be murmured across the gratings, no tender words: you have to scream to be heard above the voices of the caged men. On either side of you, along the whole row, men are shouting and smiling at their wives and telling them important things and asking question after question.

Our bear smiles. In the depths of his lair, his sunken brown eyes gleam from beneath their thick brows. He is holding onto the grating tightly with both hands—I look at the bent fingers, which are quite white, with nails filed to points and carefully polished.

He talks and talks. His powerful voice reaches us above the lukewarm clamor.

Leaning my forehead against the little metal squares, I count how many times the bogeyman goes by and try to decipher the words uttered by the veiled mouths that all look alike. Mother keeps talking endlessly about lawyers, testimonials, influence, appeals for clemency, so-and-so promised, the office, no it was no bother, law firms, plans. One after the other we send forth our few words of love across the hubbub that engulfs him.

Visiting time is running out. Doors are opening, prisoners are being taken away. We have to leave. The moment has come, if the guard is "nice," for Alice to go up to him and in her sweetest voice request a favor that is only rarely granted.

"The little girl wants to give her father a kiss."

I start to panic. It wasn't my idea. I want to get out. My heart sticks in my throat. My hands turn to ice. I want to run away, race down the stairs, jump feet first into the puddles, draw wavy lines with my hand along the walls of the maze, and retch my heart out on the cobblestones in the yard. But I stand still behind my mother, petrified. Punch looks at me over his shoulder. Through his uncertain gaze pass his suburban cottage, his wife in her apron filling his bowl with soup, the coatrack where he hangs his cap when he comes home at night, and perhaps his children running up for a hug. He answers with a nod of the head: yes.

"Go ahead," says Mother.

Stiff as a broomstick, I go ahead. People on the gallery, waiting their turn to visit, are watching me. So are Paul and Anne, both jealous. I'm the pathetic little one, and only I get to be kissed.

At the end of the hallway, after the row of cages, there is a door with an opening at the level of my forehead. I stand on the tips of my toes, the little shutter is pulled back with a snap, and my father's face fills the hatch. So as to be less frightened, I close my eyes and dream that I'm a young bear and that he is licking me.

Sir, you smell of lavender and tobacco, your beard prickles slightly, your breath is warm, and your lips soft. Please, let me go away. Don't suck me into the shadows.

I've gathered the laurels of your war. It took time; but I no longer resent you. When you came back, I was twelve years old, childhood was over, I didn't know you, you didn't know me.

So that you could be there, my first communion was celebrated a year late. None too soon, Juliette told me when you arrived, another year and you would have really looked like a bride. Even so, I was the tallest, the last one in the row, and beneath my English lace dress my breasts were beginning to show. I loathed you.

Afterward, we didn't get along too badly. We rarely talked. You were very busy looking for work. You never saw a single one of your old friends.

The word "politics" was banished from our vocabulary, together with any subject that might take you back ten years. For me, your glorious past stopped at Oran. When you talked about your days in the Middle East, you never went beyond it. It was followed by a large blank. You bravely jumped ahead to tales from prison, which had evidently left you bald and a little wrinkled, but free of aches and, even more, of bitterness. You were like a rock. I used to think, What a man!

You didn't want to tell us anything, and we didn't press you. If the word "war" or "bombardment" was pronounced, Jean's shadow would fall across our eyes, and Maman would cry.

I wasn't curious? Maybe. Alice had instructed me in silence all too well. Before finding out, I wanted to forget. For her sake, so as not to see her cry anymore.

In school I instinctively chose German as my main language. I was very good at it. I used to spend my vacations under the trees in Wiesbaden, in a house that the bombs had spared. There was no talk of the war. We fraternized. There, too, people were forgetting.

At eighteen, I knew nothing. I was hardly able to tell left-wing from right-wing—I had, in any case, no gift for history. I was barely starting to read Kafka, Gide, and Sartre on the sly. These Jews, queers, and phony philosophers had all been expelled from your library. I said to myself, it's normal enough. It's the generation gap. I understood nothing about anything.

How could I have? I saw you jubilant on your return from Moscow, with your astrakhan pulled down over your eyes and your suitcase full of caviar. The fact was that you were developing a sense of humor and starting to find these Bolsheviks less of a menace. You were beginning a new career. With a businessman in Berlin, you were arranging the sale of French factories to the Russians. It was a new German-Soviet pact of sorts. It earned you the sonorous title of Engineering Counselor to the Moscow Chemical Commission—a most impressive calling card that you displayed laughingly. If Doriot could have seen you then!

And me? I used to drink vodka with you and think, What a man! You were starting to make me laugh.

Then came that stopover in Berlin.

You were waiting in the transit lounge for the flight to Moscow. Suddenly your name is on the loudspeaker. You rush to the information desk: You must return to Paris at once, sir. Your son is dead, sir. You ask, What? Which one? You're not sure. Are you in Berlin this April morning? At Mainau? Constance? Everything is starting over again.

Paul was sick. But you didn't want him to leave—you didn't, you didn't. He just left. Even if it's too much, says Juliette, who in the kitchen is making herself sing. I had never seen you cry before.

Wait, there's more. For a change of scene, you send me off to some friends in Berlin, far away from Paris, far away from a mother's screams. I'm twenty years old. What did you expect me to understand? You send me to Berlin—blue Berlin with its lakes and forests—to bury my brother. And I forget him as I sink into the eyes of a pretty blond boy—don't know anything about Hitler, my love, but let's collaborate a little bit. In the bottom of a rowboat on the Wannsee he gave me my first taste of giddiness.

I return, unconsoled. You have aged. You're no longer there. You must be thinking, enough's enough. I agree.

For ten long months I stayed with you and held you. I watched you crack, come apart, collapse, and die.

You left me the day I turned twenty-one, just when I was learning to love you. Since then—but that's another story.

You have all died, and I have grown up. I haven't understood it all, but I'm starting to get to know you. Good-bye, sir. You may sleep in peace.

MARIE CHAIX was born in Lyons and raised in Paris, and is the author of nine books. *The Summer of the Elder Tree*, a memoir and meditation on the theme of separation, and her first book in more than a decade, was published in Paris in 2005, and will appear from Dalkey Archive Press in 2013.

HARRY MATHEWS has written over a dozen books, including the novels *Cigarettes* and *Tlooth*, along with collected stories, *The Human Country*, and essays, *The Case of the Persevering Maltese*. Mathews is also a member of the Oulipo—France's longest-lived and most active literary group. He divides his time between Paris, Key West, and New York.

PETROS ABATZOGLOU, *What Does Mrs. Freeman Want?*
MICHAL AJVAZ, *The Golden Age.*
The Other City.
PIERRE ALBERT-BIROT, *Grabinoulor.*
YUZ ALESHKOVSKY, *Kangaroo.*
FELIPE ALFAU, *Chromos.*
Locos.
JOÃO ALMINO, *The Book of Emotions.*
IVAN ÂNGELO, *The Celebration.*
The Tower of Glass.
DAVID ANTIN, *Talking.*
ANTÓNIO LOBO ANTUNES, *Knowledge of Hell.*
The Splendor of Portugal.
ALAIN ARIAS-MISSON, *Theatre of Incest.*
IFTIKHAR ARIF AND WAQAS KHWAJA, EDS.,
Modern Poetry of Pakistan.
JOHN ASHBERY AND JAMES SCHUYLER,
A Nest of Ninnies.
ROBERT ASHLEY, *Perfect Lives.*
GABRIELA AVIGUR-ROTEM, *Heatwave and Crazy Birds.*
HEIMRAD BÄCKER, *transcript.*
DJUNA BARNES, *Ladies Almanack.*
Ryder.
JOHN BARTH, *LETTERS.*
Sabbatical.
DONALD BARTHELME, *The King.*
Paradise.
SVETISLAV BASARA, *Chinese Letter.*
MIQUEL BAUÇÀ, *The Siege in the Room.*
RENÉ BELLETTO, *Dying.*
MAREK BIEŃCZYK, *Transparency.*
MARK BINELLI, *Sacco and Vanzetti Must Die!*
ANDREI BITOV, *Pushkin House.*
ANDREJ BLATNIK, *You Do Understand.*
LOUIS PAUL BOON, *Chapel Road.*
My Little War.
Summer in Termuren.
ROGER BOYLAN, *Killoyle.*
IGNÁCIO DE LOYOLA BRANDÃO,
Anonymous Celebrity.
The Good-Bye Angel.
Teeth under the Sun.
Zero.
BONNIE BREMSER, *Troia: Mexican Memoirs.*
CHRISTINE BROOKE-ROSE, *Amalgamemnon.*
BRIGID BROPHY, *In Transit.*
MEREDITH BROSNAN, *Mr. Dynamite.*
GERALD L. BRUNS, *Modern Poetry and the Idea of Language.*
EVGENY BUNIMOVICH AND J. KATES, EDS.,
Contemporary Russian Poetry: An Anthology.
GABRIELLE BURTON, *Heartbreak Hotel.*
MICHEL BUTOR, *Degrees.*
Mobile.
Portrait of the Artist as a Young Ape.
G. CABRERA INFANTE, *Infante's Inferno.*
Three Trapped Tigers.
JULIETA CAMPOS,
The Fear of Losing Eurydice.
ANNE CARSON, *Eros the Bittersweet.*
ORLY CASTEL-BLOOM, *Dolly City.*
CAMILO JOSÉ CELA, *Christ versus Arizona.*
The Family of Pascual Duarte.
The Hive.
LOUIS-FERDINAND CÉLINE, *Castle to Castle.*
Conversations with Professor Y.
London Bridge.

Normance.
North.
Rigadoon.
MARIE CHAIX, *The Laurels of Lake Constance.*
HUGO CHARTERIS, *The Tide Is Right.*
JEROME CHARYN, *The Tar Baby.*
ERIC CHEVILLARD, *Demolishing Nisard.*
LUIS CHITARRONI, *The No Variations.*
MARC CHOLODENKO, *Mordechai Schamz.*
JOSHUA COHEN, *Witz.*
EMILY HOLMES COLEMAN, *The Shutter of Snow.*
ROBERT COOVER, *A Night at the Movies.*
STANLEY CRAWFORD, *Log of the S.S. The Mrs Unguentine.*
Some Instructions to My Wife.
ROBERT CREELEY, *Collected Prose.*
RENÉ CREVEL, *Putting My Foot in It.*
RALPH CUSACK, *Cadenza.*
SUSAN DAITCH, *L.C.*
Storytown.
NICHOLAS DELBANCO, *The Count of Concord.*
Sherbrookes.
NIGEL DENNIS, *Cards of Identity.*
PETER DIMOCK, *A Short Rhetoric for Leaving the Family.*
ARIEL DORFMAN, *Konfidenz.*
COLEMAN DOWELL,
The Houses of Children.
Island People.
Too Much Flesh and Jabez.
ARKADII DRAGOMOSHCHENKO, *Dust.*
RIKKI DUCORNET, *The Complete Butcher's Tales.*
The Fountains of Neptune.
The Jade Cabinet.
The One Marvelous Thing.
Phosphor in Dreamland.
The Stain.
The Word "Desire."
WILLIAM EASTLAKE, *The Bamboo Bed.*
Castle Keep.
Lyric of the Circle Heart.
JEAN ECHENOZ, *Chopin's Move.*
STANLEY ELKIN, *A Bad Man.*
Boswell: A Modern Comedy.
Criers and Kibitzers, Kibitzers and Criers.
The Dick Gibson Show.
The Franchiser.
George Mills.
The Living End.
The MacGuffin.
The Magic Kingdom.
Mrs. Ted Bliss.
The Rabbi of Lud.
Van Gogh's Room at Arles.
FRANÇOIS EMMANUEL, *Invitation to a Voyage.*
ANNIE ERNAUX, *Cleaned Out.*
SALVADOR ESPRIU, *Ariadne in the Grotesque Labyrinth.*
LAUREN FAIRBANKS, *Muzzle Thyself.*
Sister Carrie.
LESLIE A. FIEDLER, *Love and Death in the American Novel.*
JUAN FILLOY, *Faction.*
Op Oloop.
ANDY FITCH, *Pop Poetics.*
GUSTAVE FLAUBERT, *Bouvard and Pécuchet.*
KASS FLEISHER, *Talking out of School.*

FOR A FULL LIST OF PUBLICATIONS, VISIT:
www.dalkeyarchive.com

FORD MADOX FORD,
The March of Literature.
JON FOSSE, *Aliss at the Fire.*
Melancholy.
MAX FRISCH, *I'm Not Stiller.*
Man in the Holocene.
CARLOS FUENTES, *Christopher Unborn.*
Distant Relations.
Terra Nostra.
Vlad.
Where the Air Is Clear.
TAKEHIKO FUKUNAGA, *Flowers of Grass.*
WILLIAM GADDIS, *J R.*
The Recognitions.
JANICE GALLOWAY, *Foreign Parts.*
The Trick Is to Keep Breathing.
WILLIAM H. GASS, *Cartesian Sonata*
and Other Novellas.
Finding a Form.
A Temple of Texts.
The Tunnel.
Willie Masters' Lonesome Wife.
GÉRARD GAVARRY, *Hoppla! 1 2 3.*
Making a Novel.
ETIENNE GILSON,
The Arts of the Beautiful.
Forms and Substances in the Arts.
C. S. GISCOMBE, *Giscome Road.*
Here.
Prairie Style.
DOUGLAS GLOVER, *Bad News of the Heart.*
The Enamoured Knight.
WITOLD GOMBROWICZ,
A Kind of Testament.
PAULO EMÍLIO SALES GOMES, *P's Three*
Women.
KAREN ELIZABETH GORDON, *The Red Shoes.*
GEORGI GOSPODINOV, *Natural Novel.*
JUAN GOYTISOLO, *Count Julian.*
Exiled from Almost Everywhere.
Juan the Landless.
Makbara.
Marks of Identity.
PATRICK GRAINVILLE, *The Cave of Heaven.*
HENRY GREEN, *Back.*
Blindness.
Concluding.
Doting.
Nothing.
JACK GREEN, *Fire the Bastards!*
JIŘÍ GRUŠA, *The Questionnaire.*
GABRIEL GUDDING,
Rhode Island Notebook.
MELA HARTWIG, *Am I a Redundant*
Human Being?
JOHN HAWKES, *The Passion Artist.*
Whistlejacket.
ELIZABETH HEIGHWAY, ED., *Contemporary*
Georgian Fiction.
ALEKSANDAR HEMON, ED.,
Best European Fiction.
AIDAN HIGGINS, *Balcony of Europe.*
A Bestiary.
Blind Man's Bluff
Bornholm Night-Ferry.
Darkling Plain: Texts for the Air.
Flotsam and Jetsam.
Langrishe, Go Down.
Scenes from a Receding Past.
Windy Arbours.
KEIZO HINO, *Isle of Dreams.*
KAZUSHI HOSAKA, *Plainsong.*

ALDOUS HUXLEY, *Antic Hay.*
Crome Yellow.
Point Counter Point.
Those Barren Leaves.
Time Must Have a Stop.
NAOYUKI II, *The Shadow of a Blue Cat.*
MIKHAIL IOSSEL AND JEFF PARKER, EDS.,
Amerika: Russian Writers View the
United States.
DRAGO JANČAR, *The Galley Slave.*
GERT JONKE, *The Distant Sound.*
Geometric Regional Novel.
Homage to Czerny.
The System of Vienna.
JACQUES JOUET, *Mountain R.*
Savage.
Upstaged.
CHARLES JULIET, *Conversations with*
Samuel Beckett and Bram van
Velde.
MIEKO KANAI, *The Word Book.*
YORAM KANIUK, *Life on Sandpaper.*
HUGH KENNER, *The Counterfeiters.*
Flaubert, Joyce and Beckett:
The Stoic Comedians.
Joyce's Voices.
DANILO KIŠ, *The Attic.*
Garden, Ashes.
The Lute and the Scars
Psalm 44.
A Tomb for Boris Davidovich.
ANITA KONKKA, *A Fool's Paradise.*
GEORGE KONRÁD, *The City Builder.*
TADEUSZ KONWICKI, *A Minor Apocalypse.*
The Polish Complex.
MENIS KOUMANDAREAS, *Koula.*
ELAINE KRAF, *The Princess of 72nd Street.*
JIM KRUSOE, *Iceland.*
AYŞE KULIN, *Farewell: A Mansion in*
Occupied Istanbul.
EWA KURYLUK, *Century 21.*
EMILIO LASCANO TEGUI, *On Elegance*
While Sleeping.
ERIC LAURRENT, *Do Not Touch.*
HERVÉ LE TELLIER, *The Sextine Chapel.*
A Thousand Pearls (for a Thousand
Pennies)
VIOLETTE LEDUC, *La Bâtarde.*
EDOUARD LEVÉ, *Autoportrait.*
Suicide.
MARIO LEVI, *Istanbul Was a Fairy Tale.*
SUZANNE JILL LEVINE, *The Subversive*
Scribe: Translating Latin
American Fiction.
DEBORAH LEVY, *Billy and Girl.*
Pillow Talk in Europe and Other
Places.
JOSÉ LEZAMA LIMA, *Paradiso.*
ROSA LIKSOM, *Dark Paradise.*
OSMAN LINS, *Avalovara.*
The Queen of the Prisons of Greece.
ALF MAC LOCHLAINN,
The Corpus in the Library.
Out of Focus.
RON LOEWINSOHN, *Magnetic Field(s).*
MINA LOY, *Stories and Essays of Mina Loy.*
BRIAN LYNCH, *The Winner of Sorrow.*
D. KEITH MANO, *Take Five.*
MICHELINE AHARONIAN MARCOM,
The Mirror in the Well.
BEN MARCUS,
The Age of Wire and String.

FOR A FULL LIST OF PUBLICATIONS, VISIT:
www.dalkeyarchive.com

WALLACE MARKFIELD,
Teitlebaum's Window.
To an Early Grave.
DAVID MARKSON, *Reader's Block.*
Springer's Progress.
Wittgenstein's Mistress.
CAROLE MASO, *AVA.*
LADISLAV MATEJKA AND KRYSTYNA
POMORSKA, EDS.,
Readings in Russian Poetics:
Formalist and Structuralist Views.
HARRY MATHEWS,
The Case of the Persevering Maltese:
Collected Essays.
Cigarettes.
The Conversions.
The Human Country: New and
Collected Stories.
The Journalist.
My Life in CIA.
Singular Pleasures.
The Sinking of the Odradek
Stadium.
Tlooth.
20 Lines a Day.
JOSEPH MCELROY,
Night Soul and Other Stories.
THOMAS MCGONIGLE,
Going to Patchogue.
ROBERT L. MCLAUGHLIN, ED., *Innovations:*
An Anthology of Modern &
Contemporary Fiction.
ABDELWAHAB MEDDEB, *Talismano.*
GERHARD MEIER, *Isle of the Dead.*
HERMAN MELVILLE, *The Confidence-Man.*
AMANDA MICHALOPOULOU, *I'd Like.*
STEVEN MILLHAUSER, *The Barnum Museum.*
In the Penny Arcade.
RALPH J. MILLS, JR., *Essays on Poetry.*
MOMUS, *The Book of Jokes.*
CHRISTINE MONTALBETTI, *The Origin of Man.*
Western.
OLIVE MOORE, *Spleen.*
NICHOLAS MOSLEY, *Accident.*
Assassins.
Catastrophe Practice.
Children of Darkness and Light.
Experience and Religion.
A Garden of Trees.
God's Hazard.
The Hesperides Tree.
Hopeful Monsters.
Imago Bird.
Impossible Object.
Inventing God.
Judith.
Look at the Dark.
Natalie Natalia.
Paradoxes of Peace.
Serpent.
Time at War.
The Uses of Slime Mould:
Essays of Four Decades.
WARREN MOTTE,
Fables of the Novel: French Fiction
since 1990.
Fiction Now: The French Novel in
the 21st Century.
Oulipo: A Primer of Potential
Literature.
GERALD MURNANE, *Barley Patch.*
Inland.

YVES NAVARRE, *Our Share of Time.*
Sweet Tooth.
DOROTHY NELSON, *In Night's City.*
Tar and Feathers.
ESHKOL NEVO, *Homesick.*
WILFRIDO D. NOLLEDO, *But for the Lovers.*
FLANN O'BRIEN, *At Swim-Two-Birds.*
At War.
The Best of Myles.
The Dalkey Archive.
Further Cuttings.
The Hard Life.
The Poor Mouth.
The Third Policeman.
CLAUDE OLLIER, *The Mise-en-Scène.*
Wert and the Life Without End.
GIOVANNI ORELLI, *Walaschek's Dream.*
PATRIK OUŘEDNÍK, *Europeana.*
The Opportune Moment, 1855.
BORIS PAHOR, *Necropolis.*
FERNANDO DEL PASO, *News from the Empire.*
Palinuro of Mexico.
ROBERT PINGET, *The Inquisitory.*
Mahu or The Material.
Trio.
A. G. PORTA, *The No World Concerto.*
MANUEL PUIG, *Betrayed by Rita Hayworth.*
The Buenos Aires Affair.
Heartbreak Tango.
RAYMOND QUENEAU, *The Last Days.*
Odile.
Pierrot Mon Ami.
Saint Glinglin.
ANN QUIN, *Berg.*
Passages.
Three.
Tripticks.
ISHMAEL REED, *The Free-Lance Pallbearers.*
The Last Days of Louisiana Red.
Ishmael Reed: The Plays.
Juice!
Reckless Eyeballing.
The Terrible Threes.
The Terrible Twos.
Yellow Back Radio Broke-Down.
JASIA REICHARDT, *15 Journeys Warsaw*
to London.
NOËLLE REVAZ, *With the Animals.*
JOÃO UBALDO RIBEIRO, *House of the*
Fortunate Buddhas.
JEAN RICARDOU, *Place Names.*
RAINER MARIA RILKE, *The Notebooks of*
Malte Laurids Brigge.
JULIÁN RÍOS, *The House of Ulysses.*
Larva: A Midsummer Night's Babel.
Poundemonium.
Procession of Shadows.
AUGUSTO ROA BASTOS, *I the Supreme.*
DANIËL ROBBERECHTS, *Arriving in Avignon.*
JEAN ROLIN, *The Explosion of the*
Radiator Hose.
OLIVIER ROLIN, *Hotel Crystal.*
ALIX CLEO ROUBAUD, *Alix's Journal.*
JACQUES ROUBAUD, *The Form of a*
City Changes Faster, Alas, Than
the Human Heart.
The Great Fire of London.
Hortense in Exile.
Hortense Is Abducted.
The Loop.
Mathematics:
The Plurality of Worlds of Lewis.

The Princess Hoppy.
Some Thing Black.
LEON S. ROUDIEZ, *French Fiction Revisited.*
RAYMOND ROUSSEL, *Impressions of Africa.*
VEDRANA RUDAN, *Night.*
STIG SÆTERBAKKEN, *Siamese.*
LYDIE SALVAYRE, *The Company of Ghosts.*
Everyday Life.
The Lecture.
*Portrait of the Writer as a
Domesticated Animal.*
The Power of Flies.
LUIS RAFAEL SÁNCHEZ,
Macho Camacho's Beat.
SEVERO SARDUY, *Cobra & Maitreya.*
NATHALIE SARRAUTE,
Do You Hear Them?
Martereau.
The Planetarium.
ARNO SCHMIDT, *Collected Novellas.*
Collected Stories.
Nobodaddy's Children.
Two Novels.
ASAF SCHURR, *Motti.*
CHRISTINE SCHUTT, *Nightwork.*
GAIL SCOTT, *My Paris.*
DAMION SEARLS, *What We Were Doing
and Where We Were Going.*
JUNE AKERS SEESE,
Is This What Other Women Feel Too?
What Waiting Really Means.
BERNARD SHARE, *Inish.*
Transit.
AURELIE SHEEHAN, *Jack Kerouac Is Pregnant.*
VIKTOR SHKLOVSKY, *Bowstring.*
Knight's Move.
*A Sentimental Journey:
Memoirs 1917–1922.*
Energy of Delusion: A Book on Plot.
Literature and Cinematography.
Theory of Prose.
Third Factory.
Zoo, or Letters Not about Love.
CLAUDE SIMON, *The Invitation.*
PIERRE SINIAC, *The Collaborators.*
KJERSTI A. SKOMSVOLD, *The Faster I Walk,
the Smaller I Am.*
JOSEF ŠKVORECKÝ, *The Engineer of
Human Souls.*
GILBERT SORRENTINO,
Aberration of Starlight.
Blue Pastoral.
Crystal Vision.
*Imaginative Qualities of Actual
Things.*
Mulligan Stew.
Pack of Lies.
Red the Fiend.
The Sky Changes.
Something Said.
Splendide-Hôtel.
Steelwork.
Under the Shadow.
W. M. SPACKMAN, *The Complete Fiction.*
ANDRZEJ STASIUK, *Dukla.*
Fado.
GERTRUDE STEIN, *Lucy Church Amiably.*
The Making of Americans.
A Novel of Thank You.
LARS SVENDSEN, *A Philosophy of Evil.*
PIOTR SZEWC, *Annihilation.*
GONÇALO M. TAVARES, *Jerusalem.*

Joseph Walser's Machine.
*Learning to Pray in the Age of
Technique.*
LUCIAN DAN TEODOROVICI,
Our Circus Presents . . .
NIKANOR TERATOLOGEN, *Assisted Living.*
STEFAN THEMERSON, *Hobson's Island.*
The Mystery of the Sardine.
Tom Harris.
TAEKO TOMIOKA, *Building Waves.*
JOHN TOOMEY, *Sleepwalker.*
JEAN-PHILIPPE TOUSSAINT, *The Bathroom.*
Camera.
Monsieur.
Reticence.
Running Away.
Self-Portrait Abroad.
Television.
The Truth about Marie.
DUMITRU TSEPENEAG, *Hotel Europa.*
The Necessary Marriage.
Pigeon Post.
Vain Art of the Fugue.
ESTHER TUSQUETS, *Stranded.*
DUBRAVKA UGRESIC, *Lend Me Your Character.*
Thank You for Not Reading.
TOR ULVEN, *Replacement.*
MATI UNT, *Brecht at Night.*
Diary of a Blood Donor.
Things in the Night.
ÁLVARO URIBE AND OLIVIA SEARS, EDS.,
Best of Contemporary Mexican Fiction.
ELOY URROZ, *Friction.*
The Obstacles.
LUISA VALENZUELA, *Dark Desires and
the Others.*
He Who Searches.
MARJA-LIISA VARTIO, *The Parson's Widow.*
PAUL VERHAEGHEN, *Omega Minor.*
AGLAJA VETERANYI, *Why the Child Is
Cooking in the Polenta.*
BORIS VIAN, *Heartsnatcher.*
LLORENÇ VILLALONGA, *The Dolls' Room.*
TOOMAS VINT, *An Unending Landscape.*
ORNELA VORPSI, *The Country Where No
One Ever Dies.*
AUSTRYN WAINHOUSE, *Hedyphagetica.*
PAUL WEST, *Words for a Deaf Daughter
& Gala.*
CURTIS WHITE, *America's Magic Mountain.*
The Idea of Home.
Memories of My Father Watching TV.
*Monstrous Possibility: An Invitation
to Literary Politics.*
Requiem.
DIANE WILLIAMS, *Excitability:
Selected Stories.*
Romancer Erector.
DOUGLAS WOOLF, *Wall to Wall.*
Ya! & John-Juan.
JAY WRIGHT, *Polynomials and Pollen.*
*The Presentable Art of Reading
Absence.*
PHILIP WYLIE, *Generation of Vipers.*
MARGUERITE YOUNG, *Angel in the Forest.*
Miss MacIntosh, My Darling.
REYOUNG, *Unbabbling.*
VLADO ŽABOT, *The Succubus.*
ZORAN ŽIVKOVIĆ, *Hidden Camera.*
LOUIS ZUKOFSKY, *Collected Fiction.*
VITOMIL ZUPAN, *Minuet for Guitar.*
SCOTT ZWIREN, *God Head.*